Sign up for our newsletter to hear
about new and upcoming releases.

www.ylva-publishing.com

# Other Books by Emily O'Beirne

*Here's the Thing*

*Points of Departure*

**Future Leaders**

*Future Leaders of Nowhere*
*All the Ways to Here*

**A Story of Now Series**

*A Story of Now*
*The Sum of These Things*

# All the ways to here

Emily O'Beirne

# CHAPTER 1

## Willa

"The sooner you answer the question, the better it will be for you, Brookes."

"I know." Willa smiles. Long green blades snake over her fingers, grass so springtime soft she could sink into it, pull it over her like a cool green blanket. None of that yellow stubble from camp.

They are a logjam of limbs, light and dark, jumbled under the apricot tree. It's so good to be home, back in the radius of the handful of people life has doled out to Willa. Everyone's on the map again, placed within reach: Nan's down the side, wrangling her grapevine into submission. Willa's brother, Jack, is over the road, killing digital baddies with Tyler. Her sister, Riley, is inside, supposedly cleaning her side of their room. And Kelly and Maida have her surrounded on the slip of a lawn. Even though it's interrogation time, it's blissful to lie here again in the slick of protective coating that is her nosy, beautiful best friends.

The grass tickles her cheek as a breeze cuts past, and she idly reminds herself to borrow the mower from Maida's dad and mow before Nan tries to do it herself. It can wait for a minute, though. In fact, everything can wait just one more hour. Because right now she gets to dwell in the bittersweet feeling that is a Sunday afternoon at home—Monday morning looming, but not quite there yet. At Camp Nowhere, all the days felt the same, the hours regimented by mealtimes and shower times and cabin curfews.

Willa hasn't quite left it all behind yet. It's like free-floating between two worlds. All her reference points are still about camp. She keeps thinking that at any minute a bell's going to sound, directing her to the next thing, or one of the Gandry girls is going to crack a joke about the food or the mystery fungus in the shower blocks. She keeps wanting to answer Kelly and Maida's chatter with "that's like when Amira…" or "remember when Ling…", but then she remembers that Kelly and Maida won't know who or what she's talking about, that she never talks about the people she goes to school with.

"Hey." An elbow digs at her arm. "Answer the question, Brookes."

"What was it again?" she asks, playing dumb.

"What school does this girl go to?"

"Brunswick Hill."

Kelly wrinkles her nose. "Private."

"I go to private too, remember?"

"Yeah, but that's because you're a poor genius scholarship kid."

"We're not exactly poor."

"Oh, yeah, that's right. That's me. Well, you *are* a genius."

"Is she smart?" Maida asks, twirling a dandelion between her fingers.

"Very."

"Of course she's smart," Kelly says. "Do you think Willa would date a bimbo? What would they even talk about?"

"She talks to *us*."

"She has to. We make her." Kelly turns to Willa. "Hey, she's not like that Freya chick, is she? I didn't like her."

"You didn't even meet her," Maida reminds her.

"Whatever. I didn't need to." Kelly holds a fray of black hair over her face, inspecting for split ends. "She was evil to Will."

"Finn's nothing like Freya," Willa says, smiling.

"Oh, wow, would you look at the smile," Kelly says.

But the smile's not for Finn. Not this time. Willa's smiling at these two. Because she loves them so. And she's missed them. They're the people who pull her back when she strays too far into herself, who force her to keep one foot in the land of teenager.

"Listen, you can't go around being all lovesick and gross all the time now," Kelly tells her.

Maida leans over Willa. "You know she only says stuff like that because she's happy for you, right?"

"I know."

Maida still does that—explains Kelly's behaviour. As if after all these years, Willa still won't know how to read her, won't get that this is how Kelly faces the world she was dealt, by being brash and loud and big like a bird swelling its feathers to look more ominous to predators. Willa totally gets it. In fact, she gets Kelly's automatic defence more than she gets Maida, with her sweet, slow, go-with-the-flow attitude. Kelly just dresses her fears as anger, that's all, while Maida doesn't seem to have any.

"So what's she like, then?" Maida breaks a piece of banana cake into hunks and passes it out.

Willa frowns. How do you translate a person into the slipperiness of words? Even someone who is as what-you-see-is-what-you-get as Finn? "I don't know. She's really smart and thoughtful. And kind."

"Okay, now she sounds boring. *Kind?*" Kelly pulls a face.

"What's wrong with kind?" Maida asks.

Willa pops a bit of cake in her mouth. There's an instant starburst pang, tangy and sweet. Cream cheese icing. The best kind. "Don't worry, she can be feisty too. She's definitely got opinions."

"Okay, now I like her more," Kelly says.

Maida shakes her head and swipes crumbs from her tights. "Imagine if we judged this hard on the guys you hook up with. Finn sounds nice. And Will could use some sweetness."

"Sweetness?" Kelly pulls another face. "I just threw up in my mouth a little."

This makes Willa laugh. Because Maida sounds like some honeyed meemaw from the deep South. Only she's a million miles from it. Maida's a classic inner-city Melbourne mongrel, Kelly always says proudly, just like her and Willa. Aussie, Greek, and Filipino are all tossed into the mix that made her, and somehow all these ingredients have conspired to make this doe-eyed, dreamy pixie with a haircut to match.

"Anyway," Kelly says from inside a sigh. "I know I'm being judge-y, but she could be Willa's first proper girlfriend, so I have to make sure she's picked a winner. We've waited long enough."

This is the good, the bad, and the ugly of telling them about Finn. Well, telling Kelly, anyway.

"So," Kelly nudges her and grins, "most important, will *I* like her?"

Before Willa can give that question the sarcasm it deserves, a loud, wailing "Wil-la!" rides high in the air.

Riley's on the back step, hands on hips, the ridiculously long hair she refuses to cut floating around her elbows. She's wide-eyed and brimful with all the melodrama that Willa's quickly learning that an eleven-year-old with a new, prepubescent sense of self-importance can muster.

"What's wrong, Riles?"

"I can't find one of my library books. They're due tomorrow. I've looked everywhere."

"Well, have you finished cleaning your side of the room?"

"…sort of." She gives Willa a sheepish smile.

"Then the only surprise is that you're surprised you can't find it. It'll be somewhere in that mess."

Riley clicks her tongue loudly but doesn't move. As usual, she's waiting for Willa to solve the problems she can't be bothered solving.

Maybe Willa doesn't love this part about coming home. "Look, I'll help you look for it later. But only if you haven't found it *after* you clean up."

Riley's mouth moves towards a pout but second-guesses itself at the last moment. Instead she goes for that new, helpless look she's been trying on.

"Just do it, Riles," Willa says, fighting a smile. Is it possible her sister has learned even more guile in Willa's absence? "Then you'll be able to watch TV after dinner."

The pout makes its victorious return. "You're lucky I missed you!" She spins and flounces into the house. "Your phone's ringing!"

Finn. It has to be. Willa leaps up and jogs into the shadowed kitchen. But by the time she snatches up her phone from the kitchen table, it's stopped. It *was* her. Damn. Just the fact Finn's thinking of her right now makes her blood swim harder under her skin.

The sun hits her right square in the eyes as she steps back outside, her bare feet slapping the concrete. There's a thump and curse from down the side of the house. Nan's standing in the narrow space between weatherboard and fence, glaring up at the gnarl of vine, her hands jammed on her hips. Riley all over again.

Willa edges down the path, fern fronds skimming her legs. "What's wrong?"

"Support beam's cracked, and the wire's jammed in it."

"Oh." Willa peers into the tangle of stem and bright new leaf. "Want me to climb up and see if I can pull it out?"

"No. It's going to need some pliers and a ladder, I think." Nan rubs her upper lip, where beads of sweat have gathered. She's been trying to downplay whatever illness dogged her while Willa was gone, but Willa can see traces of it in the ashy torpor of her skin. It's been setting off flickers of worry since she got home.

"Should I ask Kelly to get her brother to come take a look?"

Nan nods, but Will can tell she's only half listening as she scrutinises the tangled mess above her. "Or maybe I could just climb the fence to get to it."

"Don't do that," Willa says hurriedly. Nan will do anything if her precious jungle is at stake. "I'll ask Dave. He can mow the lawn too."

"That boy will take forever about getting himself here."

"Not if I get Kelly onto him." Willa swipes some cobwebs from Nan's back as she follows her down the path. "And not if you pay him."

"Of course I'll pay him. I always do." Nan stops every few steps, inspecting her ferns, turning over fronds and picking off dead bits, master of all the green she surveys. "This garden. More work than raising children."

Willa smiles. She always says that. "Want help with dinner?"

"It's ready to go. You can switch the potatoes and lamb on in about twenty minutes while I finish repotting the baskets out the front, if you like. Throw on some of that fresh rosemary from the garden, and tell the girls they're welcome."

"Thanks." But for the first time ever, Willa isn't excited that the girls might stay for Sunday dinner. Only because she'll have to wait even longer to call Finn. But she also knows that if she doesn't ask them, Kelly will be making her own meal, and who knows what hippie fare Maida will have to endure.

They haven't moved. Kelly's thick legs are kicked up against the tree, while Maida's petite ones are crossed primly on the grass.

Willa flops down between them and turns to Kelly. "Can you send your brother over tomorrow? Nan's got a job for him. She'll pay."

"Then I'm sure he'll find a minute in his busy schedule of doing sweet FA to help."

"Nan says you two can stay for tea if you like. Lamb."

"A Nan roast?" Kelly click her tongue. "Damn. Can't. Got to go to work."

"And my mum's making *nut* roast." Maida pulls a face.

"What the hell is that?" Kelly asks.

"You do not want to know. But apparently it's an event we must all be in attendance for."

"Lucky you," Willa says. Canned laughter from some tween sitcom spills out of the house. She sighs and adds another thing to the growing list of things to do tonight. Because Riley clearly isn't going to clean until Willa helps her. And Willa still needs to pack her schoolbag, iron her uniform, hang out her camp washing, and check that all her camp homework is complete.

Kelly yanks at a strand of her hair. "By the way, after careful consideration, Maida and I have decided that we'll permit you to date this girl. As long as we get to meet her, *stat.*"

# CHAPTER 2

## Finn

"She goes to Gandry Park." Finn opens the glove box and rummages through manuals, receipts, and odd car bits. Bingo. She pulls out a tin of mints. "On scholarship."

"Uh-huh." Her mum, Anita, is doing a woeful job of pretending to listen as she weaves the car through the tight Sunday afternoon traffic. Usually, if Finn dropped the news that she's dating someone, there'd an Inquisition-level list of carefully-crafted, not-too-nosey-but-not-too-uninterested questions. Not "uh-huh". And then there's the fact that her mother—award-winning educator extraordinaire—didn't jump all over the Gandry scholarship info. That's a dead giveaway that Finn's words are just gliding right past.

So Finn gives up. Flinching at the hot peppermint slide in her throat, she watches the slow-moving scenery as they attempt to depart the inner-north. High Street inches by in a chaotic montage of apartments under construction, old ladies pushing trolleys, and hipsters leading trends and dogs and children from café to café.

Anita brakes suddenly and mutters something under her breath. Finn glances uneasily at her. Her mother's usually a chilled driver, the type to say "go team" instead of "hurry up" when cars are slow to take off at a newly green light. Not today.

Anita's sunglasses are monsters, dominating her small face. Even with their protection, she still manages to look tired and deflated. It was the first thing Finn noticed when her bus pulled into the school carpark on Friday—how small her mother looked as she stood by her car, clutching her keys. And Anita's never small. In size, yes, but in personality, she's always been a lioness.

The first thing she said as she folded Finn into a strangle of a hug was "I'm sorry."

And because Finn was so shocked by the sight of her mum looking that way, she just said, "It's okay." Even though it's not. Even though coming back to a dad-less house has made everything so strange.

Finally, they pull clear of the traffic and head for an exit that will take them to the beige boringness of the eastern suburbs. Visiting her grandmother has always been a hell mission. And not just because she lives forty-five minutes out of the city.

"So, why do we have to even visit Grandma Esther if you and Dad…" Finn doesn't know how to describe whatever it is that her mum and dad currently are. Or are not. "She's not your mum."

"Because no one else will." Anita leans forward as she speeds up to merge with the cars streaking past on the highway. "And because we are good people."

"We are stupid people."

Anita clicks her tongue and does that head-tilt thing she always does when she wants to agree but knows she isn't supposed to.

"And why doesn't Anna have to come?"

"Your sister's working."

"That's it," Finn says. "I'm getting a weekend job."

"No, you're not." Now she's listening.

"Why not?"

"We've been through this enough times, Finn. You're busy enough as it is. If you want to be a student representative and go to painting classes and do all the other things you want to do on top of your studies, that's fine. But there's not enough time to work too. I'd rather give you pocket money."

"You know, most parents would want their kids to get a job."

"Most parents want their kid to get a job because they can't provide pocket money or because they want them to learn a lesson in responsibility. We can manage pocket money, and we were also lucky enough to be born with a freak child who has the responsibility part down already."

Finn doesn't know whether to smile because her mum is being her mum again or to pout because she never wins this argument.

"You can get a job in the summer holidays. You can have three jobs then if you want." Anita pats her leg. "Besides, you have to admit, finding employment just to avoid a monthly encounter with your grandmother might be a little overreaching."

"But smart." Finn watches house roofs streak past, half hidden behind the cement slabs shielding them from the freeway. "She's going to say…stuff."

"Yes, she will. About everybody and everything. And we shall listen politely, make chitchat, eat afternoon tea, and leave in thirty to forty minutes. And then we reward ourselves with pasta and a movie. And the good news is that your cousin got suspended from school, so I'm sure the spotlight will be on your Aunt Laura's failings instead of our own."

"Yes!" Finn wriggles in her seat. "Major diversion. What'd he do?"

"Some prank with his soccer team. Damaged an equipment shed."

"Excellent. Thank you, Mark."

"And hon," Anita says, "of course, it's completely up to you, but you should be prepared that if you do mention Willa to Esther, she'll—"

"Oh, don't you worry." Finn shakes the tin to see if there are any mints left. "The less that old homophobe knows about my unsavoury love life, the better."

This time her mother laughs. Her first real laugh since Finn got home.

# CHAPTER 3

## Willa

Willa strides up the footpath, stitching her way through the crowds of blue-and-white check headed for the school gates. There are the excitable juniors, the bored intermediates, and those remote senior girls, all moving en masse towards the hulking red-brick building.

It's strange to be back among them. Willa's cotton school dress hangs weirdly after weeks of jeans and T-shirts at camp. And then there's the depressing tug of her laden backpack on her shoulders. It will be even heavier on the way home.

She puts her head down and strides, tired already. Even with all her preparation last night, the morning was chaos. Riley was freaking out because she still couldn't find her library book. It took another twenty minutes of hunting and questioning before they finally deduced it was in her book bag. At school. Then Jack spilt his cereal on the floor, and the washing machine stalled mid spin while Nan was out in the yard. All before 8am.

*Three more weeks until the holidays*, she repeats in her head like a mantra.

The first person she sees inside the school gates is Eva, standing in a wash of sunlight, staring at her phone. Just as Willa's deciding whether to stop or not, Eva spots her and smiles. She pushes her sunglasses up. "Hey there."

Eva looks impeccable, as always. Her light-brown hair is wrapped into a loose but neat bun, and her brows smoothed to perfect arches over blue eyes. Even though Willa is always Gandry-mandated neat and tidy, she never feels as put together as Eva. Or any of these girls. She thinks she looks tidy when she leaves the house, but as soon as she gets among the picture perfection of these girls, she'll notice the wrinkle in her shirt sleeve or the small spot on her blazer. No one else would notice, but Willa does.

"So, how was your weekend?" Eva falls into step with her. "Oh, and by the way, this is me making sure you don't go all aloof on us again." Willa gives her a look, but Eva just gives her an insouciant smile. "It's weird to be back, isn't it?"

"It's weird being back in uniform," Willa says, yanking at her blazer. "So, was it nice to see your family?"

"Well, well. Look at you with the chitchat," Eva teases.

"Very funny." But it is kind of nice walking into school with the closest thing she's had to a friend since coming here. On the bus ride home from camp, she learned more about Eva than she's ever known. That she lives in an apartment not far from the school. That both her parents and her brother travel all the time—the parents for work and the brother for fun. Apparently, her older brother loves trouble like Eva loves success, and she's constantly acting as buffer between him and their parents. Willa even told Eva something about her family. Not everything, though. Not yet.

The noise thickens as they enter the building, and girls desperately jam in last night's stories before the imposed silence of form assembly. The air cloys with the smell of mass-applied girl product.

"Only fifteen more school days until the end of term," Eva mutters.

"Now, that's not the Gandry girl attitude," Willa jokes, jumping as an arm drops suddenly onto her shoulders and hauls her in close.

"Morning, ladies!" Amira inserts herself between them, carrying her own personal cloud of sugary perfume and self-confidence. "Civilisation is a wonderful thing, isn't it? Nothing like a stint in the country to make you appreciate clean sheets and choose-your-own-meal-adventures. You suddenly begin to appreciate the little things."

"Like self-direction," Eva drawls.

"So true. I gotta run." Amira presses a kiss onto Eva's cheek, drops a slap on Willa's backside, and marches off into the crowds. "See you in Japanese!" she yells over her shoulder.

Eva grins at Willa's expression. "Yeah, so now you've let her in, you're going to have to learn to live with her complete lack of boundaries."

"I let her in?"

"She can slip through any friendship crack. Catch you later." Eva turns for the west buildings.

Before Willa can head through the doors to the north quad, she hears her name. She spins around, nearly bumping into some Year 8s. The vice principal is standing by her door, beckoning.

Ms Cassavetes' hair has already begun its daily escape, falling in lank strands around her head. And, as ever, her effort at corporate attire is stymied by wrinkles, what looks like dog hair, and a shaggy cardigan she keeps in her cold office but sometimes forgets to remove before leaving. Basically, she's a mess—especially compared to the parade of impeccable girl grooming that's currently marching past her door.

Willa's always figured that Ms Cassavetes made some deal with the career devil, one that sacrificed grooming skills for maximum efficiency in all other areas. Because while she slays at her job, and parents and students both like and respect her, she always looks like she woke from a twenty-year coma and had five minutes to get ready before returning to work.

"Good morning." Ms Cassavetes folds her arms and leans against the doorjamb. "I heard you girls did very well on camp. Good job."

Willa smiles uneasily. She's already had to come to terms with the fact that teachers make her unreasonably nervous. It's her lot in life. "Thank you."

"I was going to get a hold of you after assembly, but you're here now. It's late notice, I know, but could you please attend a middle-school curriculum meeting this afternoon? Just for an hour? The council has suddenly decided that there needs to be a student representative on the committee. It seems like a job for one of the academic leaders, but Stella from the seniors is busy this afternoon. Could you make it this once?"

Willa recalibrates her afternoon, biting back at the stress that's already flickering at her periphery: Curriculum meeting instead of study. Pick up Riley from Lefah's house. Then get dinner started while Nan goes to her community gardens meeting. The missed homework can happen after dinner while she helps Jack with his. She can probably get it all done if she spends lunch in the library today too. Then there's the fact she'd never say no anyway. "Sure, I can do it."

Ms Cassavetes smiles and pushes herself off the jamb. "Great. Thank you. Can you also ask one of the girls to chat at assembly on Wednesday about the camp? It would be good for the younger girls to hear about the experience. Especially those Year 9s. They can focus on trying to get selected for next year."

Willa nods, mentally signing Amira up for it. "Sure."

"Good girl. Have a great day." And she's back in her office with the door closed.

# CHAPTER 4

## Finn

She finds Dan where she can always find him on Tuesdays: in the front garden, under the weird scrubby tree that drops needles into their hair and food. Still, no one else is ever sitting there, so it's become their Tuesday lunch place.

Mondays he has drumming lessons. Wednesdays she has all-captain meeting. Thursdays she has lunch with the other intermediate student representatives to talk shop. Then he has multimedia club on Fridays, while she has extra art. But Tuesdays are inviolably theirs. Finn loves their little forty-three minutes of banter and smartassery. It gives her strength to get through the rest of the week. School gets so fast and so hard sometimes, but on Tuesdays with Dan, there's only the comfort of having completely understood nearly every single thing another person has said since the day you met them. It's been like that since they sat together in Ms Hedge's horrifyingly dull history class in Year 8 and shared a textbook and commentary on the teacher's unhinged outfit. And they've never looked back.

He rubs his palms on his grey school pants as she sits down. Then he immediately swipes his hand through his sandy hair. She knows exactly why he's being a fidgety weirdo too. His new girlfriend is sneaking off from her school today to eat lunch with them.

"You're nervous," she sings.

"Of course I am." He rubs his legs again. "My girls eating lunch together? Terrifying."

"Your girls? You make us sound like a harem." She picks up her roll and inspects it.

"What are you expecting to see in that sandwich? Have you actually ever eaten anything but a cheese roll for lunch? Ever?"

Finn shrugs. "I change cheeses. Sometimes it's cheddar. Sometimes it's Swiss." She's never been an adventurous eater. "Anyway, some of us are too busy with our more pressing life commitments to bring handcrafted meals every day." She eyes his bento-style lunchbox, jammed with a rainbow array of healthy edibles. "Your mum really needs to go back to work. She's clearly bored stupid."

"Bored *and* a post-chemo health nut. It's all raw and grains at my house." He picks up a piece of purple cabbage. "This, apparently, is food. I'd always thought it was merely decorative. Can I come to your house for some carbs soon?"

"So what you're really saying is that you're jealous of my cheese roll?"

"I'm not saying anything at all."

"Yeah, right."

In a blur of energy and wispy, dyed-blonde hair, Rosie arrives. Finn can tell Dan's really into her, because he stutters a little as he introduces them. "Y-you remember Finn, right?"

Rosie rests her hand on Dan's shoulder and gives Finn a sunny smile. "Of course. Hi. How was your camp?"

"It was great." Finn eyes Rosie's jeans and loose, long hair—the perks of going to state school.

"Finn met a lady there," Dan says.

"Awesome." Rosie drops cross-legged onto the ground and turns to Dan, "Hey, remember the community group thing I was telling you about? The one Andy was asking you about making YouTube videos for?"

"Yeah."

"They might have to shut it down."

"Why?"

She snags a piece of carrot from his lunch and shrugs. "Funding issues. Or maybe conservative assholes disguised as funding issues. Who knows?"

"That's crap."

"Totally," she says, munching. "We're trying to come up with a plan to attract attention to it. Will you help if we need video?"

"Of course."

"What's the group?" Finn asks.

"It's this queer-friendly space for under-eighteens. Down on Leight Street, near the old mattress factory. You know it?"

"No."

"The building's shitty, but the people are great. Andy's practically lived there since he came out."

"Who's Andy?"

"Oh, sorry." Rosie laughs. It's an obnoxious snort of a thing for someone so delicate, which makes Finn like her even more. "My twin. So now we're all trying to think of ways to get some attention to the cuts."

"You should help out, Finn," Dan says. "Sounds like your kind of gig."

"Why? Just because I kiss girls?" She slaps his knee. "Next thing I know, you're going to be asking me if I know every gay you meet."

"No. Because you're a crusader, like this one." He tips his chin at Rosie.

"Nothing wrong with that," Rosie says. "Not all of us want to spend our days ranting into cameras, waxing lyrical about sci-fi for fellow nerds."

"One hundred and twenty thousand YouTube subscribers can't be wrong."

"They could be, if they all have teeny tiny little brains."

"You got even more subscribers while I was gone," Finn says, eyes wide.

He gives her his best faux-modest look. "What can I say? I know my stuff."

Rosie turns to Finn. "You know, we've been together six weeks, and I've avoided watching a single sci-fi film."

"You lucky, lucky thing."

They smile at each other, and Finn knows that finally, *finally*, Dan has picked a winner.

The three of them banter for a bit, comparing school and life notes until Rosie checks her phone and jumps up.

"I've got to go. But, hey, if you do want to help, Finn, we could totally use extra brains on this. And it's a really cool place. I can let you know about our next meeting?"

"Uh, sure." How does Finn always manage to get herself roped into helping with things? What vibe does she give off that says *ask me*? "I'll try to come down."

"Cool, I'll message you." Rosie drops a quick kiss onto Dan. "And you'll help if we need you too, right?"

"Of course." He smiles up at her. "I told you I would."

Finn gets the feeling he'd say yes to anything Rosie asked.

"Good." Rosie kisses him again. "See you, guys." And she's off, bouncing across the lawn and through the front gate. Dan's smile as he watches her stride down the street is a sickening thing.

"She's great," Finn tells him before he can ask.

"Isn't she? She reminds me of you sometimes." He freezes. "Oh, wait, that's weird."

"Yep. Weird."

"I just mean because she's got all this energy. You don't look alike or anything." He's blushing. Actually blushing.

"Uh, I'm aware of that." There's no avoiding the fact that Rosie's a babe in a way that Finn could never be.

She has to laugh, because Dan still looks creeped out. "It's okay, don't freak. We're clearly pretty different. For example, she thinks you're hot."

He smirks but doesn't say anything.

It's not like this stuff hasn't come up before. When they first met, Finn sometimes worried that Dan was into her in a way she wasn't into him. She liked this skinny, nervous sweetheart with a biting sense of humour, but he didn't give her the tingles. But if he did like her back then, he never said or did anything about it.

It's annoying, when she tells people her best friend is a guy. They always ask her if she's ever "gone there" with him, like it's an inevitability that things will get complicated. But it never has. It's been a point of vague awkwardness from time to time, like now, but Finn only knows that she loves him to death and has no desire to touch him. And she's 99.999 per cent sure he's always felt the same.

"Hey, so Rosie and I had the commitment talk this weekend," he tells her, shutting his lunchbox. "I don't know why she thought we needed to have it. I'm not looking anywhere else. *Ever*."

"That's sweet. And gross." She hands him the rest of her roll. "Willa and I haven't talked about anything like that."

"Yeah, well, you have to give it some time before you talk about that stuff. Just let it happen for a bit, and see what's what."

She shoots him a look. "Hey, Wisdom Boy, don't do that thing where you get all sage and advice-y because you've been in a relationship for, like, a minute. Before Rosie came along, it'd been a long time between drinks for you too."

"Can't you just let me have this one thing? You're better at everything else."

"I guess." She elbows him. "By the way, that is so spectacularly not true."

"Whatever. So, what's she like? You barely told me anything the other night."

"That's because your mum kept yelling questions the whole time. You should have just given the phone to her."

"She missed you."

"I know. I'll come see her soon. Anyway, Willa's awesome. She's super serious and tough, but then she's kind of a secret softy. It's cute."

"So when can I meet her?"

"First *I* have to see her."

"When's that?"

"We're supposed to meet Friday." A hum of impatience crashes through Finn. It's only Tuesday. She lets out a little moan.

"What's wrong?"

"Friday's ages away."

He stares at her. "Wow. This girl's made you all weird and needy. Now I really want to see her."

"One, shut up. Two, get in line."

# CHAPTER 5

## Willa

Willa's in the library, using every minute of her free period to bury this maths chapter in her past. It will be one less thing to do tonight.

Behind her, a group of Year 8 girls back and forth between complaining about some group project they're supposed to be doing and discussing Melinda's chances of making up with Joel. Willa has no idea if Melinda is someone from TV or a girl who goes to Gandry, but either way the debate is intense.

She blocks them out and works steadily through the next forty minutes. With five minutes until the bell, she's only got one equation left to do. But right at the last hurdle, the temptation's too much. She slips her phone out of her pencil case and slides it under the cover of her maths text. It wouldn't exactly look good for an academic leader to be on her phone in study period, but she can't resist. She used to be able to leave her phone in her bag all day and not even think about it. Not any more.

But it's worth it because there's a message from Finn.

*Confession…*

Willa smiles. *Do share.*

The response is instant. *Waiting until Friday is really, really hard.*

*Tell me about it.*

*Two more days…*

*I know.*

*Unless…*

*What?*

*What time do you get back from school?*

*My bus usually gets in just after 4.*

There's a pause. *I have school council until four. What if I met you? Could you hang out for a minute? Or do you need to be home straight away?*

*I have to pick up Jack from soccer at 4:30 in Prince Park*

*Oh.*

Willa frowns. It's always like this. There's always something she's supposed to be doing. She's about to text *sorry* when there's another message.

*What if I met your bus and walked you there? I live near the park, remember?*

Willa can't help grinning. *Persistent, aren't you?*

*Oh, sorry! I don't mean to be pushy. I can totally wait 'til Friday.*

But Willa can't. *Don't be sorry. I was joking. Please meet me.*

*Okay. I'll be the weird, stalkery one lurking at the bus stop.*

A thrill jets through her as the bell rings. The girls behind her instantly start to complain they didn't get enough done. Surprise.

Willa didn't finish her work either. And it was totally worth it.

~ ~ ~

She finishes the last sum on the way home, working a dicey balance of textbook, notebook, and calculator on her lap.

The bus lurches along the busy roads, returning her to the northern suburbs. By the time they get to her stop, there's only a handful of Gandry girls left, crowded out by a horde of nonnas and their shopping trolleys who got on at the markets halfway between school and home.

When her notebook slips off her lap at a sudden stop, an old man next to her picks it up and mutters approvingly at her studiousness. She thanks him politely and wonders what he'd think if he knew she's sprinting through her homework so she can meet a girl in the park. A girl she hasn't stopped thinking about whether she's going to get to kiss in the park.

The bus swerves into her stop. She hauls her bag onto her shoulder and peers through the window. Finn's leaned against a brick wall, hunched over her phone. Willa just stares for a moment, struggling to compute the exquisite knowledge that the girl in the striped school dress, her hair blowing forward in the wind, is waiting for her. Just for her. Because that girl couldn't wait another two days.

They meet in the middle of the footpath. Finn squints into the sun, smiling and clutching a small, white takeaway cup. "Hi."

"Hi." Willa smiles, thinking how Finn looks different. Maybe it's seeing her here with the heavy urban grey as backdrop, instead of the strident green of camp. Maybe it's the demure pinstripe of her school dress and her hair looking like it knows what a brush is. Maybe it's the hint of eye make-up. She's like the smoother, city version of Finn.

They eye each other for a moment, and then Finn, ever the brave one, folds her into a brief hug. It's awkwardly platonic. A hug that feels like a lie, because it's pretending they are something they are not.

Willa panics at the strangeness of it all. Like she suddenly can't find their *them*-ness. This is exactly what she's worried about each night, in those lights-out moments when

Finn inevitably invades her thoughts. What if they can't find what they had at camp? What if it can't be shifted and still hold its form, instead collapsing like a piece of clay moved before it's solidified?

"You know," Finn says, "I usually hate it when people state the obvious, but I'm going to say it anyway: it's really, really good to see you." And that candid smile pulls Willa back from the brink. Because there she is. And here they are.

They stroll the asphalt stretch that splits the cool, green centre of the park. Finn checks her watch. "So, by my calculations, we have about fourteen minutes before you have to go get Jack."

"And how many seconds?"

"Don't tease. A good stalker always knows these things."

They drop their schoolbags and settle onto a bench. Finn turns and gives her a bashful smile. "Sorry I was all weird and desperate and couldn't wait to see you."

Willa laughs and shakes her head.

"Why are you laughing?"

"You shouldn't be sorry. I wanted to see you too." Willa's face is instantly hot. Why does she have to be so self-conscious?

"Good." That's all Finn says as she plucks Willa's hand out of her lap and weaves their fingers together on the bench.

Willa stares at the sudden cacophony of colour between them: the clash of blue check and purple stripe, the chipped bottle-green of the bench, the silvery residue of worn graffiti, Finn's freshly mulberry nails and her plain ones.

She looks up to see Finn smiling at her like it's a question. Like she's asking if it's okay to hold her hand here. Probably because Willa's the private one. But all Willa knows is that Finn's holding her hand on a bench in the park and how incredible it feels. It will have to be okay.

A clutch of kids stalks by in Willa's old school uniform. A guy with a straggling effort at a goatee leads the pack, mouthing off about some argument with a teacher as he tosses his bag high in the air and catches it. A pair of girls trails them, school shoes in hands, cutting straight through the pond that surrounds the broken fountain. As they clamber out, wet footprints ghost their steps. One of them eyes Finn and Willa and mutters something to her friend. She turns and stares, then shrugs.

"I wonder if they're talking about the fact we're holding hands or the fact that we're in two different school uniforms," Finn muses.

"Probably the uniforms." Kids at Willa's old school hated the Brunswick Hill kids on principle. "An interschool relationship? It's very Montague and Capulet."

"So, how is it being back in Gandry's clutches?"

They talk quickly, making a feast of the minutes. They even talk about the things they've already talked about on the phone, because it's different when they're together. Better.

It still stuns Willa how easily talk comes to her when she's with Finn. She never feels tongue-tied or too earnest like she does with girls at school. She tells Finn about Riley's meltdown over some science project about plants last night, and how it just got worse as Willa struggled to explain it simply enough so her sister will get it. "I'll never be a good teacher."

Then Finn tells her how a group of kids at her school got in trouble for making a GIF of the principal shaking his finger at them and putting it at the top of the online school newsletter. "I thought it was genius," she says.

"No one would dare do anything like that at Gandry."

"Kids at mine dare and then get detention for weeks. Hey, so is your nan feeling better now?"

"Well, she's not sick anymore."

"That's good." Finn's thumb grazes the back of her hand. "Right?"

"Yeah." Willa doesn't tell her that the worry's not gone, that even though Nan's better, she doesn't seem completely right. Sometimes Willa catches her stopping and taking long breaths as she works or sitting in her chair when she'd usually be buzzing around her garden. But Willa doesn't want to talk about it because that makes it real. Instead, she focuses on the sooth of Finn's thumb sliding across her hand.

They sit and watch the world trudge past until Finn checks her watch and clicks her tongue. "That went too quickly. So, are we still going to hang out on Friday?" she asks as Willa heaves her bag onto her shoulders.

"Do you still want to?" Sometimes she's scared Finn's going to change her mind, going to realise this was all just a dumb camp thing.

"Of course. Should we take your brother and sister to the movies, still? Some Disney Pixar whatever?"

"Are you sure?"

"Why not?"

Willa smiles. "Wait until you meet them."

"The Willa siblings don't scare me."

"They should. Hey, you don't have to walk me all the way there," she says as Finn turns for the soccer fields.

"Yes, I do. My place is on the other side of the fields, remember?"

"Of course." *Damn.* Because what Willa really means is they should say goodbye here. Because here, she can do it properly and not in front of a whole lot of gawking boy children and a brother who knows nothing about Finn.

Finn starts walking, but Willa grabs her hand, pulls her back to her, and kisses her. A whisper of a kiss, really, because she's too shy to dare anything more.

A slow smile spreads over Finn's face. She plays with Willa's blazer lapel, pulling her closer. "You look younger in uniform."

"Well, you look girlier in yours. I mean, not to say you don't look like a girl..." Willa blushes. "I just meant—"

"It's okay. I know what you mean." Finn takes hold of both her hands. "You kissed me first."

"I kissed you first." Willa leans in and does it again, like she means it this time. "And second."

"Good." Finn drags her back onto the path. "You're nearly caught up."

# CHAPTER 6

## Willa

"Shower and change, okay?" Willa pushes open the front door. "Then we'll start homework."

"Okay." Jack bolts upstairs, his too-big soccer shorts flapping around his knees.

She aims straight for the kitchen and the food smell. Nan's at the bench, stripping stems of basil, a loaf of bread cooling on a board on the stove. "How was school?" she asks without even looking up.

"Good." Willa dumps her bag by the dining table and leans over to sniff the loaf. One of her favourite smells. "We could buy bread. They have sourdough at the market."

"Doesn't taste the same."

"I know, but it's so much work, and y—"

"Hush, or you won't get any of my cashew pesto. Made with basil from the garden and biodynamic nuts from the market." Nan tosses a handful of leaves into the food processor and frowns. "Someone should bloody ask those climate change deniers why if the world isn't getting any warmer, I have basil thriving in late September."

Willa takes a branch and slowly adds to the pile of green sacrifices. "You should call the papers. Maybe they'll write about it."

Nan swats at her with a ravaged stem. "Don't be smart, my girl."

Every female under sixty is 'my girl' to Nan, a leftover of thirty years of wrangling girls into obedience at a country boarding school. It's always said in this part affectionate, part remonstrative way, as if she expects you're being naughty and she's onto you but can't help liking you anyway. And her students must have adored Nan's frowny affection, because they still write letters and send her Christmas cards and baby photos.

"Want help with the rest of dinner?"

"Helping like you are now?" Nan gestures at the one stem that Willa's managed to strip in the time it's taken Nan to finish the rest of the pile. "I'll be fine on my own. Anyway, you'll want to do your homework."

True. There's no avoiding the pile of books in Willa's bag. She tosses the stalk in the compost bin and heads for them.

"Did you have to stay back? You usually come home and get changed before you pick up Jack."

"No, I hung out in the park."

"You don't just hang out."

"I do sometimes." It's annoying how well Nan knows her.

"By yourself?"

Willa traces a crack in the chopping board so she doesn't have to meet Nan's eye. "No. With a girl I met at camp."

When she finally looks up, those grey-blue eyes are on her. Nan nods slowly and turns to run her hands under the tap. "Do you have something to tell me, Willa Brookes?"

"No." Willa heads for the stairs as if she suddenly remembered something vital she has to do. Something not-coming-out-to-Nan vital. But before she even reaches her bedroom, the guilt grabs her by the scruff of the neck and marches her back downstairs.

In the kitchen, Nan gives her a look. "So you do have something to tell me."

"I guess." Willa stares into the sunlight streaming through the back door.

"You met someone at camp?"

"Yes."

"And are you seeing this girl?"

If Willa were Riley, she'd tell Nan no one calls it that anymore. But she's not. She's Willa. Stilted and weird and making this as awkward as she possible. "Yes."

Nan pushes a bowl of beans at her. "Right, then. You'd better top and tail those and tell me about her."

# CHAPTER 7

## Finn

"Yo, Finn!" It's Hana bustling at them at lightning speed.

"Hana!" Finn smiles wide. Besides Amy, she's barely seen her fellow Camp Nowhere survivors since they got home. The closest she's gotten was waving at Craig and Jessie in the hall yesterday.

"Hey, girl!" Hana folds Finn into a huge hug. "We miss your face." She high fives Amy. "You too," she tells her, then turns back to Finn. "Where've you been?"

"Catching up on schoolwork. Where's Zaki?"

"Talking to Ms Griggs. Hey, I just heard about the captain thing," Hana says, all undertone.

"What captain thing?" Amy asks.

Hana's hands go straight to her hips. "You guys didn't hear yet? Zehra told Zaki—whoa that's a mouthful—that she overheard the admin staff talking about it. They're picking the all-school captain from the Year 11s instead of the Year 12s next year."

Finn's eyes widen. "Really?"

"Yep. So you better get ready, girl. Now you won Camp Nowhere, there's no way it won't be you."

"There's plenty of ways it might not be me, actually, but thanks. So why are they changing it?"

"Don't know."

Amy shakes her head. "The kids going into Year 12 are going to be so pissed."

"Probably." Finn wonders how she'd have felt if her year missed their chance to take charge of the school.

"Hey, there's Zehra. Let's ask. Hey Zehr! Come here!" Hana waves furiously.

Finn turns to see Zehra, her vice captain, striding over to them. She towers over Finn with her long legs and high, frizzy bun. Glittering badges cover her lapel, announcing her worth to the school. Her smile is thin. "Welcome back."

"Thanks. It's good to see you," Finn says, even though she's pretty sure Zehra's anything but happy to see her. She's also certain Zehra loved her Finn-free month of playing captain. There's always been this tension between them. Well, it's mostly from Zehra. Finn's tried her best to just be all normal and "we're on the same side", but she knows Zehra thinks of her as the competition. Has done since they first turned up on the student representative council as hungry Year 7s.

"So, that thing about about the captain being a Year 11 next year?" Hana asks. "Did they officially decide?"

"I don't know, Hana." Zehra shoots her a look. "You weren't exactly meant to be spreading it around."

"It's *Finn*. And Amy won't tell."

"I honestly don't care enough to gossip." Amy shoots Finn a grin. "Sorry."

"And considering Finn's probably going to get the job, she might as well know, right?" Hana adds.

*Whoa.* Finn holds her textbook tighter and wishes she were anywhere but in this conversation. Hana's not exactly the queen of tact, but that was way klutzy. "That's not true. It could just as easily be Zehra next year," she says, trying to save face and feelings. "Or someone else."

Hana scoffs and goes to say something, but Finn fires her a look. Hana *finally* seems to get the picture and scrambles a recovery. "True, could be anyone. Anyway, I better find Zaki. See you guys." She bustles off down the hallway, leaving Finn to curse her very name.

"Yeah, I'm out," Amy says, not even bothering to make an excuse. "See you in labs."

Left alone, Finn turns and gives Zehra an awkward, conciliatory smile.

"So…" Zehra makes a show of checking her phone. "I was actually going to message you to see if you wanted me to go to the staff-student committee this Thursday. Seeing as how I wrote up the student brief before you got back."

"Uh, that's okay. I'm back now." Finn sees the flicker of disappointment in Zehra's eyes and backpedals. "Actually, maybe we should both go. You know, you can present the brief, and I'll catch up, ready for the next one."

"Good idea." Zehra sounds flat, though. "I better get to class." Another thin smile and she's off, leaving a trail of that sweet musk perfume that gets up Finn's nose every single time.

The minute she's out of sight, Finn beelines for the Humanities block. She follows the familiar passage past the Year 7 classrooms with their childishly cheerful posters and timelines and along the ranks of "favourites" display shelves. Then she ducks around the bend to the little alcove office where she knows they'll be hiding right up until the bell rings. She's just never figured out who they're hiding from more, the students or the other teachers. Maybe both.

When Mr Granger sees her, he drops his iPad onto his lap. "Thank God you're back! Zehra's been driving me crazy. That child is far too fond of lists."

Finn laughs and leans on the filing cabinet that keeps them partially hidden from sight.

"Dave." Ms Lehrer gives him a lip-pursed look over the essay in her hand before offering Finn a perfunctory smile.

Finn returns a nervous one. Ms Lehrer's so impeccable and remote with her perfect outfits and her perfect hair. Finn's glad she's not in any of her classes, because she doesn't know if she could actually conjure words in the face of all that hotness.

Mr Granger, on the other hand, is all pointy and shaggy and passable at a push. Finn's pretty sure the two of them have got something going on. A shacking-up kind of thing. They bring the same lunches every day. Dead giveaway. Not that she'd ever ask Mr Granger, or that he'd ever tell. Finn's relationship with the student-council advisor is strictly workplace. They have the perfect arrangement: Finn supplies student gossip within the bounds of loyalty, and he keeps her posted on the teacher-parent machinations that the other students aren't privy to.

"I know I'm not supposed to say things like that about the esteemed intermediate vice president," Mr Granger says. "but there are levels of earnest that even I, a student politician of many years in my own past, cannot endure."

Finn chokes back another giggle. Granger's always dropping truth bombs about and *to* the kids. But he's also kind and funny, so they take it pretty well.

"Zehra's a gun," he told Finn once. "And probably more efficient than you. But she's needs too much validation. No one has time for that in this world." He also said that the teachers like Finn because she's mature and gracious without being a suck. Finn not sure if the fact that he made those two comments in the same breath is inferring that Zehra *is* a suck.

"Hey, so I just heard that they might be picking school captain from the Year 11s next year?"

He scratches his cheek and nods. "It's as good as decided. After Emma Bale's little flip-out last year, the parent-teacher group decided it would be better that the Year 12s focus on their studies without all the extra responsibilities."

"Is next year's group upset? I mean, Emma was…" She hunts for a polite way to say it.

He grins. "A high-maintenance stress head who never should have been put in charge of anything?"

"Uh." Finn eyes Ms Lehrer, but she's either utterly engrossed in her essay or pretending to be. "I was actually just going to say a special case."

"Sometimes I think you two should swap roles," Ms Lehrer suddenly says.

"That's because Finn's a far more diplomatic person than I'll ever be." He picks up his iPad and plucks his jacket from the back of the chair. "Anyway, you'd better get cracking with the teacher-wrangling, because Zehra's been busting a gut since she got a whiff of this." He gives her a wide-eyed, theatrical stare. "She's after the crown, Harlow."

Finn laughs and salutes him. "Yes, sir."

"Now, get to class," he says in his best teacher voice.

# CHAPTER 8

## Finn

Willa's grandmother has laser eyes. It feels like she's scanning Finn for any faults or irregularities as she smiles her welcome from the wide green armchair. Willa told Finn that Nan used to be a schoolteacher, and looking down the barrel of her stare, it's not surprising.

"It's very nice to meet you, Finn," she says after what seems like a zillion years of scrutiny. She turns to Riley and Jack. "So, did you two enjoy the movie?"

They both nod, staring at the TV, their eyes deadened from the post-sugar comedown.

"Good. Then toilet, teeth, and bed."

"But it's Friday," Riley moans, tipping her head back in protest.

"Well done. They manage to teach you something at school." Nan swats at the back of her legs. "It's also late. Bed."

"Night, guys," Willa says pointedly.

Jack rips his eyes from the TV and gives his grandmother a half-hearted hug. "G'night."

"Good boy."

"Night, Will." He hugs his sister and gives Finn a timid smile as he edges past. He's barely spoken ten words tonight. He's adorable, though, with his little helmet of cropped black hair and his big brown eyes that stare like they're trying to take in absolutely everything at once.

Besides, Riley more than made up for his silence. She not talking now, though. She's standing in the middle of the living-room rug, pretending to be utterly transfixed by whatever is on.

"*Night*, Riles," Willa says in her warning voice.

"Yes, goodnight, madam," Nan adds, even firmer.

Finn would be scuttling to bed if these two were telling her to, but Riley just lets out a slow huff and drags her eyes from the screen. "Night," she mutters, doling out an unwilling peck on Nan's cheek. She drags her feet across the living room, the picture of despair.

"It was nice to meet you," Finn says, trying not to grin at the theatrics.

Suddenly Riley's all sunshine and smiles. And the next thing Finn knows, her skinny little arms are wrapped around her waist. "Night, Finn. Thanks for the movie." She turns to Willa. "Thanks, Will," she says, way less enthusiastically. And she's gone.

"She seems to like one of us," Nan says.

"Finn said she's into some TV show Riley likes, and it was insta-love," Willa says, rolling her eyes.

"She didn't talk to me for the first half an hour, but then…" Finn smiles and shakes her head. "Boom."

Nan settles back into her chair and appraises Finn again. There's a sweetness to her stern, though. Not one you have to burrow for, like you do with Willa.

"Need the kettle on?" Willa picks up an empty cup from the table next to Nan.

"No, thank you, my girl." She takes Willa's wrist and shakes her arm affectionately.

The sight gives Finn this warm feeling. She likes seeing Willa in this house with her family. She seemed so alone at camp.

"I know what you can do, though." Nan turns to Finn. "Do your parents cook?"

Finn nods.

Nan shakes Willa's wrist again. "Take Finn out the back and cut her some of the basil and new parsley. I've got hoards of it, and I'm sure her mother could use it. Oh, and cut her some of the kale too." She turns back to Finn. "It's all one hundred per cent organic."

"Wow. Thank you," Finn says, because she has no idea what else to say. But then she never thought she'd be granted the gift of that leafy hipster manna from someone's grandmother.

The back of the narrow little house opens into a kitchen and dining area. It's lamp-lit and cosy with green walls. There's a solid wooden table by the sliding back doors. Bunches of herbs and garlic and chillies hang from the windows.

Willa grabs a plastic bag from a drawer and shoves the sliding door open. "Nan's got this thing about organic food. I don't think a pesticide has darkened these doors for at least five years. She's sure she's going to save us all from cancer."

"I hate kale," Finn whispers as they step out into the night. "It's so rabbit-y."

"I don't like it either, but I'm not about to admit that to Nan." She grabs Finn's hand and draws her into the garden.

As soon as they're standing in the shadowy sprawl of a tree, Willa pulls Finn to her and kisses her. It's fierce and soft at the same time and makes Finn lean hard into that silken feeling she gets when Willa's pushed up close like this. Her eyes drift closed as Willa presses a chain of small, sweet kisses up to her ear and back before dropping another onto her lips.

"I think you're finally all caught up."

Willa's answering smile is a lazy, beautiful thing.

Finn idly sketches the sweep of her cheekbone with the tip of her finger before nuzzling her face into Willa's neck, breathing deep. She loves that Willa doesn't wear perfume, doesn't obscure the truth of herself with canned girl smell. Instead she's musk, skin, and clean-clothes smell. It's honest, like Willa.

"So, how are you feeling about seeing your dad tomorrow?" Willa asks eventually.

"Good, I guess." The last time Finn saw her father, she was marching away from his car, struck by a storm of anger. "It'll be weird, though."

"Do you miss him?"

"I do," Finn admits. Of everything, she misses just hanging out with him. Sitting around after school, chatting about whatever. Doing the things that they always did, like plotting dinner and watching the news. Now, when she gets home, the house is silent.

She elbows these thoughts out of the way and concentrates on what's right in front of her. On the electric feeling that comes with kissing Willa.

Tinny pop music suddenly trickles out an open window, and Willa steps back, rolling her eyes. "That's Riley. We should stop before she sees us. She likes to dance while she gets ready for bed."

Finn has to smile. Riley's everything Willa said she'd be and more. All sass and mouth for an eleven-year-old, but kind of sweet to boot. "I didn't think she was going to talk to me at all at first." When Finn met them at the park, Riley just stared curiously at Finn from the swings, and then kept her distance on the tram, sitting on the other side of Willa. But later, by the time the movie was over, high on sugar and soft drink, she chattered at her all the way home.

"I knew she'd do that." Willa crouches over a garden bed and then passes her a handful of leaves. "She asked a billion questions about you before you came and then went completely shy the minute you showed up."

"Well she's definitely over it now." Finn inhales the cocktail of green smells and drops the bunch in the bag. "Does she know you're gay?"

"No. I never thought of telling her. I guess because there's been nothing to tell." Willa holds out a handful of kale.

Finn wrinkles her nose and holds out the bag.

"It's good for you, remember? Riley asks me why I don't have a boyfriend sometimes, and I say I just don't. And because she loves the sound of her own voice and because she thinks I'm socially useless, she just starts giving me advice on how to get one."

"She's funny."

"Sometimes. I guess I better tell her now."

"Not until you're ready."

Willa smiles and hands her another bunch of kale. "I'm ready."

# CHAPTER 9

## Willa

If Willa was asked, she'd probably would have predicted that life after camp would just be more of the same. Maybe she'd have some new outdoorsy skills under her belt and a few more clues about what being a leader means. But she wouldn't have expected anything to actually change. And not in the delicious, earthquake ways it has. Just another thing she's gotten wrong lately.

For starters, she wasn't expecting to have actual friends at Gandry. But apparently she does. Yesterday Ms Ikenishi announced to Willa's Japanese class that they need to prepare five-minute dialogues in groups of three to present next term.

As soon as she was done talking, Amira nudged Eva and turned to Willa, who was sitting at the desk behind them. "We've so got this."

"Hey, maybe ask Willa if she wants to work with us first," Eva said.

"But why wouldn't she?" Amira was a picture of disbelief.

"Yes, why wouldn't I?" Willa added, straight-faced.

Amira grinned. "See?"

That made Willa feel a slide of relief. Group projects have always been awkward territory. It's not that people don't want Willa in their groups. Of course they do. She's academic leader and top in three subjects. Willa's pure value-added. But she's always been a strategic choice. Before camp, no one would ever have automatically turned to her or nudged her, like working together is a given. Not just because they *want* to.

Then there's the staggering (still) fact that there's a girl in the world who likes Willa so much that she misses her when she's not around, in the way Willa used to hope a girl might one day. And this girl is every bit the breath stealer Willa hoped she'd be. Yesterday she got a text from Finn when she was on the tram home with Kelly. It was a photo of Finn's legs stretched high up on a rock somewhere in Tasmania, the sweeping view of ocean laid out in front of her. It said, *There's a space on this rock next to me. It's very annoying you're not in it.* Willa smiled so hard that it made her blush and glance nervously to see if Kelly noticed.

And now there's the fact she's about to come out to her little sister.

Riley doesn't even look up when Willa comes in to the bedroom. She's on Willa's bottom bunk, eyeballs deep in her tablet, her curtain of dark hair muting all the little bleeps and sploshes coming from whatever non-homework thing she's doing.

Willa perches next to her. "Hey, Riles?"

"I'm going to start in a second, I swear."

"No, it's not that." Willa traces the swirling purple pattern on the doona cover. "I want to talk to you."

Riley's eyes stay glued to the screen. "Yeah, what?"

Willa frowns. These things never go like they do on TV. Isn't Riley supposed to recognise there's a meaningful moment in the making and pay immediate sisterly attention? Nope. It looks like Willa's on her own. "Um, so, you know how some people are gay?" She cringes. Wow, clumsy.

"Uh, yeah," Riley drawls in her best 'duh' voice. "We're doing a project on it at school."

"A project on gay people?"

"I don't know. A thing on equal rights or something."

"Hang on, you don't *know* what you're studying at school?"

"It's not my fault. Mrs Roland makes everything so boring. I miss Mr Majhidi."

"I know, but even if you don't like your teacher, you still have to concentrate. You're in Grade Six next year. Then it's high school."

"I *know.*" Riley sighs impatiently and taps at her screen. "Because you keep telling me."

This conversation is seriously straying. "Well, anyway, I just wanted you to know that *I'm* gay."

"*Really?*" Riley's small, brown eyes are suddenly bug wide. Now she's paying attention.

"Really." Willa's face burns.

"Since when?"

How do you answer that? How would Willa even know? "Probably always."

Riley keeps staring, like she's busily rearranging her view of Willa around this. "So am I allowed to tell people?"

"Like who?"

"Like people at school. My friends."

"I don't know. I guess you can if you want." Isn't this the part in the TV show when Riley's supposed to say something astonishingly sage and accepting for her age, not ask if she can gossip?

"Awesome." Riley settles back over her tablet. "Brittany's got a gay uncle, and Lefah's neighbours are lesbians, but no one's got a sister. They're going to freak."

"Right." Trust Riley to see this little bomb-drop as beneficial to her popularity power base. She goes back to her game, like Willa's confession is just a ripple in her day.

When Willa gets to the door, she turns. "And Riles, you know Finn?"

"Yeah?" Riley's head springs up again. "Oh, wow, she's your girlfriend, isn't she?"

"Yeah."

She bounces up and down. "That is so cool. Finn's really cool. And cute." She nods approvingly. "You did good, Willa."

"Gee, thanks." Something tells her Riley won't catch the sarcasm. But as she trots down the steps to find Jack, Willa has to smile at her sister's total nonchalance. If only everyone were like that.

# CHAPTER 10

## Finn

Finn stares, sleepily mesmerised by the water lapping at the wood below her dangling boots. The thought of its temperature makes her shiver, though. Even with her jacket zipped to the neck, it's arctic here. Tasmania apparently has no idea that spring sprang weeks ago across the water.

A takeaway coffee cup is dangled in her face. "Double shot, no sugar."

She clasps it reverently. "Thank you."

"You're welcome." Her dad, Martin, settles on the weather-greyed wood next to her. He takes a long sip, chased by a sated sigh.

This is something they've always done together well: mainline coffee and ease into the morning.

"You can see the peak today," he says, tipping his chin at the mountain.

She stares back at the city, overlooked by its hulking, rocky sentinel. They drove up there yesterday. They'd gone for the view of the city but found themselves above the clouds, unable to see anything but a sea of white.

The thrill of being higher than the weather, of sitting under a blue sky with those fluffy masses rolling below kept them there until they were chilled to the bone. And just before they left, the skies finally cleared, revealing the sweep of land and ocean below. Finn couldn't resist taking a picture and sending it to Willa.

Afterwards, they thawed out in the gallery across the harbour and then walked on a wild, windswept beach, where both rain and sun happened in the space of an hour. They tried clumsily to catch up and to ignore the gaping hole in their conversation: the fact that he is here and she and her mum are there. And that this state of things is an excruciating—and apparently ongoing—limbo. Still, it feels good to be with him again. A home of sorts, even if it's not *home*.

The wharf is empty for once. All the other tourists have gone to the market. Finn and her dad, creatures of habit they are, woke early and wandered through as the stallholders set up. Then they read the paper together in the only open café they could find.

They've finally found their groove. Just two hours before her plane makes the short leap home, she can feel them coalescing again. In their own way. Finn's mother comes at her hard, all loving nag and advice. It's mild to very annoying, depending on the case. But with Dad, it's always been like they're old friends, coexisting side by side.

Maybe it was because he worked from home so much. He was the one to pick her up from kinder and primary, and so he was there to tell the day's stories to. And he always, always talked to her like she was a grown-up. He was the one who explained the world to her.

She almost wishes they hadn't found this place again, because now it's going to be even harder to leave him. Especially when he seems to be liking this place so much, even if the weather's crap and the coffee subpar. It scares her that he so obviously loves Tasmania. Every time he says something good about it, she gets this gnarl in her chest and wants to turn and snap at him, "Well, you can't stay." Wants to remind him he has a life elsewhere.

He's been writing. Some kind of big project, but he won't say what. He's always wanted to write long-form articles. Used to talk about it with his friends, a few beers in. But he was always too busy. Not now.

He tips up his cup, draining the last drops.

"Wow, that's got to be some kind of speed record." Her own coffee is still a warm weight in her hand.

"Probably." He shifts closer, his heavy brown boots hanging next to her smaller ones. "So, tell me, this girl you've met?"

"Mm?" Finn tips her face as the sun makes a fleeting appearance.

"You know what I'm going to ask you, don't you?"

"Who would she vote for if she was old enough?"

"No, smart-ass."

She doesn't have to look at him to know he's smiling. "Okay, then, does she know how to use proper grammar and punctuation?"

He laughs. "No. Well, I'd ask both those eventually, but not yet."

"What, then?"

"Is she special?

"That's kind of a cheesy TV-dad question coming from you," she says.

"Can't help it. I just have a feeling it needs to be asked."

How does he know that? She hasn't spoken much about Willa this weekend. Even though she's thought about her. A lot. "Yeah, she is."

"Good. I hope I get to meet her."

"Well, if you ever plan on coming home, you might."

Her words drop like weight between them. She clenches her jaw and waits for him to fill the silence with a response. He doesn't. All she sees in his reaction is that same clenched jaw and the tightening around his eyes he'd get after a fight with her mother.

Guilt makes her veer topics. "And, FYI, I don't know who she'd vote for, but I can tell you that even her text messages are painfully grammatically correct."

"Well, that's a relief." He smiles but keeps his eyes fixed on the water.

A tourist boat lurches in to dock on the other side of wharf, the cartoonish sound of its horn filling the air. Windblown tourists step off the gangplank and turn straight for the markets. A little girl chases a seagull, screeching louder than the bird she's terrorising.

"So, how's your mum?"

"You should ask her yourself."

"I do. We talk most days."

Finn has to work to cover her surprise. "Well…good."

"I miss her a lot."

"Good," she says again. Then she looks him square in the eye so he can't avoid her this time. "So when are you coming back?"

Another silence hangs. "I don't know yet."

"Well, hurry up and know." She stands. "We should get going. My flight's soon."

He stares up at her. "I'm sorry, Finno."

"Yeah, you both keep saying that." She folds her arms and watches another boat coming in. "But you know it doesn't really help, right?"

"I know."

"Then let's go." She turns and walks towards the car without waiting for him.

# CHAPTER 11

## Willa

Amira's late.

"She had some fight with her brother about him driving her here or something," Eva tells Willa as she leads her to the living room.

Eva's family's apartment is light and white and display-home tidy. Kind of like Eva. Or so Willa thinks until she witnesses Eva's room.

"I know," Eva mumbles as she hunts out her textbook from a towering pile on her desk. "It's a mess. Believe it or not, I tidy it all the time. But it just ends up this way again."

"This way" is catastrophic. Like, Riley-level catastrophic—if Willa let Riley have her piggy way. There are piles of clothes on every surface, and books and papers and girl stuff wherever there are not. And, for reasons Willa can't fathom, a potted palm sits in a dish in the middle of what may or may not be a rug under the piles of crap.

She's staring at it when Eva turns around. "Oh yeah, I haven't quite decided where that should go yet."

Willa wants to say, "So putting it in the middle of the room seemed like a good idea?" but doesn't. She stares at Eva's impeccable hair and outfit. How did that come into being in this hell-den? It seems scientifically implausible.

They arrange their books on a large table in the living room, where leafy tropical plants nudge the windows and a small deck overlooks a park.

The apartment is silent. At this time of day, Willa's house would be alive with sound. Nan's talkback radio. Riley singing. Jack's games. Footsteps running up and down the stairs. She's not sure she would know how to live in such calm.

Eva brings in a plate of biscuits and dried fruit from the kitchen. "Mum and Dad are still at work. Jason's in Thailand." She pushes the plate closer to Willa.

"Thanks." Willa takes a dried apricot, biting into its sunshine taste. "What's he doing?"

"Nothing. Being a professional slacker."

Sounds like Kelly's brother. Except Dave's idea of doing nothing is gaming and smoking until his eyes fall out, not holidaying in exotic locations. Willa's sure he would do it that way if he could afford it.

The minute Amira arrives, she grabs a biscuit and launches into an epic tale of her fight with her brother.

It's kind of entertaining, how chaotic and extravagant Amira is. Especially for someone who looks so high-maintenance, with her overblown eye make-up and just-been-to-the-salon hair. She rants through her mouthful of biscuit, her story long and loud and jam-packed with "then he said" and "so I said". Eva just listens, like she's used to it, rearranging the snack plate around Amira's grazing.

Finally, Willa checks her phone. There's only an hour before she has to catch her bus back and take Riley to the pools for swimming lessons. She starts chewing her lip, wondering if the story will ever end.

"Hey, come on, Mir. We should get started," Eva says finally. "Willa's only got a little time." She grabs a pencil and then frowns. "Crap, I forgot my vocab. I'll be back in a sec." She dashes off to her room.

Amira gives Willa a sly grin. "Did you see it?" She points towards Eva's bedroom. Willa nods.

"It's terrifying, isn't it?"

"What's terrifying?" Eva asks as she sits back down with her book.

"Nothing." Amira's all innocence.

Eva turns to Willa, eyes narrowed. "What was she saying?"

"She just asked if I'd seen your room."

"And what did you say?"

Willa purses her lips.

"It's okay. Stop being polite. You can say it."

"I don't know how you find your way out of it in the mornings. That's what my nan would say."

"Yeah, it's next level," Amira says. "They could make a whole season of a reality show about cleaning that pigsty. A total makeover while you confront your inner-hoarder-chaos monkey." Then she jumps and shimmies, veering to another topic as only Amira knows how to do. "Hey, Will, how's it going with your little blonde? Have you seen her since we got back?"

"Little blonde?" Eva says before Willa can. "You are a testament to feminism. Her name is Finn."

Amira sighs loudly, like now Eva's the one wasting time. "How is *Finn*?" she asks dutifully.

"She's good," Willa replies.

"So it's on? You're all serious and stuff?"

"I guess." Willa shrugs. "We went out on Friday. And I'm supposed to meet her mum this week."

"Oh, wow. That's serious. Mothers hate me. Something about me just screams bad influence, apparently."

"Maybe your mouth?" Eva suggests.

Willa can't help laughing, even though she's found herself playing third wheel to yet another best friendship. It's Kelly and Maida all over again.

Amira slaps Willa's leg. "Don't worry. As long as her mum's okay with the gay bit, she'll totally love you. I mean, what's not to love? You're a parent's wet dream. All mature and responsible and academic leader-y."

"She's totally right," Eva tells her.

Willa hopes so. She's been trying not think about the dinner invite, sent by the Finn Mother herself. Just the thought makes her all fluttery, and not in the good way.

When she checks her watch, another ten minutes have slid by. "Guys, we really need to get started." How can she explain everything she needs to do when she gets home? How she can't just rock up twenty minutes late, and everything will be okay?

"Yeah, we do," Eva says. "Mir, anything else you just need to get out of your system before we start?"

"Me?" Amira looks wounded for a split second. "No, well, except did you hear about Georgia B? She—"

"Stop!" Eva pushes Amira's textbook at her. "Don't worry," she tells Willa. "She's actually really good when she finally gets started."

"She'd better be," Willa mutters. "I need the marks."

"Ooh, I've poked the bear!" Amira opens her textbook and dutifully picks up her pen. "I promise I'll be good. *Kitto umaku ikuyo!*"

Willa has no idea what she's saying, and she's not sure if that's a good sign or not.

# CHAPTER 12

## Finn

Dan's girlfriend Rosie may be a sweetie, but she sucks at introductions. When they arrive at the big brick building, she just flaps her hands at the small crowd sitting around the boardroom table and says, "Everybody, this is Finn. Finn, this is everybody." Then she darts off to chat to an older guy standing by an ancient photocopier.

The community centre is a partitioned section of some sort of larger warehouse space, like it used to be the office for a factory. Somewhere beyond them, Finn can hear thuds and bangs and a weird grinding sound. Maybe it still is a factory.

She's standing and staring, hands thrust in pocket, when a girl with a short shock of curly black hair and the biggest hoop earring Finn's ever seen on a human smiles and gestures at a seat next to her. She's mid-diatribe at a guy at the end of the table, though, and doesn't stop when Finn sits beside her.

A group of ten kids around Finn's age sits at the table, chatting and waiting for the meeting to start. She wonders if the boy talking to the black-haired girl is Rosie's twin. He's the only other Asian kid there, and he has the same delicate Cupid's bow and high cheekbones as Rosie.

"Hi there." The girl that leans over the table towards Finn is a welcome splash of colour in the industrial bland of the warehouse. She has brown eyes, ringed with the kind of eye make-up that pulls them surprised wide. Her dress is peacock blue, her lips a deep fuchsia pink.

"Hi. I'm Finn."

"I'm Bea." She points to a girl next to her. "And this is Nona." She curls a pale arm around the much smaller girl's neck. Nona looks up from her phone, wraps her arms around Bea, and kisses her cheek. "Say hi to Finn," Bea tells her between kisses.

Nona readjusts her cap over her short hair, eyes Finn up and down, and nods. "Hi."

"Hey." There's a brief silence as the three of them appraise each other. "I love your dress," Finn says to Bea.

"Thanks." Bea smooths her fingers over the deep neckline. "I made it myself." She rolls her eyes. "Plus-size designers seem to think fat girls only like floral or neon. Why is that?"

Finn laughs. "No idea."

"Neither do I." Bea leans forward. "But thanks for laughing. Most people get funny when I used the dreaded *F* word."

"I've never seen you here before," Nona says suddenly to Finn. It sounds like an accusation.

"You haven't. I only just heard about this place when Rosie invited me to the meeting."

"Rosie's recruiting?" Bea raises an eyebrow. "For a het, she's the biggest gay enabler I know."

"I used to be so sure she just didn't know she was gay yet, but now she's got this *boyfriend*, apparently." Nona wrinkles her nose. "Gross."

"A boyfriend who's my best friend," Finn tells her.

Nona screws up her lips, as if to say "noted", and then sits back, arms folded, eyeing her again. And Finn can't tell if her stare is hostile, flirty, or just plain rude.

There's a silence. Finn hunts down some conversation. "So, Rosie says they want to close this place down?"

"Which would suck," Bea says. "I've been coming here for a year, and it's amazing. Not everyone's here today, but during school holidays there's a heap of us, and we do some really cool stuff." She jerks her thumb at Nona. "This one's been coming here since she was, like, twelve."

Nona nods. "Best place to hide from my parents."

"They're really not okay with the gay," Bea tells her.

"Really not okay," Nona says. "I had to hide at a friend's house for a week after I cut off my hair."

"Are they okay about it now?" Finn asks.

"Hell no. But there's nothing they can do."

"I'm lucky," Bea says. "My dad's somewhat cool. What about your parents?" Then she holds up a hand. "Oh, wait, you're not straight, are you? I mean, it's cool if you are.

This place is open to "and friends". But except for Rosie, it pretty much tends to be a queer catchment zone."

"I'm bi," Finn says. "And except for a bigoted dinosaur of a grandmother, everyone's pretty cool."

Nona sits up. "Hey, I heard a great joke the other day. What's the best thing about being bisexual?"

"What?" Bea asks while Finn grits her teeth.

"Double chance of a date on Saturday night."

Bea pulls a face. "That's not a good joke. Who told you that was a good joke?"

"Me." Nona pouts. "It is a good joke."

"No, it's lame."

Nona turns to Finn. "You liked it, right?"

"Not even the first time I heard it," Finn tells her.

"Ha." Bea jabs a finger into Nona's side. "See?"

Nona folds her arms and digs her chin into her chest. "Whatever."

"Aw, baby's sad because no one likes her joke," Bea coos. She leans in and kisses Nona's cheek over and over until Nona melts, giggles, and grabs her. Next thing Finn knows, they're so deep in PDA, she has to look the other way.

When they're done, and Nona's bouncy and kiddish and pleased with herself again, she turns back to Finn. "So, are you more into girls or guys?" She wags an eyebrow up and down.

Why does Finn get the feeling she's asking this more to get a rise than out of actual curiosity? "It doesn't really work like that."

"But you must—"

"Hey, sorry." Rosie drops into the seat next to Finn. "I had to talk to Costa about something before the meeting. You okay?" She waves a hand at Bea and Nona. "You've met these guys?"

"Don't worry, we took care of her," Bea says. "Nona's currently interrogating her about her sexuality, but I planned to intervene before she got too nosy or ridiculous."

"Too late," says the earrings girl, joining the conversation. "I heard that terrible joke."

Nona holds her hands up. "Look, I just never got bisexuality, okay?"

"What's for you to get, dipshit?" Earring Girl leans over the table and slaps Nona's cap down over her face. "I don't get why you baby dykes have to act like mouthy little teenage boys just because you dress like them."

Nona cackles and readjusts her hat. "At least I don't think hula hoops are jewellery."

"Ooh, them's fighting words," says the boy who may or may not be Rosie's brother. He grins at Finn. "Welcome! I'm Andy." Case closed. He points at Earring Girl. "And she's Kayah."

Bea grins at Finn. "And we're just one big happy family."

"I'm sensing that," Finn says.

~ ~ ~

Finn traipses home from the community centre, exhausted and strangely charmed by the bombastic little bunch of people she just met. They spent the hour brainstorming ideas to attract attention to the centre's plight, and even though they didn't come up with anything, she's already tempted to go to the next meeting.

Actually, maybe it's because they *didn't* come up with anything. If there's one thing Finn can't resist, it's a challenge. And it's kind of fun talking to other gay kids. Finn doesn't really know any of the handful at her school, except to say hi,

Her phone starts ringing as she turns into her street. It's Anna. Finn picks up, grinning. "Yes, hello, who is this please?"

"Very funny. I'm so sorry we haven't caught up. Worst sister in the world."

"Half-sister," Finn reminds her.

"Oh, that hurts."

"Okay, you don't completely suck. Not yet."

"My excuse is that I've been on night shift. And believe me when I tell you I've now seen enough babies being born. Thrill's gone."

"I don't know if it would ever have been there for me." Finn stops and sniffs a fat orange rose listing over a fence.

"I feel really bad," Anna says. "I haven't even spoken to you about what's happening with Dad and your mum—which I only just found out about when I rang Dad the other night, by the way. I'm so sorry, Finn. It must suck."

"It does. A lot."

"Are you okay?"

"I'm okay. Just scared."

"They're solid. They'll figure it out."

Finn plucks at a dry leaf, rubbing it to pieces between her fingers. "I hope so."

"Look, let's meet up sooner rather than later. How about Friday? I'll have slept all day, so I might be a bit groggy, but we can grab dinner before I have to go back on shift?"

"I can't. Willa, this girl I met at camp is coming over to dinner. You know how my mum likes to do the embarrassing invite-them-for-dinner thing?"

"You met someone? Anything else major that I should know about? Any career changes?"

"No. That's it, I promise."

What about Sunday night?"

"Sure," Finn says. "That'd be great."

"Great I'll see you then. I gotta go to work."

Finn hangs up, smiling. Because she cannot wait to see Anna. Because no matter what Finn says to Anna, she'll get it. She always does. Finn didn't even know she was missing out on having a sister until she found out she had one. Now she wouldn't give it up for anything.

There's no sign of life when she reaches her house. No lamplight or flickering blue promise of the television shining between the curtains. Her mum's at work late again.

Staring at the darkened windows, she wishes she'd gone to Dan's for dinner. Too late now.

# CHAPTER 13

## Willa

Finn's mum, Anita, is the source of Finn's grounded energy and her small, compact build. She shakes Willa's hand when they meet, her brown eyes vice-principal keen.

Willa does her best to smile, even through a clenched jaw.

The house is modern and small, busy with books and stacks of paper and a large dog bed by the window, filled with fur. It takes Willa a little while to realise the pile of white is actually two dogs and a cat curled up together.

"They say threes never work, but those guys?" Finn shakes her head as one of the small white dogs opens one eye, regards Willa, and closes it. "It's like a weird cult love-in."

They eat takeaway at the counter that separates the tiny kitchen from the living area. Willa's questioned over dinner, of course. But Finn must have briefed Anita already, because she asks about Nan and her brother and sister but not her parents. And Willa's grateful. It's awkward enough without that conversation.

Once the requisite getting-to-know-you questions dry up, Willa relaxes enough to eat more than a grain of rice at a time. She tunes in to Finn's workshopping over whether to help her friend with a project at a local community centre.

"I don't know if I'll have time to help and try and do my captain stuff," Finn says. "Especially now a Year 11 is going to be captain next year. I only just found out, and Zehra's been all over it while I've been gone."

"Is there a student vote for captain?" Willa asks.

"No. Just the teachers and the principal." She prods at a piece of chicken with her fork. "I've got so much catching up to do if I want them to even consider me."

"That can't be true." Anita serves herself more rice. "You've been captain all year. You've been away on camp, being an ambassador for your school. *And* you won a prize for them while you were there. You've hardly been lazing around. The staff will recognise that."

"I guess. I just don't know if I can manage both."

"Well, what's more important to you?"

"I don't know. I want to help at the centre. It's fun, and—I don't know—it feels *important*. Some kids really need that place. I'm lucky. Imagine if Grandma was my mum? I'd need it too."

Anita sighs. "Possibly you would. She thought Martin's sister having a baby before she was married was a criminal act. I don't know what she'd have done if one of them had been gay."

"My grandmother's still holding out hope it's a stage," Finn tells Willa. "Anyway, I want to help. It's just a time thing, figuring out if I have enough to do both and everything else."

If there's one thing Willa can sympathise with, it's the pain of prioritising. "Just remember, being senior school captain looks really good on paper," she reminds Finn, thinking of all the uni and job applications they'll need to do in a couple of years. Willa already knows what she'd do. It wouldn't even be a decision, let alone a hard one. But, then, she's not Finn.

"But good for what? Isn't it better to do something that's good for the world?" Finn asks. "If I'm just being school captain for resume fodder, isn't that kind of self-serving in comparison to helping keep a space that's *needed*?"

"I guess." Willa would still choose captain.

"You're certainly your father's child," Anita tells her.

Willa can't tell if that's meant to be a good thing or a bad thing, the way Anita says it, all resigned and quiet.

"I'd personally say that you should focus on being school captain," Anita says. "You're already doing that role. Don't bite off more than you can chew." She smiles wearily. "Like there's ever been any point in telling you that. Anyway—" She gets up from her seat. "I must go and do some work. Are you two doing anything tonight?"

"We'll probably just hang in my room and watch a movie or something," Finn says.

Willa pushes a forkful of food in her mouth, trying to smother the instant, delicious flicker of anticipation at having some time alone with Finn.

"Okay, well, it was very nice to meet you, Willa." Anita rests a hand lightly on her shoulder as she passes. "I'm glad you could come over."

Willa hurriedly tries to chew and swallow her food in time to reply. "Y-you too," she mumbles, hand over her mouth. "And thank you for dinner."

"Don't choke," Finn teases as her mother carries her laptop to the sofa and drops down on it with a sigh.

When they've tidied away their plates, Finn grabs Willa's hand. "Come on."

"Remember the rule," Anita calls from the couch.

"I know." Finn leads Willa down a short passage and into an orderly, colourful little space. Half the bed is covered in a rainbow chaos of pillows, and her bookshelf is piled neatly with books. Willa can tell from the stack of slender kid-book spines on the bottom that all Finn's lifetime literary treasures have a place there.

There are posters on the walls, mostly art prints, but Willa's eye is immediately drawn to a small one pinned to the wall above the desk. It's painted on a piece of paper about the size of two postcards—a landscape, sort of—but everything is done in this swirling watercolour, like the edges of everything are made from coloured wisps of smoke. It's fragile and lovely.

"This is one of yours, isn't it?" she says.

"Yup." Finn switches on a bright yellow lamp and shuts her curtains to the night. "It's one of my favourites. I've been meaning to get a frame for it so it doesn't get messed up, but I keep forgetting."

"You should. It's beautiful. Nothing can happen to it."

"Yes ma'am," Finn says as she slides her arms around Willa's waist.

"You're so stupidly talented." Willa turns to face her. "So, what's the rule that your mum was talking about?"

"Door-open policy."

"What's that?"

"When I have, uh, *special guests* over, the door stays open." Finn grins and rolls her eyes. "Not that I have, like, a parade of people coming through or anything."

"Oh." Willa feels like such a child. Of course that's what it means.

"No rules like that at your house?"

"It hasn't really been necessary." Willa blushes. "I'm such a boring innocent."

"No, you're not. You're…" Finn shakes her head like she can't finish her sentence.

For the millionth time, Willa wonders how this girl happened to her. She wants to kiss her, but instead she stands, head tipped, listening for movement in the rest of the house.

"Don't worry. Wooden floors. You can hear her coming." Finn taps Willa's nose. "You're cute when you're nervous."

If there's one thing no one ever calls Willa, it's cute. But she might like it when it comes from Finn.

"Come here," Finn whispers, pulling her close enough to press her lips to Willa's.

In minutes they're sprawled on her bed in a kiss so deep Willa has to drag herself up for air. "Isn't this exactly what we're not supposed to be doing?"

"Mum knows we're together," Finn says. "She expects us to be kissing. I think the whole open-door thing is more of a make-sure-the-clothes-stay-on-while-we-kiss thing."

"Right." Willa's cheeks flame as she smooths her finger along a pale stretch of Finn's throat. This is a whole new world for her. Parents. Bedroom rules. Policing the potential of sex. All of it.

"So don't worry," Finn whispers, reaching for her again. "And come here."

And Willa obeys. Because this is where she knows she holds her own. In the social, normal stuff, Finn runs rings around her, while Willa is all awkwardness and patchy silences. But when the two of them are like this, curled around each other, Willa is just as capable. Somehow, without ever being aware she did, she knows how to make Finn pull in a breath. She knows the ways, with the right kind of kiss or with a finger slowly tracing a stretch of skin, to make Finn slide an urgent arm around her and pull her even closer. Here, Willa feels equal to the task of being in this thing they've become.

As they plunge into another kiss, Willa decides she almost likes Finn's mum's rule. Because while she's confident about what she can make happen, she's less confident about what she *should* make happen. Willa already knows, after camp, that Finn's cautious about moving too far too fast, but she's not sure exactly where the line is. Only that it exists. This way, with the door wide open, it's firmly drawn for them. Hands roam but never go truly astray. Breath gets heavy and limbs tangle, but it all happens in the enforced safety zones of over the clothes and above the waist.

And Willa's happy in the knowledge that she can just lie here and trace and retrace the smooth, half-moon curve of Finn's waist through her T-shirt, learning the lay of this land by heart and not worrying about what should happen next. With the door open, she can just wallow in the deliciousness of here and now, and not overthink a thing.

They kiss and kiss, and they don't stop until a rainbow avalanche of pillows ends in a pile on their heads. Willa giggles and bats one off her face. "Are you sure you've got enough pillows? Is there one each for all your special guests?"

"Very funny." Finn tosses them to the side. "I like to have a lot. When I was a kid and I'd get scared at night, I'd put them all around me, even under my feet." She snuggles in next to Willa. "They were like this magic protective ring. I used to steal them off the bed in the spare room. Even the sofa cushions. Then, finally, Mum bought me a heap of my own so our guests would have something to put their heads on when they stayed."

"What were you scared of?"

"I don't know. Just kid things. Witches, ghosts. Monsters I saw on TV."

That's slightly adorable. Willa's never been scared of imagined things. Just real stuff. She wraps her arm around Finn's waist and stares at the little painting again. She already loves being here, snug in this nest of Finn-ness. Willa's bedroom is a jam of her and Riley's things—mostly Riley's—and Willa's attempts to keep the chaos at bay. There is no space in the world that's just hers.

There's a sudden skitter of claws on wood, and a small, scruffy white dog leaps onto the bed. Then another. The scruffier of the two snuffles in, sniffing at Willa. She pats the ruff of white hair around his neck, and instantly he collapses onto his side next to her. She scratches his warm belly. "He's sweet. What's his name?"

"Banjo. He's twelve. This is Patter, his little brother. He's eight." She rubs Patter's ears. "And the cat's called Son. Are you sensing a pattern?"

"As in Banjo Patterson? The poet?"

"Yeah, my dad's a dag, what can I say?"

"So where's the cat?"

"Oh, she'll be here. It can get kind of crowded in here at night." Finn rolls over and pulls her laptop from under the bed. "Want to pretend to watch something? So when Mum drops by soon with the inevitable intervention in the shape of an invite for dessert, we can at least maintain a charade of innocence?"

Willa laughs. "Sure."

"So, what do you want to pretend to watch?"

"I don't mind."

Finn puts some sitcom on, and they ignore it, curling in close, the dogs pressed to their backs.

Canned laughter erupts around them as Willa eyes her shyly. "Hey?"

"Hey what?" Finn says dreamily and traces Willa's jawline with her index finger.

"You know I've never had a girlfriend, right?"

"Neither have I." Finn's nose wrinkles. "Well, there was this girl last year. From my painting class. We ended up kissing every time I went to her house for a while there, but that doesn't really count."

Willa has to bite down on the bitter spring of jealousy that accompanies the thought of Finn's lips near another human's. She wonders what Finn would think if she knew about the jealousy that ripples through her when Finn mentions her ex, Matt, or now this girl she hasn't heard of before. Would she be flattered? Or put off? "But you've had boyfriends, right?"

"A couple."

"So…" Willa bites her lip. "So, how do you know when you've gone from hanging out to something official? Like, when you've actually become serious boyfriend and girlfriend?"

"I don't know. Matt and I never made it official. It just *was* eventually. I guess some people have a conversation or formally ask each other out. Dan and his girlfriend did that whole commitment talk recently."

"Like when people used to ask each other to go steady in old movies?" Willa cringes. Why do her only cultural references have to be from films she's watched with her sixty-six-year-old grandmother?

But Finn doesn't blink. "Mum told me that when she was at school, they used to call it 'going round' with someone."

"That's kind of vague."

"Totally."

"But there are no rules about this stuff?"

Finn smiles at her. "You know, this isn't something you have to study for, Will. Or plan."

"I know that," Willa mumbles. "Don't tease me."

"But you're so tease-able." Finn's about to nuzzle in and kiss her again when the sound of heels against floorboards invades their world.

"Girls?"

"Yeah, Mum?" Finn sits up. So does Willa, and then Patter and Banjo in a chain reaction of wide-eyed.

"Would you like some sweets? I got some fancy ice cream."

Finn's grin is sly as she mouths *I told you*. "We're coming!" She shuts the laptop. "Come on. You can finish impressing my mum."

But before Willa can make it to the door, Finn grabs her by her belt loops and pulls her backward. She presses herself against Willa's back, sliding her arms slowly around her waist. "Hey, Will?"

"Yeah?"

"Want to go round with me?"

"Maybe," Willa says, walking out the door like it's nothing. Like there's no treacly, happy sensation surging like a tsunami through her. "I'll think about it."

# CHAPTER 14

## Finn

Nona's got her eyes shut and her cap pulled down low.

"Hard day?" Finn asks as she sits down at the table.

Bea leans in and pats Nona's leg. "Baby, wake up. We're starting."

"Huh?' Nona sits bolt upright, blinking. "Oh, right," she says slowly, looking around the warehouse. "We're here."

"What's with you?" Kayah snaps her fingers in front of her Nona's face. "Get it together, child. We've got a community centre to save," she says in her best after-school-special voice.

Nona rubs her hands over her face and mumbles, "Didn't get a whole lot of sleep last night."

"Party too hard?" Rosie asks. "No, wait, it's Wednesday. Can't have partied that hard on a Wednesday."

"Oh, you poor, misguided child." Kayah pats Rosie's arm. "Wait until you get to uni. You won't be saying that."

"Yeah, but Nona's in Year 10. So unless she's got fake ID…"

"True. I can't exactly see that baby face passing for eighteen," Kayah admits.

Nona gives Kayah the finger. Kayah cheerfully sends one back.

Kayah's the black-haired girl with the huge earrings who showed Finn a chair at the first meeting. She's in first year at uni, studying communications. She's smart and opinionated and knows everything that's going on in the world. She's got pretty, dark eyes and wears blouses with wild, colourful prints. She's seventeen, bi, and studying marketing with her boyfriend. Finn may already be harbouring the mildest of crushes on her. Not a serious one—no one stands a chance against Willa. It's more one of those "I want to be as cool as you when I'm at uni" ones more than anything.

"I didn't go out last night," Nona mutters, resting her head on Bea's shoulder. "My parents kicked me out, and I had to sleep in a friend's garage."

"What for?" Finn asks, eyes wide.

Nona shrugs, like it's no big deal. "Mum found a ticket from a queer party I went to and told Dad. They tag-teamed losing the plot at me for hours, and when I fought back they kicked me out." She grins. "No regrets, though. That thing was lit. Full of babes."

Bea raises a perfectly shaped brow. "Excuse me?"

"Just looking." Nona curls her arms around Bea. "You were grounded, remember?"

"You're not going to be living in a garage for long, are you?" Finn asks. Poor Nona.

"No, they'll let me back in a week or so."

"How do you know?" Rosie asks.

"Nona gets kicked out once every couple of months," Bea tells Finn. "Like clockwork."

Nona grins. "Every time a bit of my gay leaks out."

"Isn't that all the time?" Kayah grins. "Listen, we could probably push some reprobates off the couch at my place and make room for you for a few days."

"Aw, thanks, big sis."

"No problem. Come to mine after this." She straightens the papers in front of her. "But we should get to work. Otherwise you won't have this place to hide in either."

"What about using stories like Nona's for whatever we do?" Bea asks. "I mean, everyone's probably got one about why this centre's so important for them. Unsupportive parents, safe places, all that. If we could share those somehow, surely someone would listen."

Finn nods. She loves that this place exists, and she also knows she's lucky enough not to need it as an escape from anything. Not so far, anyway.

"Sure, but then what do we do with the stories?" Kayah taps her fingers against the table. "If we include them in media releases, we'd only fit one or two short quotes at best, and that can't tell a real story."

"What if we made a little book or something? We could give out copies," Rosie suggests.

"But can we afford it? Hey, Costa!" Kayah calls out to the youth leader. "What's our budget?"

Costa turns from the kettle and laughs like she just made some hilarious joke. Then he makes a circle of his thumb and forefinger.

"Oh, right," Rosie mutters.

"Awesome!" Nona does a little fist pump. "Zero budget. This is getting easier all the time."

"Doesn't matter," Kayah says. "I think we'd be faced with the same problems if we made a book: how would we get the media to cover it?"

"Chain ourselves to the centre?" Nona suggests.

"That would definitely get their attention," Finn says. "But possibly on the extreme side."

"Just a touch," Andy agrees.

Rosie flops her head down on her arms. "This is hard!"

"No, it's not," Kayah says. "We just have to come up with something that *demands* attention."

"Like she said," Nona mutters, "hard." She shuts her eyes again.

# CHAPTER 15

## Willa

It's Riley who finds Nan.

One minute she's screeching about getting a form signed for a school excursion, and the next she's just screeching. It's shrill and terrified enough for Willa to instantly know that it's not just the usual intruding spider or rodent melodrama.

She bolts down the stairs, her socks slipping against the wooden floor. Riley's in the yard, standing over Nan, screaming.

Nan's sprawled sideways on the patch of concrete. There's no movement, apart from the slow, reassuring up-and-down drift of her ribs. There's blood too, pooled stickily on the paving, a cut on her head, already on its way to drying. It takes Willa only a stomach-clenched moment to put the scene together. The hanging plant basket lying on its side, potting mix scattered all over the ground. A broken plant, splayed on its side. The stepladder akimbo on the ground, one leg at rest against Nan's foot.

"Don't touch her!" Willa pushes past Jack, who's now white-faced and silent in the doorway, and sprints for the phone.

～ ～ ～

The nurses make the businesslike scurry of examinations and X-rays and doctor-waiting seem almost mundane. It's a forceful calm, and Willa's grateful, because it forces her to be the same. Outwardly, anyway.

Inside her, there's still the panicked residue of the frantic calls to Kelly and Maida, searching for someone to take care of Jack and Riley, and then the torturous wait for a taxi to the hospital after the ambulance took Nan away.

When she left, Riley and Jack were both in tears. Kelly, still in her netball uniform, stood at the door, her arms around both of them, telling her not to worry.

Willa pulls out her phone and punches out a message to her.

*Are they okay?*

*They're fine. They're watching TV with us. Maida's calling for pizza.*

Willa doesn't know why that makes her want to cry, but it does.

*How's Nan?*

*They say she's got a broken hip, bruised ribs, a sprained wrist, and a concussion. But she'll be okay. Can you tell the kids?*

*Of course. Maida's asking if you want her to come down and sit with you?*

*No, I'm fine.*

Willa doesn't want anyone. Not even gentle Maida, colonising with her kindness. She just wants to stay here, frozen, and wait for her grandmother to be her grandmother again. She slips her phone into her pocket and sits rigid in the corner, watching the nurses do their thing around Nan's unconscious form.

Why didn't she go to the kitchen first instead of going upstairs to change out of her uniform? Why did she eat that leftover muesli bar on the way home? Otherwise she'd have gone for the pantry like Riley did. Then it would have been Willa that found Nan, not her little sister.

A grey-haired nurse places a water jug on a table by the bed and turns to Willa. "Are your parents coming soon?"

Willa shakes her head. "We live with Nan."

"We?" She spreads a blanket across Nan's legs.

"My brother and sister and I."

"Older or younger?"

"Younger."

"And your grandfather too?"

"No. Just with Nan." Her grandfather died when Willa was two, the first to go in the incredible shrinking family.

The nurse wipes her hands on her slacks and sighs. "I'll grab the social worker."

Willa's eyes widen, and the icy sludge of panic creeps back in.

~ ~ ~

When they've covered the stitches on Nan's head with a white bandage, finally Willa drags her eyes to her phone buzzing in her hand.

It's Finn, her voice all low and concerned. "Hey, I got your message. How's Nan?"

"Okay." Willa recites the injury list again.

"Are you still at the hospital?"

"Yeah."

"Who's with you?"

"No one."

"The kids?"

"With Kelly and Maida."

"Do you need anything?"

Numb still, Willa shakes her head.

"Will? Are you there?"

"Yeah, sorry. I'm fine."

The nurse tidies bloodied bandages from the table and leaves, giving Willa a reassuring smile as she passes.

"Do you want me to come down? I could—"

"No, it's okay. Don't." She can't say yes. If she sees Finn, she will want the world to stop. And Willa can't afford the softening that comes with Finn. Not now that she has to get through a meeting with a social worker. "I'll talk to you later, okay?" She hangs up before Finn can say anything else.

~ ~ ~

They sit in the hallway on some plastic chairs as people pace and scurry by them.

The social worker is young, with an undercut and a tattoo of a flower peeking out from under her blouse sleeve. Willa stares at it for a moment and then pulls her eyes away.

"Call me Eleni," she says, with a thick accent.

Will nods, her fingers pressed to the edges of the plastic seat.

Eleni smiles gently as she flips a notepad open. "You're okay, Willa. Maggie just wanted me to check in with you because she says you're home alone with a younger brother and sister. How old are they?"

Willa considers lying, saying they're older, but can't bring herself to. "Nine and eleven."

"And where are they now?"

"My friends are looking after them."

"Okay." She nods and writes something down. "Who else looks after them when your grandmother can't?"

"Usually me."

"That's good. But you're in school, yes? What year?" She looks Willa up and down. "Ten? Eleven?"

"Ten."

"So you're sixteen?"

She nods.

"Is there anyone who could come and help you?"

"I don't know." Willa chews at her lip as she mentally lists the handful of people she could call. There's Nan's old student who came while Willa was on camp, but she's looking after her sick daughter. There are her church friends, but they're too old and doddery. It would be unfair to ask them. Maida's house is full to brimming, and Kelly's flat is a no-go zone for Riley and Jack. "Not really," she admits finally.

Eleni nods and writes something else down.

Willa notices she's wearing the same deep-purple nail polish as Finn's and immediately thinks what a dumb thing it is to notice right now. She swallows hard. "What's going to happen?"

The social worker's hand is a sudden warm weight on her arm. "Willa, this is not a movie. I'm not here to throw you in a foster home or split you up or anything drastic like that. But I am here to see you have the support you need."

The relief flooding Willa is embarrassing. Because that's exactly what she's been imagining.

"But what worries me," Eleni continues, "is that even if you could find someone to check in on you and offer a little support while Nan's here in hospital, usually people of her age who get hip surgery need time in rehab afterwards. And with her anaemia delaying surgery, and the wrist injury complicating her use of physical support, she certainly will. It will be more than a month, I think." She squeezes Willa's arm and lets it go. "So we need to figure out some kind of solution. Because it's too long for someone your age to take on this kind of responsibility. And I don't think your grandmother would like it much, would she?"

Even though she shrugs, Willa knows there's no way Nan would like it. She purses her lips and finally gives in to the only other option. "There's my dad. He's in Queensland."

"Do you think he'd be able to come down for a while?"

"Maybe."

"Call him, okay?" Her hand is on Willa's arm again.

Willa fights the urge to shake it off. "Okay."

"Good girl." Eleni gathers up her papers and gives her a warm smile. "I will pop back in half an hour and see how you went." With that, Eleni strides down the hall.

Willa feels oddly bereft now that she's gone. She sits there, phone clutched, staring at a poster warning people about diabetes. When was the last time she even spoke to her dad? Maybe it was Nan's birthday, back in March, or Jack's in February. Why would she remember something like that? The conversation would have been like all the others, brief and stilted and full of yes/no answers, because they both have no idea what to say or how to talk on the phone. They barely know how to speak to each other in person.

She reads the poster over and over again, stalling. There are over four thousand amputations performed per year due to type 2 diabetes in Australia, the poster warns. *Get tested*. Willa's pretty sure Nan's hippie diet puts her out of risk, but it also puts this phone call in perspective on the scale of sucky experiences. She grits her teeth and dials his number.

"Willa?" He sounds like he's outside, all echo and distance. It makes sense to her. He's not made for indoors.

"Hey…Dad."

"Is everything okay?"

"No." Why else would she be calling? Just to chat? "Nan's in hospital."

There's a short silence, and when his voice returns, it's clearer, sharper, like he's moved under shelter. "What happened? Is she okay? Are you guys okay?"

Willa tells him the things she has learned but still can't quite compute. "They said she'll be fine but that I need to call you because she'll be in hospital a while."

There's another short silence. "Okay, I'll talk to my boss and get on a flight."

She grips the phone hard, learning that it's possible to feel relief and dread at the same time. "Thanks." Why is she thanking him? This is what he's *supposed* to do, isn't it?

"I might not get there until the day after tomorrow, though, by the time I get into town. Will you be okay until then?"

"Yes." The longer the better. Then she can get used to the idea.

"Okay, I'll see you soon." And he's gone.

Back in the room, the doctor's with Nan, tapping and testing with efficient touch. Nan was awake for a minute, she tells Willa, but slid back under. It's the painkillers, the doctor assured her, not the head injury, as if that's what Willa was thinking. But she speaks so fast Willa didn't even have time to think it.

Her throat aches at the thought of a missed moment with Nan.

"She was very groggy. But she said to tell you to go home and have your dinner. That she'll see you tomorrow. *After* school." The doctor smiles. "It sounded like an order to me."

She guides Willa outside and sits with her on the same plastic chairs Willa sat on with Eleni and talks even faster. Her gaze flicks down the hall every few seconds, as if she's expecting something to happen somewhere else any moment. She tells Willa the same stuff the nurses did. Fracture, concussion, a replacement surgery when her head is better and the anaemia they just discovered improves. "And your grandmother is right to tell you to go home. She probably won't wake again tonight, and she needs the rest so she can get strong for surgery. You go and get some rest too."

Willa can't help flinching as the doctor pats her knee. Why do these people think strangers touching her will be somehow comforting?

Outside the hospital, the dusky, peak-hour world is an assault. Willa pulls her school blazer around her and edges her way onto a crowded tram. When she reaches her stop, she strides through the park, back to her brother and sister.

# CHAPTER 16

## Finn

Finn paces, retracing the journey from her bedroom to the kitchen and back again. It doesn't help, though. Neither does the painfully brief "yes" from Willa when Finn messages to ask if she's home yet. Brevity is never a good sign from Willa. Not when Finn knows how easily she can slip inside of herself when something's wrong.

"Mum?"

"Mm?" Anita's at the kitchen counter, frowning at her laptop.

"Can I go over to Willa's? Just for a minute? I'll come straight back."

Her answer is automatic. "It's a weeknight, and it's too dark to be walking around."

"I could ride my bike?"

"I don't think so, hon. It's too late. Call her."

"But…" Finn stops and sighs. Willa will just say she's fine, no matter what. Finn doesn't have the time to explain Willa-level reticence to her mother right now. "Please, Mum. She's on her own."

That wrenches the vice principal out. Anita looks up, still frowning. "What do you mean she's alone?"

"Remember? They live with Nan."

"So there's no adult with them now?"

"I don't think there *is* anyone."

Anita taps her fingernails against the counter. "No one?"

"Well, I don't know for sure, but her dad's in Queensland, and there's no other family. Her friends were looking after her brother and sister while she was at hospital."

Anita shuts her computer and lets out a brisk sigh. "Grab my car keys. I'll drive you over."

When they're stopped at a traffic light by the park, Anita says, "Remember, we're just dropping by to check in. Then you have to come home and do your homework."

"Got it." Finn doesn't care. She just needs to see Willa for a second.

The girl who opens the door is solid and striking, with dark eyes and broad features. She frowns as she holds the door half-open.

Finn gives her an uneasy smile. "Um, hi. Is Willa there?"

The girl's stare lingers. "Hey Will!" she finally calls down the hall. Then it's back to staring. This girl could compete with Willa in the scrutiny stakes. "You're Finn, right?" she finally says.

"I am. And this is my mum, Anita." Finn gestures behind her.

The girl nods, her mouth edging towards a smile but never quite getting there. She doesn't introduce herself, but she opens the door wider. "Willa's okay," she says. "We've got her."

Even though Finn can't tell if she's being reassured or told to go away, she smiles and nods, because all she knows is that she can see Willa coming down the hall towards her.

Willa's eyes widen when she gets close enough to see Finn. And they widen even more when she sees Anita there too.

Before Finn can stop herself, she darts forward and folds her into a tight hug. "Hey. You okay?" she whispers.

Close up, Willa looks taut and tired. She just nods, her hands still at her sides, like the hug and the words have barely touched her.

Finn retreats, blushing, wondering if she's done the wrong thing coming here.

"Willa." Anita moves closer. "Finn told me about your grandmother's accident. I'm so sorry to hear that. We just wanted to check in and see if you need anything?"

Willa gives Anita a polite smile, but before she can say anything, her name is called from inside. It's Riley, in a ratty nightie, peering down the dark hall.

"Finn!" She dashes towards them, darting between the girl and Willa to stand next to Finn.

"Hey." Finn smooths a hand over Riley's hair. "You doing okay?"

Riley nods, her mouth pursed into a frown. She looks just like her sister when she does that. "I found Nan," she says in a small voice, leaning against Finn.

"That must have been scary." Finn wraps an arm around her shoulders, saddened by the sight of uppity Riley collapsed back into little girl.

"It was."

They all stand there a moment, saying nothing. Finally, Anita shakes her keys. "So, Willa, are you going to be okay here by yourselves tonight? Because you'd be quite welcome to—"

"We're okay," Willa says, adding quickly, "but thank you."

"All right." Anita nods slowly and smiles at the girl standing guard behind Willa. "Well, it looks like you have your friends helping you."

The girl nods.

"Thank you for coming," Willa says in her best polite, talking-to-adults voice.

"You're welcome." Anita runs a hand along Willa's arm. "Don't hesitate to call if you do find you need anything? Even if it's just a lift to the hospital. We can help."

"Thank you." Willa stares at her feet, pressing her lips into a thin line. She looks like she can't wait for them to leave.

Finn tries not to feel the hurt. Tries to tell herself it's just because Willa's not good at being looked after. She gives Riley another squeeze. "Bye, sweetie." She looks up at Willa. "I'll see you soon, okay?"

Willa nods, holding the edge of the door next to her body like she can't wait to close it. Her smile seems to come from a continent away. "Bye."

The minute Finn's off the steps, she hears the door shut quietly behind her. Tears prick at her eyes. Why does she feel like she just did something completely wrong?

# CHAPTER 17

## Willa

At first when she wakes, Willa isn't sure what to do. Is she supposed to go to school? Or to the hospital? Then she remembers Nan's instructions. Come *after* school. And because she has no idea what else to do, Willa just does as she's told.

The morning is the usual scurry to get everything done. She pours cereal and checks schoolbags and gives yawning Jack and Riley money for lunch from Nan's purse. But while the scramble is the same, the feeling is different. There's no smell of Nan's morning coffee. No talkback radio or commentary on what's happened in the garden overnight. No ever-present voice, chivvying them through their routine. It's weird. Lonely, somehow, even with the three of them there.

When she's watched the kids get on their tram, Willa trudges to her bus stop, walking as slowly as possible. Mostly because she's dreading the conversation with her English and History teachers about why she didn't get her homework done. Her skin crawls at the thought of their sympathetic concern. Maybe she can get it done on the bus. Then she won't have to tell anyone.

Part of her wishes she could stay home. She's so tired. Sleep did not love her last night. Worry about Nan prodded at her. And there was guilt too.

"Are you mad at Finn or something?" Kelly asked as they walked back to the lounge room last night.

"No," Willa said quietly, although she was already feeling the slide of shame because she knows she was weird last night.

"Well, it kind of seemed like you were."

Willa wasn't mad. She was just paralysed by the sight of both Finn and her mother standing on the doorstep, their expressions so sympathetic and searching. It was too much. She didn't mean to be rude, though. She really didn't. It was just her awkwardness hardening into paralysis, like it always does.

Still, Kelly's question picked at her. And later, after she replayed the scene in her mind over and over, she wanted to text Finn, to explain that the minute she saw Finn, all Willa had wanted to do was to be absorbed into Finn's comfort. But she couldn't. Not with Kelly and Anita there. Not with all those worried eyes on her. But Willa didn't know how to put that into text, so she didn't.

Willa nearly stops in her tracks when she spots Finn up ahead, waiting at Willa's bus stop in her purple school dress and blazer. This time, she forces herself to keep moving towards her.

When she gets close, Finn gives her a small smile. "Hey. I wasn't sure if you were going to school."

"Nan said I had to."

Finn smiles. "Still a teacher, even in hospital. My mum would do that too."

Willa forces a return smile, but it fades fast. They stare at each other as people rush around them, intent on their mornings. Willa tries to urgently to think of the right thing to say, but it isn't coming.

Finn gets there first. "Listen, I wanted to say that I'm sorry about last night. I just wanted to see if you were okay, but then Mum would only let me come over if she came too. I really didn't mean to impose."

"You didn't," Willa manages to say.

"Oh, okay, well...good." Finn gives her a diffident smile, but it fades quickly. "Anyway, I don't want to get in your face, but just...let me know if you need me." She stares at her feet, kicking one shoe against the other. "I'll be there."

Why does Willa feel like crying? "Thank you," she manages to whisper. It comes out stiff and formal, though. Like a lie.

"I better go. You'll be late. I just..." Finn bites her lip, hesitating. "I hope you're okay. I'll see you." Her smile is watery as she walks away.

A sadness seeps through Willa. Why doesn't she know how to ask for things? For what she wants? Before she can talk herself out of it, she takes off at a run. "Finn, wait!"

Finn's face is tense as she turns at the entrance to the park. But because she's Finn and her heart's so damn big, it dissolves into a smile at the sight of her.

Willa comes to a halt in front of her and fidgets with her prefect badge. "What are you doing later? After school?"

"No plans. Why?"

"Want to come over and study with us?"

Finn smiles. "Of course."

"We're going to see Nan straight after school, but we'll be back later. You could stay for dinner, maybe?"

"Okay. Just message me when you're heading home, and I'll come over."

Relief replaces sadness. How does Finn make things so simple, when all Willa seems to do is make them hard? *This* is what Willa actually wants, what she wanted all along. For Finn to be smiling at her. To be able to hold the promise of seeing her again all through this day. "I will."

Unable to relinquish this moment without touching her, Willa takes a tentative step forward. But Finn's coming at her already.

"I'm sorry," Willa whispers as Finn folds her into a hug. "If I was—"

"Sh." She squeezes Willa tight. "Don't be sorry. Just…need me if you want to. Okay?"

Willa swallows hard and presses her cheek to Finn's hair. "I'm not used to it."

"I know. Get used to it."

# CHAPTER 18

## Finn

She's about to hang up when finally he picks up.

"Finn-o!"

"Hey, Dad."

"Sorry, I was out the back. Why aren't you at school?"

"I am. It's lunchtime. I'm waiting for Dan, but he's late."

"So you're only talking to me because Dan's late? Don't I feel special?"

"No, I'm ringing because I need to ask you something." Finn settles onto their bench in the front yard.

"Shoot."

"How do you get journalists to write a story about something? Like, how does it get to the papers?"

"I thought you were going to hit me up for money or permission to do some reckless teen thing."

"Hilarious. Have you met me? I don't do reckless. I barely do mildly adventurous."

He laughs. "So why do you want to know?"

"I just do," she tells him, drumming her fingers. "I'll explain in a minute."

"Okay," he says slowly, in that way he always does when she asks him a question. It drives her crazy. "Usually, unless it's something we're looking for and we contact them ourselves, organisations and companies send us media releases about stories they want told or news they want people to hear."

"Right." She's heard Kayah talking about media releases at the warehouse. "It's that easy?"

"Well, it's that easy to send one, but it doesn't mean we'll write about it. It depends on whether anyone thinks there's a good story in it."

She stretches out on the bench, sunning her bare legs. "So how does they decide if it's a good story?"

"I don't know. You just know after a while."

"Helpful."

He laughs. "Okay, well, when I was at university, they taught us about these things called news values. It's like these unspoken criteria about what makes an event newsworthy."

"Like what?"

"Well, the most obvious one is that it has to be new, or it isn't news. It has to be about someone prominent or important, or about a place or people we have some kind of relationship or affinity with. Or it has to involve some kind of conflict. Journos love a conflict story. Politicians arguing, wars, athletes fighting on the field. Then there's the stories about weird things no one expected. Like that story this morning about the woman who killed her husband in Croatia. We probably wouldn't even hear about that here except that she used a soup ladle to do the job. That gave the story a reason to be told. Then there's the fluff pieces."

"Fluff pieces?"

"You know, the story at the end of the news, right before the weather. The one that gives you the warm and fuzzies. The sick children who are cured. Police or firemen rescuing cats from a tree. Stories that make us feel good about the world. We need one of those to balance out all the bad news we've just heard."

"Right." Finn chews her lip. She has no idea where their story would fit into all of this. "I still don't know what to do."

"I've got an idea. Why don't you actually tell me what you're *trying* to do?"

She fills him in on what's happening at the centre, and their so-far useless attempts to attract any media attention.

He loves it, of course. Her dad's never not loved an uphill battle or a cause. One of Finn's first memories is going to a protest about protecting journalists' jobs. She remembers holding his hand tight as they walked Bourke Street, surrounded by towering adults, electrified by the wall of sound and movement that only a group of people passionately believing could make.

"Okay," he says. "So you have a cause and you need to get it into the public eye. Trouble is, there's more competition for attention when it comes to a cause than anything else. You have to find a unique way to attract attention. That's why organisations are always finding off-the-wall means to promote things, like getting people to shave their heads to support cancer research or to grow moustaches for men's health, or getting people to not eat for forty hours to help countries in famine. The media love stuff like that. There's photo ops and human interest, so it's an easy story to write."

"So we have to figure out how to do something like that to get noticed?"

"It'd help. On your plus side, you have the marriage equality debate going strong, so LGBT issues have a bit of currency right now, but on the downside, you're always going to have lost dogs' homes full of puppies, and sad babies trumping cute gay teens in your attempt at being the fluff piece."

"Great." Finn gnaws at a fingernail and watches Dan stroll towards her, lunch in hand. "This is hard. I just thought we could get a reporter to come down or something."

"No paper's got the time or money unless you give them a good reason to come down. The way the industry is these days, most journalists are doing three people's jobs. You have to hand them a story on a plate. Then some local papers might consider it."

"Great," she says with a sigh. "I feel so much better now."

"Don't give up, Finn. Just come up with something to make them look. You're smart. You'll think of something."

"I hope so," she says as Dan drops onto the edge of the bench, clutching a greasy bag of chips and a can.

"I'd make a couple of calls to the guys at my paper, but I'm not so popular right now."

"I should go," she says. "Dan's here."

"So when are you coming for another visit?"

"I don't know. Soon. See you, Dad. And thanks." She puts her phone in her pocket and gives Dan a weary smile. "Hi."

He holds out his bag of chips drowning in tomato sauce. "I couldn't take any more of mum's salads."

She shakes her head.

"Was that your Dad?"

"Mhm. Needed some journalism advice."

"He still in Tasmania?"

"Yep."

"Does it still suck?"

"It really, really does. Do you know what I'm most scared of?"

"What?"

"That the longer he stays there, the more they'll just get used to this. Used to being separate. Then it'll be easier for them to never get back together." She watches a chip packet whisking past in the breeze. "At least when they were in each other's faces, fighting, they could actually remember what it was like to be together, to be in the same room." She frowns. "Does that make sense?"

"Yeah, it does." He gives her a sympathetic look. "I'm sorry, mate."

She smiles at him, glad it's Dan Tuesday.

"There's one upside to this week, though."

"What?"

"School holidays next week."

"Oh yeah." She'd totally forgotten about that. Bring it on. "That's the best news I've heard all day."

"Happy to be of assistance."

# CHAPTER 19

## Willa

Onions hit the pan with a thick sizzle. Willa breathes in the beautiful familiarity, the overture of so many meals in this house. If Nan isn't here to make this smell, Willa will make it for her.

Nan was awake today, restored to her ineffable, glorious Nan-ness, even with the bandages and the hospital sheets. She was pale and slightly shocked, but she acted like everything was normal while she interrogated them about school. She didn't give Jack and Riley a moment to give into their unease at being in the stark ugliness of a hospital room. It was like nourishment to see her alive to the world again. And even though Willa's so tired her eyeballs hurt, she feels better than she has all day.

Jack wanders into the kitchen, standing at arm's length, the way he always does these days. Close but not too close. At the hospital, though, he let Nan clasp his hand the whole time. He smiled at her little jokes, brave before the frail truth of Nan. Sweet, solemn Jack.

He fiddles with the clutch of oregano that Willa has gathered from the garden for the sauce. Usually, she wouldn't have bothered, because Riley has this annoying habit of laboriously picking out all "green stuff" from sauce before she'll eat, but tonight Willa's showing off for Finn, so flavour wins.

Jack puffs his cheeks as he thinks whatever he's thinking and stares at the mess of dinner to be on the counter. Willa has to fight the urge to wrap her arms around him— to smother him with love—because she knows he'll slip away. So she slings a casual arm around his shoulder and pulls him to her side for a millionth of a second before letting him go. "You good, Jackling?"

"Yeah," he says in that shrugging, laconic way he learns from the older boys at school. She sees so much imitation in her sister and brother these days, nascent echoes of teen girl drama and boy taciturn. The prepubescent shall inherit the teenage earth.

When she releases him, he immediately steps away.

She smiles and pushes the onion around the bottom of the pan. There was a time when she couldn't go anywhere without him pinned to her side, his hand a constant warm presence in hers. "Homework?"

"Spelling and writing."

"You should do it before dinner."

"Okay." He retreats to the kitchen table where Riley and Finn are already sitting in a small sea of books, including the ones Willa hasn't had a chance to touch yet. Seeing them makes her stir a little faster.

"We have to write about the marriage equality vote," Riley is telling Finn. She stumbles over the word.

"Really?" Finn raises an eyebrow at Willa. "Your class is writing about the marriage equality vote?"

"Kind of. It's part of this big project we're doing on equal rights and…stuff."

"And *stuff*," Finn teases. "Well, I for one think a marriage equality vote is a rubbish idea, letting the entire nation decide whether we should have equal rights we're already supposed to have. The government should just do their job and make it happen."

Willa wants to laugh, because she can see Riley's hanging on to Finn's every word, but she's probably not actually following any of them.

"Why do you even want to get married?" Riley screws up her face. "It's dumb."

"That's not the point. Shouldn't anyone be able to if they want to?"

Willa flings a handful of peppers into the pan. The air turns sweet and smoky. She can't imagine being married. Can't even picture adulthood. If she really tries, she can muster some blurry images of herself at university, strolling between classes on a leafy campus, but that's about it.

Riley crosses something out in her book with wide slashes of her pencil. "I'm never getting married."

"Even to the biggest hottie in the world?" Finn waggles an eyebrow at her.

"We can just live together. That way, if things don't work out, it's easier to split."

Finn turns to Willa, mouth open. Willa shrugs. Yep. This is her eleven-going-on-twenty-five-year-old sister.

"Hey, do you know this song?" Riley's shoulders veer from side to side as she sings a few lines of some girl-power rap.

"How could I not?" Finn says. "It's *everywhere.*"

"Willa wouldn't know it."

"No, I don't," Willa says cheerfully. There are some ineptitudes she can live with. "You should let Finn study. She came here to do homework, not listen to you."

Riley pays precisely no attention. "Do you know this one, then?" Riley sings a couple of lines in her reedy but surprisingly tuneful little voice.

Willa's never heard that one either. This is why Riley has given up on her: she is a pop-cultural lost cause.

There's hope for Finn, apparently. "Of course I know it. Do you think I go home to the sixteenth century after I see you or something?"

"Seriously, don't you have homework to do?" Willa says.

Riley leans into Finn, conspiratorial. "Why do you date Willa? She's so uncool. I mean, she's the best sister in the world." She's backpedalling like she always does when she remembers where dinner is coming from or who might wash her favourite T-shirt so she can wear it to dance class tomorrow. She's nothing if not strategic. "But she's kind of like an old lady."

"Wrong." Finn points her pen at Riley. "You just have a very narrow definition of cool."

Even with her back to them, Willa knows Finn's smiling at her. And that makes her smile too.

"Maybe." Riley sounds doubtful, though. "Hey, do you know this one?" She sings another few lines.

"This is slightly embarrassing," Finn says. "I have it on my phone."

"Really? Can I listen?"

"Of course."

Next thing Willa knows some sugar-sweet pop thing is blaring out of Finn's phone. She turns, a stem of oregano hanging from her fingers. "You *own* this?"

Finn just shrugs and smiles winningly at her. "There's no accounting for taste."

"Lefah's got this whole album on hers. She's allowed to have a phone," Riley says pointedly over her shoulder at Willa, as if it's Willa who decides these things. "We dance to it every day at lunch."

"Show us your moves, then," Finn says.

Riley never needs to be asked twice. The world has been her stage since the day she was born, the patch of floor in front of the sliding doors her personal one. Willa doesn't know how many woeful tween-angst pop songs and wildly age-inappropriate dance moves she and Nan have had to endure in here. Today's no different.

Actually, it is different. Because by the time Willa returns from the pantry with a packet of spaghetti in her hand, Finn's up there too, dancing in the sunshine that glides through the glass doors, hamming it up with her little sister. She's laughing hard, clearly enjoying being this ridiculous. But, of course, she doesn't look that silly, because she's Finn, and she's endless charm. She'd be adorable dancing with a bucket on her head. Riley shrieks with laughter and dances even harder. Even Jack's smiling.

"You two are nuts," Willa says.

"Yup." Finn darts over and grabs Willa's hand. "I'd ask you to dance with me, but I bet I know what you'll say."

"And you are one hundred per cent correct."

Finn sidles up close, smiles flirtatiously, and then shimmies away. And it's everything Willa can do not to abandon the pan and follow her.

Willa doesn't hear the doorbell. All she knows is that Jack suddenly says, "I'll get it!" and dashes from the room.

When he returns, his eyes are saucers. And trailing him is that familiar figure, a large navy bag slung over his arm.

She stares. They all stare. Even Finn, though she must have no idea who he is.

Suddenly, the music disappears, and the silence only makes the moment stranger. And like too many times lately, Willa has absolutely no idea what to do with this moment. With the fact that he's here already.

Her father looks the same as always. Scary-thin and deeply tanned in that outdoor-work way. His blue eyes beam out of the dark hair and whiskers. The only difference from last time is that his wiry black hair is now shot through with a scatter of white.

"Hey, Dad. I didn't think you'd get here until tomorrow." She knows she sounds wooden. But that's how it feels, confronted with a man she sees once a year and still has to call Dad.

"I got an early ride into town this morning, so I caught an afternoon flight." He leans on the doorjamb, one leg crossed at the ankle. The place he stands in every room, like he's ready to edge out of it if necessary.

Willa can hear the rolling boil of the pasta water behind her, and she feels this sudden itch to turn her back on him and just go about the business of dinner, pretending this isn't happening. To go back to the dancing and the stupidity and the promise of herby pasta and sitting elbow to elbow with Finn. Why isn't that an option? Where did that blissful moment disappear to?

Riley's the first to break rank. She traipses over and gives him a ginger, one-armed hug. "Hi, Dad," she says, all casual, like he usually drops in around at this time on a Thursday.

"Hey. You're taller." He holds the flat of his palm just above her head.

"Yep. My hair's longer too." She pulls out a strand and drops it, letting it float back down as she slides back over the kitchen floor in her socks. "That's Finn," she says, pointing.

Before Riley can say anything awkward, Willa hurries over and gives him the barest of hugs. "Hi."

"You look well," he says, holding her at arm's length for a second. "Tall too."

"So do you." What else is there to say? You look the same only older? You look the same, even though I can't remember exactly the last time I saw you?

"I just dropped by the hospital to see your nan," he says. "Surgery next week, she said."

Willa nods, trying not to think about knives slicing into her grandmother. "Do you want some tea? I can put the kettle on."

"I think I might just go have a quick shower." He shoulders his bag. "I came straight off night shift."

"Towels are in the linen cupboard in the hall."

"Righto."

Willa watches him walk away, relieved. It's so awkward acting familiar when he's not. He's little more than a birthday phone call. He's distant memories of being taken fishing and camping because he couldn't stay inside. He's the figure driving while her mother sits in the back seat with her when she was carsick. He's the hand securing hers and Riley's while her mum holds Jack up high at an air show. He's never just standing in their kitchen, a full-bodied being, playing at being part of the scenery.

A hand squeezes her wrist, wrenching her back to the room.

"Hey." Finn's expression is both curiosity and concern. "I think I might go home."

"What about dinner?"

"It's weird me being here now. And besides, then you'll have enough food."

"Um, okay," Willa stutters, slightly relieved she won't have to juggle an extra level of social awkwardness.

When her schoolbag is packed, Finn turns back to Willa and gives her a *you've got this* smile. "I'll call you later, okay?" Then she frowns. "Unless, of course, you just want some time w—"

Willa grabs her hand. "Call me later. Please?"

Finn's responding smile is small, but Willa feels it like sunlight. "Okay, I will." She waves at the kids before turning down the hall. "Bye, guys."

And now there were four.

# CHAPTER 20

## Finn

Given the choice, Finn would have spent her spring school holidays lying around in the sunshine, reading and hanging out. Hopefully with Willa.

But these are not options. Instead, she is third wheel to last-minute marital crisis talk arrangements.

This means flying to Tasmania with her mother for eight long, windy, and Willa-less days. Finn doesn't even bother trying to get out of it when her mother springs the newly hatched plan. Because she knows there's no way her mum is leaving her alone that long. And Anna's housemate is going through some personal crisis and won't want little sisters around, so Finn knows she's along for the angsty ride.

So are the dogs. Their usual kennel was full, and Fatima, their neighbour, will happily look after Son any time they go away, but she's terrified of dogs. Even small, white, lazy ones. Banjo and Patter emerge from their airline crates, dazed but frantically excited to see her. Finn feels the same. She gets the feeling she'll be hanging out with them a lot in her role as genetic appendage to this "holiday".

They don't go to the tiny east coast town where her dad has been staying. Instead, they have created some kind of neutral territory in a rented three-bedroom cottage by the sea. It's a rugged, rocky place a mere fifteen-minute drive to the city. Apparently, you can have it both ways in Tasmania.

During daylight, they go on nature walks or into the city for food and culture. During daylight, they play nice and normal. Then, at the end of the day, they come back to the cottage. A bottle of wine is opened, and her parents reconvene on the deck and talk for hours. Or sometimes they're just silent. They don't fight, but Finn can sense the intensity every time she passes them on her way to the bathroom or the fridge.

Later, when it gets dark and cold, they move to the living room by the fire and switch the TV on, attempting to resume nuclear family status. But when they try to draw Finn out of hiding, the air still feels too thick, so she plays up adolescent apathy and floats back to her room. There, she curls up with the dogs and watches old movies on her laptop.

Even worse, the internet is wiggy to nonexistent. Especially when there's weather. And there's weather all the time in this elemental place. Sometimes she just sits there and watches the reception bars on her phone come and go, looking for a window to get a text through to Willa, dogged by that electric longing she always gets when she wants to be near her and can't be. Nan's having her operation this week, and it's an obnoxious hurt that Finn is stuck here, unable to be there for Willa.

Poor Will. She was paralysed the afternoon her father arrived. So was Finn for a moment. Willa may resemble her mother in skin colour and hair and eyes, going on the photos Finn's seen, but Willa's father is the framework that props it up. He is the genetic material that squared Willa's shoulders, widened her mouth, and granted her the gift of long legs. No one would ever believe for a second they weren't father and daughter.

They looked so similar, but the distance between them was continental as they greeted each other. Even though Willa was the one who called him to come down here, she seemed so shocked by him, his presence just another seismic shift in her life—in her *week*.

"Are you getting used to him yet?" Finn asks her when she finally gets a call through.

"I guess. It's all just kind of weird," Willa says. "You know, I didn't even know that he drank his tea black or that he's allergic to eggplant."

Finn knows by now that what Willa really means is by that is that he's still a total shock to her, and she hates it. Finn's getting used to Willa's need to downplay everything, like she thinks she doesn't have the right to feel bad or conflicted about things, that she must always be the stoic one.

She's even stiff with Finn at first on the phone, like she's already forgotten in just a few days how to be the Willa she lets herself be when they're alone. But Finn just waits it out, and Willa finally comes back to her.

"I miss you," Willa says softly as they say their goodbyes.

And Finn smiles, because she always feels this exquisite radiance when Willa uses her words with her. "I miss you too."

Finn can't imagine what that would be like to have a stranger of a dad suddenly flung on you. Or to not know your own father to the point that when you see each other, it's stilted and bloodless. Her own parents are being weird enough. One morning, she wakes to the absence of Patter in his usual spot at the crook of her knees. She leaves Banjo snuggling into the warm residue of her sleep and goes hunting.

Down the hall, her mum's room is ajar, but when Finn edges it open, neither she nor Patter are there. Finn stands there, blinking away sleep, staring at the made-up bed, slowly finding the obvious in her mother's absence. Anita doesn't do early walks. And she definitely never gets up first on holidays. There's only one place she could be. What Finn doesn't know is what to do with the feeling it gives her.

She hunts down Patter in the living room, snatching the last of the heat from the dying fire. When they pile back into bed, sleep eludes her. She has no idea how to put the jigsaw of factors together: the civil family days, the tense evening conversations, the sharing of a bed. How is all that supposed to fit together into a cogent clue about what comes next? Because that's all Finn wants—a spoiler on this life episode.

On the last weekend, her half-sister Anna flies over, and for one night, she fills the place with the kind of easy mood that exists wherever Anna is. She brings air and light, and Finn can breathe again.

On the Saturday, the two of them go to the city for a girls' night.

"Thanks for saving me." Finn flops backwards on the hotel bed. "There's nothing like feeling like an intruder with your own family."

"I'm so sorry you couldn't come stay with me instead."

"It's been so weird." Finn stretches her arms out across the wide, white spread of bed and counts the pillows. Four. "They're deciding whether they want to be married still, but they're sleeping together." She tells Anna about Patter and the empty bed.

"Yeah, but you can be sleeping with someone and not be okay." Anna slides open the balcony door and examines the view. "Sex is easier than the other stuff sometimes."

Aside from the fact that Finn doesn't want to think about her parents and the act, she doesn't really get it. How can she? She hasn't used sex for anything but sex yet. Well, she used it to lose her virginity, she guesses. And look how well that turned out.

"So, are you and Willa doing the deed yet?" Anna asks her later. They're drinking hot chocolates outside the movie theatre after an insanely long French film about teenagers working at some beachside camp. It was chock full of romantic angst and the awkwardness of first sexual encounters. Totally cringe-y and real. Not that Anna needs a movie to prompt these questions. Her conversation knows no boundaries.

"Not yet." Finn stares at the trickle of blinking, sun-dazed people coming out of the cinema and fights a blush. They could be, though. It's between them all the time. Well, a lot of the time. Sometimes when they're kissing, it's all indulgence, a sweetness. Other times it turns to sex. But because they're not having sex, it's more a kind of delicious frustration, a friction. It's *not* doing it. It's all hot kisses, fingers dancing close to places but retreating quickly. It's stealth touches of skin bared by clothes riding. It's chaste, but the intentions are not. And when there are no more places they can go that wouldn't cross the unspoken line that Willa never goes near and Finn knows that she drew, they falter.

They haven't talked about it, but Willa seems to have absorbed the things that Finn told her that night at camp and is letting Finn lead. Finn doesn't say anything or move the line, because she feels safe in this nowhere zone. Because she's still stuck in the rut of knowing she stupidly rushed into something once when she thought she knew better. And she never wants to be that wrong again.

But that doesn't mean she doesn't feel the constant pull of it with Willa, a girl who is as inexperienced as her but who kisses like she's been making girls feel like this all her life. A girl whose hands always know the right places to go, and how to make Finn feel hot and liquid and electric all at the same time.

But there's always a moment when Finn's brain kicks in, taking over from the greedy instincts of her body. And before she knows she's going to, she calls an end to it by pulling away or pretending she's scared to miss her curfew.

She doesn't tell Anna this. It's too raw and way too confusing. She just lets her sister accept the "not yet" as a simple fact of not arriving yet at what's supposed to be an inevitable destination. Because Finn doesn't know how to choose the words she'd use to describe the conflict between the feelings she gets when she thinks about being naked with Willa and what she does when it's actually a possibility.

If she knew that, she'd know how to talk to Willa about it too.

# CHAPTER 21

## Willa

Willa was eight when they went to live with Nan. They'd spent the year after her mother died living in a house on a winding road that led to the forest and, beyond that, the mines.

She missed their small flat in the northern town they'd lived in before, with the yellow-wallpapered room she shared with both Riley and Jack. Her favourite spot was the tiny balcony. She'd hang her arms and legs through the gaps in the railing so the wrought iron pressed against her chest, holding her in place in the sky. This is where she liked to eat fruit, dripping juice onto her feet and the garden below.

"How did you get such sticky toes, little one?" her mother would chide as she held Willa's small brown feet under the tap.

The new house was rangy and weatherboard and too big for the four of them. Jack and Riley were tiny still, and the rooms so big they looked lost in them. Spiders loved the corners, and Willa spent her days leading her brother and sister from tight, dark spaces where they'd inevitably wander. The backyard was a jungle, and out the front a poinciana tree littered its rage of red petals all over the lawn.

Every day, their father went to work early, and they'd go next door to the corpulent, indulgent woman who dropped them at school and crèche each day and picked them up later and fed them their tea. They'd watch TV at her house until he came home, smelling of earth and smoke.

Willa doesn't remember knowing they were going to leave. What she does remember is her father staring at them. On weekends, he'd sit on the edge of the veranda's sprawl and smoke and tap his foot and watch them play. Or he'd take them to the safe water and let them paddle. Even when they were quiet, and they'd just draw or read or collect up petals together, he'd stare. Somehow, she knew he was trying to solve a problem. And her eight-year-old brain knew the problem was them.

Then, one day, there was a rush of packed bags and the roar of a plane and Jack crying in Dad's lap. Probably because his ears hurt, the woman sitting in front of them told them. She handed them boiled lollies from a plastic bag. Willa sucked hers dutifully and felt her ears snap, crackle, and pop as the plane bounced its way south.

That first night at Nan's, she sat in the kitchen with Jack pressed to her side, eating toasted sandwiches made of Nan's baked bread and the tomatoes that she let Willa pick from the yard. When Willa pulled the ruby fruit from the vine, they smelled dusky, like sun dust might. Her small brain reasoned that if there was moon dust, there surely could be sun dust. But the bright-red flesh inside her sandwich tasted like the place she'd left behind, rich and sun-drenched.

The back door was wide open to the yard as they ate. Sunlight hit Riley where she crouched on the rug, tired and listless and refusing a chair. Nan didn't seem to care; she just handed her a placemat and her plate and let her pick over her dinner on the floor. Outside, her father smoked, staring at the sky over the tall fences that divided Nan's yard from the world.

After dinner, Riley erupted into tears for no reason that Willa could fathom.

"Poor thing's tired," Nan said to no one. She picked her up and rocked her in her arms, Riley's long legs dangling from Nan's hip. "A bath. That's what you need. A bath and your bed." Riley pressed her face to Nan's neck, and her crying became a quiet grizzle. "You three are going to be good and do what your Nan says, aren't you?" She said it like it was a fact, not a question, and Willa nodded. It had never occurred to her not to be.

When they were done with their sandwiches, Nan replaced their empty plates with bowls. All Willa could do was blink at the bouquet of riches before her. One small, perfect scoop of each of the Neapolitan ice cream flavours.

Nan's house was like that. The perfect combination of treats and rules. It was fresh fruit, and it was ice cream, and it was greens gathered from the garden. It was clean sheets and being tucked in to bed early and one hour of TV doled out after school. It was scented cuddles and chides to pick up after themselves. It was everything life had not been the last year. Dinners were meals, not toast and orange spaghetti from a can. School lunches were thick sandwiches and crisp apples eaten from plastic boxes they washed themselves after school every day.

Melbourne was loud, and it rang in Willa's ears in a way that both unnerved and fascinated her. The neighbours' houses pressed strangely close, and at the end of the street, trams cranked by. Willa liked to stand on the front footpath, one hand on the gate, and watch them pass. The weather was confusing too. She missed the tropical consistency of where they lived, the way the air always pushed against you, thick and warm like a blanket. She missed bare arms and legs against the air all year round.

She doesn't remember what her father did in those first days, except smoke and stare and do odd jobs with hammers and drills while he listened to Nan's chat. But she remembers him coming to their room that last night to say goodnight. He leaned against the railings of the bunk beds he'd put together the day after they arrived. "I have to go to work," he whispered to her as Riley snored below. "You kids cost money." He pulled the doona to her chin and grinned. "But I'll come see you, okay?"

She'd nodded, round-eyed, wondering what job he had found here. What did people do to make money at night, she wondered as he kissed her forehead, his whiskers grating her skin. She was that small and stupid that she didn't take his promise to visit for what it was: a goodbye.

It took Willa a week to work up the courage to ask where he was. She stood by Nan's side as she hosed the vegetable patch, because she liked watching how the slide of the sun made rainbows of the spray. And she also just liked being near Nan.

"When's Dad coming?" she asked.

"Probably in a few months." Nan turned the hose at the eggplants. Drops of water gathered at the southern corners of the leaves, clinging a moment before plunging to the soil. "Or maybe Easter."

Willa gasped, taut with confusion.

Nan looked down at her and clicked her tongue. "God's bloody gift to communication, that boy. I wonder how he even managed to find the words to propose to your mother." Then she took Willa's hand and held it firmly in hers. "He's gone back to Queensland, because that's where his job is. You'll stay with me here. You like it here, don't you?"

"Yes." Willa said, because she did like it, and she never lied. But that night, the weatherboard house, the fiery poincianas, and even the spiders danced by her eyes as she willed her way to sleep. They never came again, though.

# CHAPTER 22

## Willa

Hard hospital chairs again. Not the same ones, but the same, in that way that the floors and passageways always look identical in places like this. If they removed the signage, you could be anywhere and everywhere.

They sit in a line, first her dad and then Jack, bent over his tablet. Then there's Riley, slowly threading her hair into a cluster of small plaits while she chomps on some gum. Then Willa, stuck in time, back here in a hospital hallway, her stomach as rudely knotted as last time.

Even in the fluorescent clarity of this place, everything feels slightly smudged, like the lenses of last summer's sunglasses. In Willa's bags are books waiting to be read and a script for her Japanese assignment ready to be memorised. But there's no room in her brain for knowing new things. For now, she can't do anything but sit here and be stillness itself, as if Nan's getting through this surgery depends on her ability to stop time with her inertia. It makes no sense, and Willa doesn't even try.

The doctor was all confidence as she talked them through the process earlier. But the whole time she talked, Willa's mind cagily circled around *ifs* and *buts*, as if her mind is programmed only to look for the ways in which things could go wrong.

Even though the doctor said it could be up to four hours until Nan is awake again, they stayed, on the long watch. Because what else are you supposed to do while someone you love—someone who holds the key to your existence—is being sliced open and rearranged? You can't do anything but sit and wait and watch fate take over. Sit and let the question that has ruled the roost in Willa's mind for days completely dominate: what will happen if any of the other possible variables occur?

Willa looks at her brother and sister, slouched in their seats. They're so chilled they could be on the couch at home, just hanging out. She supposes it's good they aren't scared, that they don't even know they could or should be. Because they only know the soothing things that older, sager people tell them.

Maybe Willa's even a bit jealous of their innocence. What if she got to coexist in that kind of assurance with them? That would be blissful.

Instead, she's terrified. And she can't talk to her dad about it. Even if she wasn't strangled by her own awkwardness, she has no idea how to articulate her fears to him. To tell him that this is about Nan, but it's also about the next part of their lives. Because she can't broach this without having to dance around the fact that it is him who has made their life this tenuous thing. Because he left them here and all but disappeared.

It doesn't help that he acts like a stranger. He spends most of his time out of the house. And when he is there, he sits in the yard, smoking his skinny hand-rolled cigarettes and staring, just like those first days, years ago, when he brought them to Melbourne. The rest of the time he fixes things in the yard or on the roof—mysterious, important tasks that Willa doesn't understand but which seem to keep him out there for hours, tinkering and hammering.

When their paths cross and they're trapped in conversation, he fidgets, his eyes on the exits. He'll roll a cigarette or check the tap for drips as he speaks so he doesn't have to meet her eye. He tries, though. He asks questions about her day, but it's like he doesn't seem to know what to do with her answers, so he just nods, and the moment curdles quickly into silence.

And Willa lets it default to that silence, because it's so exhausting trying to summon familiarity where it doesn't exist. She wishes she could be more like Riley. She's just taken his presence in her stride, acting like he's some distant family acquaintance she doesn't need to pay too much attention. Like she can't remember a time when their dad was their dad and not a stranger, so she doesn't know it could be any other way.

Jack's different. He hovers at a ginger distance, fascinated, like he wants to initiate contact but isn't sure how. Sometimes their dad notices and lets him help with whatever he's doing, teaching him boy tricks with tools and measurements and logic. Or sometimes she finds them in the living room, watching sport in silence together. Other times, he doesn't seem to notice Jack at all. But Jack just waits, infinitely patient on the sidelines, until he does.

Willa's filled her school holidays with visiting Nan and doing housework and shopping and cooking. In the long stretches of afternoon, she takes her brother and sisters for stints in the park. When they're playing at friends' houses, she hides out in her room to avoid more awkward encounters than necessary, wishing her friends were around. But Kelly's working extra shifts, building her quiet stack of savings and her plan to get out, and Maida has gone with her family to their new block out in the bush somewhere.

And to make sure these holidays truly sucked, Finn's been in Tasmania, wedged into her own family awkwardness. They've talked and messaged, but it's been patchy and frustrating and nothing like it is when they're together, where Willa can spill dangerous thoughts in the one place they're safe. Finn will finally be home tonight. Every time Willa thinks about seeing her, her stomach tightens into an urgent little knot.

"I'm hungry," Riley says loudly. Their dad doesn't even look up from his paper.

Willa sighs. It's annoying. He never seems to notice things like dinnertimes and bedtimes and dirty dishes. It's like he doesn't know that they are things that need doing at all. Maybe it's because he lives most of his time on a fishing boat or at a boarding house. Maybe there's no such thing as housework on a boat.

"I'm going to get them some lunch," she says, getting up.

He blinks up at her. "Oh, okay. Here." He pulls a couple of notes out of his pocket.

"I've got my own money." She sounds sullen, and she knows it.

"Take it." He holds it out to her.

She takes it. Because she knows it's the only thing he knows how to do. Every time she mentions going to the shop or taking the kids somewhere, he thrusts money at her. He can't cook, and he can't talk to his kids, apparently. But he *can* provide money. So he does. And she lets him because she doesn't want to make things any weirder than they already are.

She buys them soggy pies from the teeming cafeteria, and they eat them in the playground, a small square of fenced false cheer at the edge of the car park. Willa sips a can of drink as Jack and Riley eat. Then she watches them play half-heartedly on the swings because they know time must be slowly slaughtered with slides and swings and rope ladders. No one's heart is in it, though.

Eventually, they congregate on some benches near the entrance to the hospital and watch the twin tides of grief and relief roll in and out the hospital doors. Willa clenches her jaw and wonders if the world is willing to give her what she wants just one more time: for Nan to wake up in an hour or two, awake and alive to the world again.

# CHAPTER 23

## Willa

The doctor blinks at Nan, her pen stopped in mid-flight. "You're *hungry?*"

"I'm hungry." Nan punctuates her declaration with a single nod of her head.

"Well, that's lovely news." The doctor shuts the clipboard with a snap and turns on her heels. "I'll ask the nurses to bring you a sandwich." She gives Willa a reassuring wink as she strides out.

Riley swings her legs on the end of the bed. "Lefah said her mum threw up for three hours after her operation."

"Well, I feel completely fine. A bit tired and a bit peckish, but perfectly chipper." Nan tugs at Jack's sleeve, drawing him closer so she can inspect him. "You're shooting up again. He's going to be as tall as you," she says to their dad.

He appraises Jack. "Yep, he is."

Jack folds his arms, smiling self-consciously at the attention.

Willa stands at the end of the bed, arms folded too, and watches them all. At Nan, pale but alert, her blue eyes shining as she prods Jack into a smile. At Riley staring at the TV, already camped at end of the bed. Her dad by the window, keeping watch.

Instead of feeling relief, something sickly and electric rushes through Willa. She swallows hard. Suddenly, the room is too full and too hot, so she backs out quietly.

In the hall, she pushes her back against the coolness of the wall and pulls in a deep breath, but it only makes her hyperaware of how hard her heart is hammering, like when she's finished a sprint in PE. Like there's not enough breath and too much breath at the same time. Her vision fuzzes a little at the edges, and for a moment she wonders if she's going to pass out.

Pacing down the hallway, Willa forces air to move in and out of her lungs, slow and controlled. Hands clenched, she focuses on putting one foot slowly in front of the other, fighting back at the panic storming her perimeter. And she doesn't stop until she is certain that whatever this wave is that's threatening to break over her has passed. It takes a few minutes of pacing and breathing, but traces of calm return. Still, her insides feel hollowed and quaking.

What was that about? She paces, eyes downwards, avoiding eye contact with anyone passing. And why did she freak out *now*, when she knows everything going to be okay? When Nan is awake and theirs again? It makes no sense.

As soon as she can finally call her breath and her body her own again, Willa returns to the room. Riley's still staring at the TV, eating a pear from a fruit basket sent by some of Nan's garden-club cronies. Jack's standing next to her, devouring grapes. Her dad's not there. Willa's blood stills. Did he see her in the hall, freaking out?

Nan beckons from the bed. "Come here, my girl. You look peaky."

"I'm fine. Just tired." Willa lets herself be enfolded in a deep, matter-of-fact Nan squeeze. It's almost embarrassing how much comfort can still be found in Nan hugs.

Nan rocks her a little from side-to-side. "My good girl. Is everything okay with you?"

"Everything's fine."

Nan kisses her cheek and pushes her away in that way she always does after she's shown affection. "I don't suppose you've had very fun school holidays, have you?"

"It's been fine."

"No, it hasn't." She pulls the blanket up and peers at her. "How's it been with your dad?"

"Okay." Willa folds her arms and eyes her siblings. They're brain-sucked into TV Land. "A bit weird."

"It's strange for him too, you know. He's not that comfortable around people."

"You don't say."

Nan smiles and peers out the door. "Where do you think that sandwich is?"

"Want me to ask?"

"Oh, that's okay. I suppose we're not at the Hilton. The poor nurses probably have a hundred more important things to do than find an old lady something to eat."

"Want me to get you something from the cafeteria?" Willa asks.

"I can wait. I'll tell you what you can do for me next time you're in, though. Bring me some biscuits and some peppermint teabags, would you?" Her eyes are suddenly bright. "That organic stuff from the pantry. And bring that Finn along to see me too, if she's got a minute."

Willa smiles. Finn's going to laugh about being lumped in with the groceries. "Okay."

"Finn's Willa's girlfriend," Riley says.

Willa shoots her a look, but Riley just grins at her.

"And what's that to you, Riley Jane Brookes?" Nan asks in her sternest voice.

"Nothing." Riley pouts. Not the effect she was going for, clearly.

"Jack, you be sure to mouth off on all your sister's personal business when she gets older, won't you?" Nan tells him.

Jack swings his legs from the bed and grins. "Okay."

"You better not." Riley fires him her best death stare.

"That's what you get for being a tell-tale," Nan says. Riley gives her a wide-eyed, innocent look, but Nan just laughs. "You don't fool me, child."

A small crawl of happiness makes its way through Willa. Because this feels like normal again.

A nurse breezes in on her shiny white sneakers. "Rumour has it that someone's hungry." She waves a Glad-wrapped parcel. "I've got you a nice chicken sandwich here." She makes a show of unwrapping it and setting it on a plastic plate. "Enjoy!" She bustles out.

For a minute, they can only stare. It's a thin, white bread thing with a sog of mayonnaise oozing at the edges and some sort of green hanging from the seam. Nan peels back the bread, peers inside, and looks up at Willa. Her expression is disgust itself.

Willa laughs and heads for the door. "I'll go get you something edible."

# CHAPTER 24

## Willa

"You're back?"

"I'm back."

"You're back." Willa sinks onto the wooden bench, letting the hose spray hit whatever it hits. Because Finn's voice is finally speaking to her from the same state. This is sit-down material.

"But Mum won't let me come over and see you because it's a school night and it's getting dark, blah blah. She says I can wait until after school tomorrow," she grumbles. "I'm tempted to turn brat and tantrum."

"Don't do that." Willa smiles because she's never heard Finn do sulky before. It's a little bit cute. "Will she let you see me if I come to yours?"

"Of course. She won't let me wander the city streets in the dark alone, but it's perfectly fine if other people do. Come over. *Please.*"

"It'll probably only be for a minute, though. I have to make sure Riley and Jack get to bed, and finish my maths."

"A minute's enough. Hurry up."

Willa finds her dad watching some current affairs show from Nan's armchair "Are you going to be here for a bit?" she asks. "For like, half an hour?"

"Yep. Why?"

"I just need to run over to a friend's house quickly."

He frowns at the screen. "Are you allowed out at night?"

"I'm just running there and back. I'll be thirty minutes, tops," she says, totally avoiding the question. Because if he gets to start parenting all of a sudden, she gets to start teenager-ing. "You'll be here for Jack and Riles?"

"I'll be here."

"Okay, I'll be back soon." She runs upstairs and yanks on a cardigan and her runners, ignoring Riley's questions. "See you in half an hour. Get ready for bed," she calls over her shoulder as she sprints down the stairs and takes off into the night.

As Willa turns down the street, she can see Finn perched on the brick post out the front, her feet dangling over the letterbox.

Banjo and Patter tear towards Willa. She leans down to pat them as they sniff and lick at her hands frantically, their small paws scrabbling at her legs.

"Leave her alone, guys. She's mine."

"Ha, cute." Willa hurries the last few steps to Finn and doesn't stop until she's standing between her knees and wrapping her arms around her neck. "Hi."

Finn's arms slide around her waist, pulling her close, her smile miles wide. "I'm *so* happy to see you. And not just because you're the only person I know who had crappier holidays than me."

"They were pretty sucky."

"But Nan's okay?"

"She is. She asked if you'd visit."

"Good, I've got a souvenir for her." Finn digs around in a little bag next to her and plucks out a jar, holding it up proudly. "One hundred per cent organic, biodynamic Tasmanian honey. No cancer here."

"Oh, she's going to love you." She tells Finn about the sad hospital sandwich. "She'll take anything edible right now."

Finn laughs and rustles around in the bag. "I've also got chocolate Tassie devils for your sibs. Less nutritious, but way more fun."

"They too will adore you. At least during the sugar high."

"And don't be jealous, because I got you something too."

Willa plays at a pout. "Lucky."

Finn's teeth are clamped on her bottom lip, and she hands Willa a small green bag. "Please don't pretend to like it if you don't."

"You will never know." But Willa doesn't have to pretend to like the delicate chain bracelet with the two slender silver eucalyptus leaves hanging from it. She loves it. It's too perfect. Because it's camp all over again. It's the beginning of *them*. It's their sunrise mornings, it's Finn's painstakingly pretty sketches under the trees at the creek, and it's that beautiful, urgent feeling that would take over whenever Finn sought her out. It all storms back in a delicious rush.

Finn clips the chain onto Willa's wrist, right next to the worn friendship band that Riley made her promise not to take off.

"I'm not pretending to love it." Willa runs her finger over the tiny links. "I just do." And even though she knows she's probably being a little loose about what constitutes half an hour, she can't help pulling herself up to perch next to Finn for a minute. "So, how was your weekend with Anna?"

"Great. She rescued me from the Mum and Dad tension. How was today at the hospital?"

"Okay. Weird." Willa tells Finn about what happened after the operation, about her little freak-out in the hallway. "It was like I couldn't breathe."

"Scary." Finn grabs her hand and holds it tight. "It sounds like you had a panic attack. Dan used to have them when he was younger."

"I don't know what it was, but it was horrible. And it was so strange, because I knew Nan was fine. I mean, she was asking for a sandwich. Why was I freaking out?"

"I think," Finn says slowly, her thumb sliding over the back of Willa's hand, "it's because you hold on so tight to being okay. So this time, when you finally let go, it *forced* you to feel it, you know?"

Willa watches the dogs snuffle around on the nature strip and lets the idea leaven. "Maybe." Whatever it was, she hopes it never happens again.

"I like it when you tell me things." Finn's head drops onto her shoulder, a sudden warm weight. "I don't like that it's happening to you, but I like that you tell me."

They sit in silence as a plane roars past, low, on the way to the airport.

"I missed you so much," Willa whispers. "All I wanted today at the hospital was to see you." She bites hard at her lip. "Is that too intense?"

"No." Finn squeezes her hand. "It was just the right amount of intense. Because it's what you felt."

"Stop being so amazing. Because I have to go home now."

Finn lets out a little groan. "Too soon."

"Do you want to come and see Nan with me after school this week?"

"Of course."

"Great." Willa drops onto the footpath, but Finn grabs at her as if she's not ready to let her go. Willa's not ready either. She throws her arms around Finn and squeezes her hard, gathering all the Finn feelings she can get to keep her going until next time. "Night," she whispers.

"Night, Will."

Willa takes off down the street, feeling the delicate weight of her bracelet gift at her wrist. For the first time in a week, happiness streams through her like a light.

# CHAPTER 25

## Finn

Today is one of those days Finn can't seem to get ahead of. Or even *with*. Instead, it's just happening all over her, stomping on her head.

She hunches over her books, frantically scribbling answers to her history homework. And as she summons half-assed answers from the unfamiliar lines of text, her mind dances around the ways her current behind-the-eight-ball status may or may not be her own fault.

It probably doesn't help that after their visit to Nan yesterday, she let the late-afternoon sunshine lure her to the park. Instead of home and to her desk and a pile of homework. Nope, instead of doing the sensible thing, she did the awesome thing. Even Willa was willing to leave her textbooks in her bag for once and hang out on the grass with the kids.

And whenever the guilt crept in, Finn told herself there was always time after dinner. Because how could she leave the kiss of sun on bare legs? Or Willa's sleepy smile and the summer taste of lemonade icy poles? Finn's strong, but she's not Wonder Woman.

Besides, why bother going home? It's depressing. Either the house is empty, or her mum is all head-down, "I just have to finish this last thing" into her work. She always stops to ask Finn about her day, but the instant Finn's done telling her, she's back at it again, and the house lapses into silence.

So instead of going home when Willa left her to go make dinner, Finn dropped by Dan's house, which resulted in the inevitable dinner invite. She stayed there until late, watching some new reality singing show with Dan and his mum. They sat around, picking on all the auditions and laughing at Dan's brother's attempts to prove he should have been a contestant.

But the end result of that indulgent afternoon was having to scramble out her Bio homework on the tram this morning and rushing through her English assignment in Maths. And now she's devoting her lunchtime to History. And then, when she gets home tonight, she's going to have to go over the maths she missed in class on top of today's homework. It's been the ripple effect from hell.

"Yeah, man, but the sequel was stellar, you have to admit." Dan and Craig are in deep movie-rant mode on the bench next to her. She introduced the two of them on Monday, and it's been nerd-boy perfect match ever since. It's funny how that can happen at school. One minute someone is bare recognition in a hallway and the next you're making bff plans for movie marathons.

It's been pretty cute, watching them geek-bond, but right now, Finn's got a Gold Rush to pretend to know something about, so she forces them back to background sound status and continues hunting down phrases that will pass for cogent answers.

She's on her second-last question when Dan elbows her. "Hey, Rosie said to remind you about the meeting tonight."

"I know. I'm going."

Another elbow. "And do you remember what you promised me? A photo. Considering you haven't been able to produce the girl in person. She has, like, no social media presence. It's creepy."

"No, stalking is creepy."

"No, it's necessary. Your general, weird coyness has made it necessary." He turns to Craig. "You've met her, right?"

"Willa? Yeah, at camp."

"Is she as hot as Finn says?"

"I suppose she's very pleasing to the eye," Craig says slowly.

"Dude, you're allowed to say she's hot if she's hot."

"Finn's going out with her. *She's* allowed to say it. I'd just be a gross, leering bystander."

"And this is why Craig's a classy guy and you're…" Finn flaps a hand at Dan. "And you're *you*."

Dan leans in close, making a megaphone of his hands. "You promised me a photo."

If there's one thing Finn knows about her best friend, it's that he has an outstanding ability not to shut up until he gets what he wants—top-of-the-resume kind of skill. So she flicks through her phone and finds an appropriately cute photo of Willa from a couple of weeks ago at the park. Willa's standing over Finn, smiling and holding out her hand, trying to make Finn get up and walk instead of taking photos of her.

"Happy?" she says, passing it to him.

Dan hunches over the screen, blocking out the light with his hand. "Oh. I thought she'd be scarier looking. She looks positively angelic."

"You sound disappointed."

"Nice one, Harlow." Dan holds up the phone. "So, Craig, would you call this an accurate representation of said human?"

Finn hits him with a pen. "What do you think I did? Photoshopped it? This may come as a surprise you, but I'm not that invested in *your* opinion of her."

"But *I* am. She's hooked my bestie. I have to approve. Ooh, hang on, you got a message. Is it her?" The excitement in his voice fades. "Oh, it's Zehra."

Dan and Zehra are enemies from way back. Something about a Year 7 Geography project, maps of Africa, and Dan not colouring in the lines. Real hold-a-grudge material. If you're a stubborn idiot, that is.

He passes the phone to her. The message is just three words. *Are you coming?* Finn frowns. And then her stomach plunges. "Oh shit. Shit! *Shit!*" She grabs up her books and pens and uneaten sandwich and shoves them into her bag.

"Please explain your current meltdown," Dan says.

"Monthly year-level brief. I freaking forgot."

"I'm pretty sure you're not supposed to forget those, Cap'n."

"Feel free to shut up." She turns and smiles at Craig. "It was nice to see *you*, Craig." She spins on her heels.

"Oh now, that's not fair," Dan calls out as she marches away. "I'm the best friend, remember? I said your girlfriend looks angelic!"

~ ~ ~

Finn shuts the door quietly and scuttles to the empty seat next to Zehra.

Mr Granger clocks the late entry but doesn't react. He's too busy listening to the junior captain reel off the Year 7 and 8 report.

Finn drops her bag to the floor, ignoring Zehra's questioning look. That's when she realises she doesn't have the brief with her. In fact, there's a strong chance it's on the kitchen counter, where she ignored it this morning in favour of staring blankly out the window while she waited for coffee to happen.

"Hey, can I borrow your brief for a second?" she whispers.

Zehra's narrowed eyes slide over her.

"Left it in my locker." Zehra doesn't need to know Finn doesn't have it because she's apparently determined to make this a benchmark day in Finn underperformance.

Zehra slides hers from a neat, blue folder and hands it to her.

Finn quickly scans it, committing as much as she can to memory, and passes it back. "Thanks."

"No problem."

"Thank you, Edward," Mr Granger says to the junior school captain, sounding about as interested as someone who is not that interested in his job as student council support can be. "Okay, Harlow. Intermediate school. Impress me."

No pressure or anything. Finn dives into her recap/comprehension/memory exercise, scrambling through the news from the different groups and committees she's supposed to talk about.

"And that's about it for this week," she says as she winds up, wishing she was allowed to put her head down on the desk now.

Zehra nudges her and says, loud enough for everyone to hear, "Um, what about the uniform drive?"

Oops. The uniform drive. Probably only the biggest student activity the Year 9s and 10s are involved in right now.

"Oh yeah. It's, uh, going well," Finn stutters, wishing she could remember just one exact detail. "We've raised about..." She looks for the sheet, but Zehra's put it in her bag.

"Five hundred and eighty dollars," Zehra says quietly. Off the top of her head. The way Finn usually does.

While her skin crawls, Finn smiles confidently. "Sorry about that. I don't have my notes in front of me. As Zehra says, we're heading towards six hundred dollars and hoping to get it to a thousand by the end of the term." Now she's just making it up as she goes along.

Mr Granger looks at her for a long moment and then nods. It's not an admonishing look, but it's definitely not a "well done, top job" look either. "Okay, good," he says. "And I suppose the next thing on the agenda for you folk is Speech Night?"

Finn nods. Speech Night. Crap. She needs to get onto that too. The Year 10s always organise it for the graduating seniors. It's a tradition. She goes back to treading water. "That's right. I'm planning on holding the first committee meeting next week."

Zehra turns to her. "But—"

"Great." Granger turns to Mark. "All right, what've you got, seniors?"

Finn sits back in her seat and shuts her eyes, ignoring Zehra's nudges. This day has officially reached full-capacity crap.

# CHAPTER 26

## Willa

*So, in conclusion, we can no longer go out. You're too distracting. And I think
I should be officially stripped of my future leader status while we're at it.*

Willa grins and types, *Okay.*

*What, you're not even a little bit upset?*

*Sh. Don't you have work to do? Haven't you learned your lesson from
today?*

All Willa gets in response is the middle-finger emoji. She smothers another smile
and slides her phone under her book.

Opposite her, Eva opens her can of Diet Coke and sighs at her work. She's been
quiet since the holidays. Not that she's that much of a talker. Especially when Amira's
around, filling every silence. But Eva looks different too. Tired or something.

Something's definitely up. For starters, she's taken to studying with Willa at
lunchtimes, instead of hanging with Amira and Holly and the others. Willa suspects it's
got less to do with her company and more to do with whatever's making Eva quiet. It's
kind of nice to have the company, though. Maybe she's fighting with one of them.
Willa would have no idea if she was.

Today they're working on their history essays in the study lounge. There'll be no
chance for Willa to do it tonight. She needs to do the grocery shopping on top of
everything else. And Riley will want to come too, just to be annoying, and it will make
everything take twice as long.

Willa pulls out the container of blueberries Maida brought over last night from her trip to the country. They're delicious. Sweet and chocolate-y in the way Nan says blueberries should always taste. She pushes them towards Eva. "Hey, try these. They're amazing."

"Thanks, but I'm okay."

The warning bell rings. While Willa packs up her books, Eva just winds and unwinds a strand of hair around her finger and stares into the middle distance.

"Is this silence some new technique to get more chitchat out of me?" Willa jokes. "Because I'm not falling for it."

There's a hint of a smile. "I'm sorry. No, it's not about you."

"I know." Willa hesitates. "Is everything okay?"

Eva rubs her finger across her bottom lip and shrugs. "Rough holidays."

"Me too, if that's any consolation."

"Really? I'll trade you." Eva leans back, arms folded, a challenge. Gandry style.

"Okay." Willa sits up. "So my Nan had an accident and went to hospital. Then she had surgery and has to be in this rehab place for three weeks while she recovers. Meanwhile I had to get my Dad, who I see maybe once a year, to come down from Queensland to look after us. Only he just kinda hangs around and doesn't talk and fixes stuff in the backyard, so I have to do everything in the house and look after my brother and sister all the time. Oh yeah, and did I mention Finn was stuck in Tasmania the whole time?"

Eva nods slowly. "Not bad, Brookes. Okay, my turn. My brother got arrested in Thailand for some stupid fight that happened in a bar. He wasn't really involved, but then he got involved trying to help someone and ended up arrested—only Dad doesn't believe that part. Now Luke's in jail over there, waiting for court. Mum and Dad flew over there a few days ago so they could find him a lawyer, but they wouldn't let me come. Dad completely lost it. Says Luke has to move out and get a job and sort himself out. And I'm scared he'll just take off and not come back at all if Dad makes him do that."

"Oh, wow." Willa just blinks at her for a moment. "Okay, I think you win."

"It's not a competition, Willa." Eva grins, because they both know it always is.

"Is your brother going to be okay?"

"Oh, sure. No one over there—including the lawyer they can barely afford—thinks he's going to get in real trouble, but he'll have to leave Thailand. And things are going to be ugly around my place for a while."

"So who's staying with you while they're gone?"

"No one. They trust me not to party." She sighs and points at her books. "I don't have time to party."

"I know what you mean." As if Willa would even know how to party.

"How are things with Finn?" Eva asks. "Still good?"

"Really good." Willa plays with the lid of her pen. "It's like Finn's the one *right* thing at the moment, if you know what I mean?"

"Yeah, I do." Eva smiles. "I'm happy for you. Just remember, if it wasn't for me, you two might still not be talking to each other."

"True," Willa says, remembering that night at camp when Eva told her that sometimes you just have to compromise if you're really into someone. "Thank you for that. I owe you."

"You're welcome."

They smile at each other as the bell sounds across the library. Girls rise like a flock of checked birds, ready to migrate to class.

"I'm really sorry about your brother and everything," Willa says as she gathers her things. "That all sounds really stressful."

"Me too." Eva smiles. "I mean, I'm sorry for you too, about your grandmother and your dad weirdness."

"Nan will be okay. I just can't wait for her to get home." Willa holds out the blueberries again. "Sure you don't want some? They're good."

Eva sighs like she's relenting, plucks a single berry from the tray, and pops it in her mouth. "Yum. Let's go."

# CHAPTER 27

## Willa

"Stop it," Finn murmurs, pushing Willa away. She starts piling up her books and shoving them into her schoolbag. "Mum will be here in five minutes."

"You two are gross," Riley says from the top bunk. "I can hear you kissing, you know."

"You'll be this gross one day too, Riles," Finn tells her cheerfully.

"No, I won't."

"Put your headphones in, then." Willa lies back against her pillows, clutching her maths text, and pouts as she watches Finn pack her schoolbag.

"I've officially finished all my homework." Finn does a little fist pump. "Which means I've totally made up for being a slacker."

Willa wishes she could say the same. She's still got Lit and Japanese to do tonight. But first she has to make dinner.

Finn drops her bag on the floor and leans in close, pouting right back at her. "Bye."

Stubborn, Willa pulls Finn right down over her until she's a delicious weight, a Finn blanket. "I wish you could stay for tea," she whines.

"So do I. We're going to Anna's. So you should feel terrible for me, because she's an awful cook." She drops a kiss on Willa's neck.

The feel of Finn's lips makes Willa's blood ripple, and for an electric second, she wishes they were alone and she could send her hands all the places they would like to go right now. Why can't they have some time? And why doesn't she have her own room? "I'm so sorry all we do is hang out here and do homework," she whispers.

"It's not your fault. Anyway, I still get to hang out with you, and it's not like I didn't need to catch up on homework." Finn kisses her once more and climbs off.

Willa sighs, feeling the absence of her body like a loss.

Finn holds her hand out. "Walk me downstairs?"

"Of course."

"Bye, Miss Riley. Behave," Finn tells her.

Riley doesn't hear her. She's staring at her tablet, headphones on now, doing some lip sync thing with her friends online. She shimmies, her mouth moving to the words of some song only she can hear. How great it would be to be eleven and have twenty minutes of homework every night? Willa taps Riley's knee, thinking how Nan hates it when they spend too much time on their tablets. "Hey, Finn said goodbye. And you can come help me with dinner."

Riley drags her eyes from the tablet and stares at Willa like she hasn't understood a word.

Willa raises an eyebrow at her. "Don't even bother."

Instant pout. "Okay, but can we make homemade pizzas? I've always wanted to do that."

"Not tonight. I've still got a lot of homework to do. Maybe on the weekend."

"You've always got homework."

"You should be grateful she even makes you dinner." Finn steps up on the edge of Willa's bunk and taps Riley's nose. "If it was me looking after you, it'd be vegemite toast every single night."

She grins. "But at least it would be fun."

"Hey, that's not very nice."

Riley has the decency to look contrite. Only because it's Finn telling her off, though.

Willa wishes Riley's comment didn't sting, but it does. It's not as if she doesn't want to make pizzas with her little sister. To do something fun with her. But she knows she'd be up until late cleaning up and making up for lost study time.

"Thanks for defending my honour," Willa says as they traipse downstairs.

"She doesn't really get it, does she? How much you have to do?"

"She's only eleven. She's not meant to get it."

"Well, I see everything you do, and I think you're an okay sister." Finn gives her a winning smile.

"Oh, gee, thanks."

~ ~ ~

109

Riley pushes a cutting board of roughly—incredibly roughly—chopped cucumber towards her. Riley's knife skills are horrible. It probably didn't help that Willa gave her the bluntest knife she could find, but she'd rather hacksawed salad than another hospital trip.

"Okay, you're done," Willa says. "You can go watch TV."

"Yes!" Riley spins in a circle, grinning. "What's for dinner, anyway?"

"Spaghetti and salad."

Her shoulders drop. "*We always* have spaghetti."

"That's because it's one of the only things I know how to cook," Willa reminds her. "And you can't cook anything, so you don't get to complain."

Riley stalks off into the lounge room, looking disgusted.

Willa's throwing the pasta in to boil when her dad enters stage left. Awesome. More awkward small talk.

He fills a glass with water. "I watered the veggies."

She nods. What does he want? A medal?

"Your friend gone?"

"Yeah." She didn't even realise he notices Finn's coming and going. Or anything, really.

"She's new, right? I remember that Kelly kid always being around, but not her."

"Her name's Finn." Willa considers telling him the truth. But does she want to make things potentially more awkward? For the sake of honesty? A second later, she hears herself saying, "She's my girlfriend, actually."

Yes, apparently she does.

He nods slightly, but there's not a shimmer of a reaction in his expression. He just puts the glass down on the sink, slides his tobacco from his pocket, and goes straight back out into the yard.

She frowns and watches the spaghetti surrender to the roiling water. What the hell was that?

~ ~ ~

"Nothing?" Kelly frowns. "He said nothing?"

"Nothing. Like, I don't even know if he heard me. No, he *did* hear me." Willa thinks of that tiny nod. "But maybe he just didn't get it."

Kelly shakes her head. "No, he got it. What's not to get about 'she's not my friend, she's my girlfriend'? Seriously?"

"I guess."

"Do you think he's a homophobe?"

"I don't know. I don't know anything about him." Willa kicks at a pebble. "I hope not."

"You know what? Who cares? He's a shitty dad. Just another thing to add to the list."

"He's not that bad," Willa says, because she knows Kelly's just packing all her bitterness about her own useless father into this character assassination. Willa's dad hasn't proved himself a bad dad, he's just been a *non*-dad. "He always sends Nan money, and he's here now, isn't he?"

"Stop making excuses for him," Kelly says. "He dumped you here and left. Just because he remembers your birthdays and came down here to save you from the social workers doesn't mean he wins a prize."

Willa doesn't want to think too hard about how much she may or may not agree with that. She prefers to stay in a kind of stasis of *non* when it comes to her thoughts about him. It's comfy there. This way, he's just a guy in her house. An annoying but necessary presence.

"What did Finn say?"

"I didn't tell her." She doesn't want Finn to feel uncomfortable here. Because she might not come over any more. Then they'd never see each other. And it's not like he's going to say anything about it. That's pretty obvious after the dead air tonight.

Willa kicks another pebble and sighs. "I better go do the dishes so I can finish my homework. He never cleans or cooks or does anything."

"Sounds like my brother and dad."

"What are you up to tonight?" Willa asks her.

"I was going to ask if I could hang out here and watch TV, actually. It's kind of obnoxious at mine."

"Sounds like it." Willa heard the music coming from Kelly's as she set the table. You can still hear it now, the muted thrash of guitar drifting between houses.

"Yeah, Dave got paid for that three-day construction job, so they're celebrating. Like earning an actual wage is some glorious feat. I've been doing it since I was thirteen, and I'm actually going to finish school."

"Where's your dad?"

"Dunno." Kelly plucks a hibiscus flower from the bush and twirls it between her fingers.

"You can hang here," Willa tells her.

"I won't distract you, promise."

"I know you won't. There's spaghetti too, if you're haven't had tea yet." Willa's happy she can help her friend, even in this small way.

"Thanks, Will."

Kelly's so different when she smiles. It changes her face, softens that default glare she faces down the world with. Willa would tell her that, but Kelly always shoves compliments away. It's like she refuses to believe good things about herself.

"So, where's Princess Riley?" Kelly asks, following Willa into the kitchen. "I haven't stirred her up in a while."

# CHAPTER 28

## Finn

Finn shakes herself loose from a pile of cat and dog and shuffles into the living room. She can hear her mother on her phone in her room, her tone hushed and deliberately steady, the way she sounds when she talks to Finn's dad these days.

The house is a mess, signs of distraction piled up everywhere. Finn moves a stack of washing from the kitchen bench to the dining-room table. They never eat there now, anyway. It might as well become an extra wardrobe. Finn hadn't realised that this would be a gap left by her father's absence, this new trail of chaos sprouting from her mother, choking every path she takes through the house. Finn never noticed how much he did around the place. Every weekend, Anita wrangles it back into being, but it all creeps back to catastrophic by midweek.

The kettle's nearly boiled, and a pile of empty shopping bags gets shoved into a drawer when her mother comes out of the bedroom, buttoned into her work clothes, phone gripped in hand.

"That was Dad, wasn't it?" Finn asks.

Anita nods, putting her work bag on the table. "He's going to call you after school." Things move in and out of her bag at lightning speed.

Finn watches her, frowning. "Why didn't you tell me you talk to him?"

She pauses for a fraction of a second. "I guess I didn't want you to think too much about it."

"That's ridiculous. How could I not be thinking about it?" Finn plucks the milk from the fridge door. "My parents, who formerly coexisted peacefully, now live in different states. Trust me, I'm thinking about whether they talk to each other or not."

Anita's gaze drops to her bag. "I know you are."

"Or do you mean you didn't want me to get my hopes up?"

"No, of course not. I don't know what I meant." Suddenly, Anita looks small again. How does she do that? "I just don't want you to worry."

Too late.

Anita hovers, keys in hand, and Finn knows she's wondering if she should stay, if she'd be a bad mother if she left for work now.

"Have a good day," Finn tells her, turning away.

The silence is long, chased by the jingle of keys. "I'll be back by dinner, I hope. I'll pick up something up on the way home, okay?"

Even dinnertime is a gamble these days. When her dad was here, they'd eat at the regular time and save leftovers if Anita was late. Then she'd come home and bring her plate in front of the TV with them, catching up with their days while they watched whatever they watched. Now Finn eats at the bench alone half the time. Or just doesn't come home.

"Actually, I might go to Willa's." They haven't made plans, but Finn's sure it'll be okay.

"I think it would be nice to have dinner together." Anita's got her careful voice on. The "I want something to happen, but I don't want to fight over it" voice. As if tone can control the moment. "And you've been at Willa's a lot lately. Surely a night at home wouldn't hurt."

Finn doesn't respond, hoping this is just a random, rhetorical observation.

There's a shake of keys. "Finn?"

"Sorry, yeah, I know. I've been helping her look after her brother and sister. I'll try to be home by tea tonight. If you really want."

Suddenly, her mother's marching across the room, trying to smother the tension with one of her sneak-attack hugs. "We're going to be okay, you know," she says into Finn's shoulder.

Why does Finn feel like this is more for her mother than it is for her? "I know," she whispers, annoyed at the way it makes her throat ache.

Ten seconds later, the front door is closing. Finn listens to the silence drop around and switches off the coffee machine. She can't be here right now.

~ ~ ~

She spots Craig in the corner of the cafe, eyes glued to his computer screen, a huge mug of something frothy next to him.

She smiles to herself. A comrade. That's what she needs this morning. "Hey."

"Howdy." He grins and gestures at the empty seat across from him.

"Don't mind if I do." What is it about Craig that just feels so easy to be around? "What are you doing here so early?"

"Just chilling and caffeine loading. If I try and do it at home, the mother ship will default to nag mode. You?"

"Trying to catch up." She orders a coffee from a guy who looks far too harassed for the four customers total in the place and pulls out her laptop. "I am *this* close to dropping the ball."

"That's not good. Aren't you supposed to be setting an example to us lower beings?"

"Sorry." She gives him a wry grin. "Can a school captain be impeached? For being a slacker?"

"You don't even know the meaning of slack."

"Don't be so sure." Once she's armed with coffee, Finn digs deep into Speech Night planning. She reads through the notes and lists and permissions from last year's event. It's all pretty basic. Boring, actually. Organise the hall hire. Find an interesting alumnus as well as all the usual suspects—school and sports captains, the principal—to speak. She has to create a run sheet, get one of the graphic design kids to make the invite. Find some willing slaves to usher and turn lights and music on and off. Do the social media. Get Admin to send out letters. Write the letter. It's just another bunch of lists to tick off.

"So I heard about the school captain being from Year 11 next year." He cocks an eyebrow. "You ready?"

"If I get it."

"You'll get it."

Finn wishes people would stop acting like it's a given. Until lately, she probably wouldn't have cared so much. She's always been secretly proud that people think of her as *that* girl. But these days, she's not so sure she deserves it.

When she looks up, he's staring at her.

"What?"

"Do you *want* to be school captain?"

"Of course. If I get the chance. It's good to be able to say you were captain. Resumes and stuff." She sounds like Willa.

"But do you *like* doing it? I mean, it seems like a whole lot of work."

"Honestly?" She pulls in a deep breath. "Lately, I don't like it as much as I thought I would." Even as she's saying it, part of her wishes she could yank the words back into her mouth and lock them away. "Please don't tell anyone I said that."

He lifts his hands, as if to say "who would I tell?"

It's true. Craig is probably the safest repository of secrets there is. Finn's never heard a single word of gossip out of his mouth.

She stares at her screen, hoping he won't pursue her little revelation.

But of course he does. He stares at her some more, head tipped to one side. "So you're saying future leaders camp made you *less* prepared to lead? Put that in the feedback survey. No one's going next year."

"That's not what happened. Not exactly. It's been more of a thing since I got back. I don't know, I just thought there'd be more to this job." She actually got to do more for the school last year when she was just a student rep, coming up with ideas for charities and awareness events and campaigning for new programs. Back then, she had time to form ideas to make the school better. Now she's too busy being the token student at parent-teacher things, writing mundane reports, being a glorified event manager, and organising Speech Night—plan-by-numbers slave labour.

"Maybe it is a little bit about camp too, though," she muses. "After all the quick thinking we had to do at Camp Nowhere to win, this captain job seems even less exciting." She sighs. "I'm pretty sure this isn't what the teachers had in mind for me to learn, but I don't know. I'm starting to wonder if everything is really just preordained. That to be captain, all you really have to do is be a model school citizen, turn up to stuff, and do the jobs no one else wants to do."

"So you're just like their little student-bot photo op?"

"It feels like it sometimes." Finn thinks of the parents group meeting she had to go to last week, where she was asked to read a report she'd written on the Year 9 and 10 extracurricular activities. When she was done, they'd just thanked her and carried on

116

with the same petty, circular arguments they'd been having about everything, from uniforms to budget priorities. No one had asked her what she thought, or even talked about the students, really.

Finn had sat there, bored, eyes on the conversation but her thoughts floating loose, drifting through a million things: her new painting, Nona's second attempt to convince them they should have a sit-in at the community centre, the ripple of Willa's ribs through her T-shirt as they kissed against a tree in the park last night, waiting for Jack to finish soccer practice. Anywhere but on that bickering and power-playing in the room that had nothing to do with her.

"So," Craig says, "you're saying you wouldn't care if you weren't picked for school captain next year?"

"I'm not saying that," she says quickly. That hadn't even occurred to her. Maybe it will be different when she's whole-school captain. "It's just a bit…" She sits back in her seat. "I don't know, uninspiring this term. Like organising Speech Night." She rolls her eyes.

"Speech Night is just awkward."

"You've been to one?"

"Have I ever." He taps his chest. "You're looking at number-one lighting director. I'll be the one turning the spotlight on yet another earnest, heartfelt speech about school spirit from the principal—who will talk *forever* if you don't stop him, by the way."

"That's one volunteer to tick off my list." She grins at him. "I'm putting you down as confirmed for this year."

"Excellent. I look forward to it."

"Liar."

He laughs.

They work quietly, as kids and teachers run in and out, ordering coffees and cholesterol breakfasts before dashing over the road to the campus.

It's ten to nine, and Finn's stuffing everything back into her bag when Craig snickers at his laptop. "Hey, have you ever heard of a filibuster?"

"A what?"

"A filibuster. Apparently it's this thing that politicians do to buy time when they don't want to a bill to pass in a parliament. They just get up and take their turn arguing against it and try to make their argument last right until the end of the session so there's no time for the vote to be taken that day. You just talk and talk about the topic, and you can't stop, even to go to the toilet."

She pulls a face. "Who'd do that?"

"This woman." He turns his screen around to show a news article showing a photo of a serious blonde woman in a suit. "So, apparently, she's in Texas right now, in her eighth hour of talking, trying to stop some anti-abortion law from passing."

"Really? That's cool. Can you send me the link?" Her dad would like that story.

"Why? You going to filibuster Speech Night?"

"Didn't you say the principal does that already?" She yanks her bag onto her shoulder. "I'll see you later."

# CHAPTER 29

## Willa

They wait for Amira under the purple sweep of jacaranda in the library courtyard. It's Willa's favourite spot at school. She loves the way petals litter the mossy brick, creating a vivid carpet. She first saw this courtyard on a school tour with the principal and Nan. That's when she knew for sure that this place would be nothing like the brown-brick eyesore of her old school.

She opens her bag and contemplates her sad, white vegemite sandwich. It's been all pre-sliced supermarket bread and bare-minimum fillings since Nan went to hospital. Something else for Riley to complain about. "Hey, how's your brother?" she asks Eva.

"Okay. They're back from Thailand tomorrow night. He got a big fine, which Dad had to pay. So things should be nice and tense at my place for a while."

Willa gives her a sympathetic smile.

"I haven't told Amira about it, by the way. I haven't really told anyone."

"I won't say anything, I promise."

"Thanks." Eva turns her can of Diet Coke in slow circles and stares at a table of Year 9s cackling evilly about something next to them. "It's kind of embarrassing, this delinquent-brother crap. I mean, I love him, but couldn't he just...I don't know, be normal?"

Before Willa can find the right thing to say, Amira arrives, all business for once. She flips her folder open and says, "All right, let's do this."

Eva glances at Willa, one eyebrow raised. "Uh, okay, *Miss.*"

"Hey, I'm trying to keep you impatient dorks happy for once. So go with it." Amira points a finger at her. "There's a very narrow window of studious Amira today. You want her or not?"

"Bring her on," Eva says.

They inch their way through the long, boring dialogue. They're supposed to be a group of friends visiting Tokyo, meeting Japanese colleagues for the first time. It's the most basic getting-to-know-you stuff. Still, it's taken a thousand years to pull the script together, in an endless file share of editing. Amira's the best by far. She never stumbles, and her accent is good. She actually sounds like a Japanese person might be able to figure out what she's saying.

Willa knows she's the most stilted and slow of the three of them. But that's because while they were learning Japanese basics back in Year 9, she was neck deep in Italian grammar at her old school and surrounded by kids who could already speak it.

Her last line comes out completely tangled. "Sorry." Willa glares at the page. She's prepared to accept being clueless at other stuff, like small talk and netball, but not schoolwork.

"Don't worry. You've got the dialogue, and the pronunciation's mostly right. Your accent's just a bit crap." Amira gives her an apologetic smile. "Sorry."

"It's okay, I know." It doesn't stop Willa from blushing, though.

"You know what you should do?"

"What?"

"Watch a whole bunch of Japanese TV. There's stuff on YouTube. Do it right before the test. It gets you into the rhythm and the accent."

"Okay, I'll try it." Jack loves all that manga stuff. Maybe Willa can watch something with him.

Amira fans her face dramatically. "Oh em gee, I'm helping Willa Brookes with schoolwork. This is, like, life goals."

"Sh," Willa tells her, pressing a finger to her lips.

"No, I will not." Amira throws an arm around her and grins. "This is my happy place." Then she sighs loudly and releases her. "And my not-happy place is the history essay that's due tomorrow."

Willa nods. The history essay is how she's planning on spending her evening. It needs one more draft, and she still has to do her references. So much to look forward to.

"I'm done with it," Eva says, stretching her arms out behind her.

"God, you're annoying," Amira says. "I've barely started."

"No, *Ms Foley's* annoying," Eva says, "She marks you down if there's even a comma out of place in your bibliography."

"That chick is so uptight," Amira says. "Lady needs to get some."

"That is such a deeply unfeminist thing to say, Mir," Eva says.

"No, it's the truth. Anyway, she's trying to get some. Cat Nguyen reckons she saw her profile on Cupid's Arrow."

"What was Cat doing on Cupid's Arrow? It's for old people."

"How the hell would I know?"

"Um, because you know everything that's happening in this school."

"True." Amira opens up a container of salad and brandishes a fork. "Where's your lunch?" she asks Eva.

"I ate during the prefects' meeting."

Willa's sandwich stops halfway to her mouth. Because that's not even slightly true. Willa was sitting right next to Eva at that meeting. She wasn't eating. She was taking notes, like always.

There's this sickening feeling in her stomach as a series of connections make themselves in her mind. All the times that Eva hasn't eaten lunch when they've been studying. Eva being weird about eating the blueberries. Eva looking so tired and different lately. She stares at Eva, trying to decide if those pale arms are skinnier than usual, or those cheekbones sharper.

Willa's mind scrambles, trying to remember the plate of snacks that day at Eva's house. Did she actually have any of it? All Willa can remember is Eva topping it up and rearranging it. She can't remember whether she actually digested anything on it.

"Come on, guys, let's run this thing one more," Eva says, bursting into Willa's thoughts.

"Sure," Willa says slowly, dragging herself back to the task.

~ ~ ~

On her way to Geography, Willa's mentally planning her schedule for tonight, trying to optimise essay time, when she hears her name being called.

It's Cassavetes, leaning out her office door, ragged and distracted as always. She looks apologetic too, so Willa steels herself for whatever's coming.

Cassavetes launches right in, clasping her hands together. "I'm so sorry, Willa. I've been trying to find Stella, but it turns out she's home sick. Is there any chance you could come to one more curriculum meeting?"

Willa fights a sigh. "Sure. When?"

The vice principal at least has the decency to cringe. "Tonight?"

"Oh, um…" Willa thinks quickly. She'll have to call the school and get Jack to join Riley at the after-school program. Then she can pick them up on the way home. Or maybe she could chance a call to her dad. *No*, she decides. He probably won't even answer. They can eat something super basic for dinner. Leftovers, maybe. That way she can get straight to work after dinner's cleaned up. "Okay. I can do it."

"Thank you, Willa." She tips her head back and sighs. "A lifesaver again. I can't tell you how wonderful it is to have someone so responsible doing your job."

Willa muscles a smile and heads for class, feeling the slide of disappointment. Because she won't be able to visit Nan after school now. She loves going to see Nan in the afternoons. Because even in that stark, ugly rehab centre, when she's with the kids and Nan, the air thickens with home. And, even better, Willa gets to be the kid again. To tuck herself under the comforting wing of all Nan's questions and chiding reminders and to take a breath. She doesn't have to make any decisions or be responsible for anything but herself. It's like a daily minibreak. But not today. Today she's going to have to go without that comfort.

She's almost late to class. Almost. She drops down next to Eva as the bell rings and pulls out her book.

That's right. Eva. Willa sighs inwardly. What's she supposed to do about Eva? She's seen the TV shows. She knows you're supposed to say something if your friend's lying about eating. What do you say? "Hey, why are you pretending to eat when you're clearly not?" If it were Kelly or Maida, Willa probably would launch straight in like that. But she has no idea how Eva would react to that. What if Eva just denies it? Or gets angry? Then what?

The History teacher starts running them through their next assignment—before they've even finished the last. Willa shoves the Eva worry down and replaces it with this new one.

# CHAPTER 30

## Finn

"So, Finn." Nona leans across the table. "I can't believe I haven't asked already. Are you coupled up, or are you single and mingling?"

Rosie gives Finn a sly look. Rosie's totally convinced that Nona's got a thing for Finn, but Finn's convinced Nona's got a thing for every girl. A full-time flirt. It's Nona's thing. In fact, you'd think it was her superpower.

"You *have* asked me before." Finn grins at her. "I just didn't answer. I have a girlfriend."

"A hottie too," Rosie says. "I've seen pictures."

"Is that so?" Nona raises an eyebrow.

"It's almost unfair," Rosie says.

That brings a smile to Finn's face. Because that's the thing about Willa. She's the kind of pretty you comment on. And it's even prettier because she doesn't act like she is. She just wears it like she wears her clothes, simple and unfussed. Even Finn's mother mentioned Willa's looks after she met her, and she's usually all teacher and "it's what's inside that counts".

Sometimes Finn just wants to sit and stare at Willa, memorising every part. She's already got her all favourites down by heart. Drawing them is easy. Willa doesn't even have to be there any more for Finn to know exactly how to sketch the thin line of Willa's lower lip or her long hands or the athletic slenderness of her shoulders. The same way she knows their exact shape under her fingers. Life is Willa in a tank top. It's lust too.

Not that Finn would tell Nona that. Just like she would never tell anyone that she doesn't know what to do with Willa's hotness sometimes. That sometimes the pull of it makes her freeze when she knows it should make her do the opposite.

"So, when can I meet her?" Nona asks.

"You'd probably scare her off," Rosie says. "Didn't you say she's kind of quiet, Finn?"

It's funny because Rosie is *so* wrong. About the scared-off part, anyway. No way would Willa be scared of Nona.

"Oh, look at Finn, smiling to herself like a creeper," Nona hoots. "Thinking about your hottie?" She elbows Kayah to get her attention, but she's staring at her phone.

"Hey, I've got an idea," Finn says brightly. "Let's think about doing some work. You know that thing where we desperately need an idea about how to save the centre?"

Kayah puts her phone down. "Yeah, Nona, imagine how great it would be if your mouth was constantly spilling ideas instead of rubbish."

Nona pulls a face of silent, mock outrage.

"Seriously, how long do you think you could go on for?" Kayah shakes her head. "I reckon you could talk for days and still not say anything useful."

"Let's not test that," Rosie says.

Finn has to laugh, remembering the filibuster story that Craig showed her in the café. She wonders if Nona could challenge that woman who talked for nine hours. She's about to ask them if they read the article when the idea hits her. What if they held their own?

"Hey." She turns to Kayah. "I think I possibly might have an idea."

# CHAPTER 31

## Willa

The afternoon is a scramble.

Willa endures the curriculum meeting, where all she was asked for the whole thirty minutes was to give her opinion on whether the homeroom period should be three minutes longer. As soon as she's on the bus, she starts going over her essay, making copious notes in the margins, ready to rewrite when she gets home.

When the bus finally delivers her from the choke of afternoon traffic a block from the primary school, she hurries to drag the kids from the after-school program and onto a tram, thinking it might be faster than walking. Instead, it's hot and crowded as it inches down High Street. Riley insists on leaning against her the whole way as she chatters about the kiddie yoga class they just did. Willa shuts her eyes and tries to ignore the sweat gathering under the arms of her blazer.

Next to her, Jack sniffs constantly between hay-fevered sneezes. He looks so miserable that Willa tries not to let it bother her, even though it makes her want to scream. She just hands him tissue after tissue and blocks it out, still clutching the essay in her hand.

By the time they get home, the stress that's been nipping at her all day has Willa firmly in its grip. She drops her bag at the bottom of the stairs and trudges into the kitchen. Because unless her dad has finally noticed dinner is a meal that doesn't just magically materialise, she's still got food to think about.

No such luck. She stands in front of the pantry, blankly staring. Why can't it be one of those afternoons when one of Nan's cronies drops by with a casserole? Usually it's annoying, because half the time made up in not cooking is lost to polite small talk. But she'd settle for that deal right now.

The sound of cartoons erupts from the next room.

"Hey, go change out of your uniforms," she calls, "*before* TV. And have you got homework?"

"Nope," Jack mutters.

"I've got spelling," Riley yells. "Can you test me?"

"Later." The breakfast dishes are still on the sink. Willa glares at them. Why the hell was she expecting him to do something about dinner when he doesn't even seem to notice a bunch of dishes? Riley's bowl isn't rinsed, as usual, and it's become a gum of puffed rice bits and dried milk. She runs the water so hot it stings her fingers.

Jack comes in, a note in his hand. He hands it to Willa. "This is for you."

"What's it about?"

"A barbecue after soccer tomorrow night. To celebrate making finals. It says we have to bring sausages."

Frowning, Willa grabs the note. "How long has this been in your bag?"

"Since practice."

"Practice last week? *Seriously*?" She lets out a hiss of impatience as the note flutters to the bench. "When the hell am I going to have time to get you sausages?"

"Sorry." He's staring at his feet.

"It's okay," she says softly, chastised by the nervous little line of his mouth. "We'll figure it out." She squeezes his shoulder. "I'm glad you made finals. We'll come down and watch this weekend, okay? Me and Riles." Riley's not going to be happy, but Willa doesn't care.

"Okay." As he slips back into the lounge room, her mind turns back instantly to dinner. She yanks the fridge door open and stands there, blinking. Last night's mashed potato is gone. So are the lamb chops. Her dad must have eaten them. Fighting the urge to swear loudly, she turns for the bread bin. There are two crusts, stale and abandoned, inside the bag. There goes the toasted-sandwich idea. Pasta it is. Riley will have to lump it.

The sliding door opens. Her dad rubs his chin and grunts a greeting.

With a nod, she goes back to the sink. Ever since the Finn-is-her-girlfriend revelation, their communication has devolved into transactional exchanges. Willa doesn't know whether to be hurt or relieved by the cease and desist on clumsy conversation attempts.

"I'm heading out for a bit," he tells her.

Of course he is. She scrubs the last, cemented rice puffs from Riley's bowl. "Will you want dinner?"

"No. I won't be back until later. Need anything?"

"Jack needs some sausages for a soccer barbecue tomorrow. Can you bring some back?" At least that's one less thing to worry about.

"Sure." He slips out of the room.

"And maybe," she mutters as she hears the front door close, "you could make some dinner? Or just buy a freaking family-sized pizza once in a while." She tosses the sponge at the sink. It bounces off the tiles and lands on the floor. This time she swears so loudly it seems to bounce around the room.

The noisy notes of whatever cartoon Jack is watching compete with the thick strains of guitar floating in the window. No such thing as peace in this place.

It's no better upstairs either. Riley's dancing around in her underwear and singlet, humming, her uniform a pool of green checks on the floor.

"Pick up your dress. You have to wear it again tomorrow." There's no way Willa's going to be able to squeeze in washing clothes tonight.

Riley shimmies across the small patch of carpet, singing to herself. She plucks the dress off the floor and tosses it on the bed.

"That's not what I meant, and you know it." Willa pulls out her laptop.

There's an exaggerated eye roll as Riley whips a coat hanger from the wardrobe. "What's for tea?"

"It's not for an hour."

"So? I'm allowed to know what we're having."

"I don't know yet," Willa lies, frowning at the screen. Her laptop is taking forever to start up.

"Not spaghetti. I'm sick of spaghetti." Riley leans out the window, taking in big breaths of air. "It's so hot. Want to go to the park? I could put my feet in the fountain."

"Go stand under the sprinkler."

"It's boring by myself." Riley claps her hands together, eyes wide. "*Please*."

"I can't." Willa stares at the screen, waiting for something to happen. "I've got an essay to finish."

"You're boring." Stomping over to the desk, she plonks herself down on the edge and kicks her feet against the drawers.

"Can you please go and watch TV or something?"

"No." Riley starts singing under her breath, testing her.

Willa gives her a warning look, but Riley just keeps singing, the smallest of smart-ass smiles dancing behind it.

She bites down on her irritation. Why does Riley have to pick today to pull an evil-little-wench act? "Go downstairs, please."

"No, it's my room. I can be in here."

"I'm trying to work." When she taps at a key, nothing happens. The start-up window just blinks at her, unchanging. "Go downstairs to play."

"But there's nothing to do. It's boring. You *never* do anything with me."

Something spills over inside Willa. "Yes, I know I'm boring. Completely freaking boring! But you," she points at her, "you're being a spoilt brat! I'm boring because I spend all my time looking after you. I have to scrub your cereal bowl because no matter how many times I ask you, you can never just rinse one dish. Then I have to make your dinner and help you with your spelling, and then I have to listen to you whinge about how you don't want to eat this and that and how you're not allowed to stay up late enough and how you don't want to go to bed. Believe me, you're just as boring! So, please, go downstairs and let me do my essay." She picks up her sister's schoolbag, which she's dumped in the middle of the small stretch of carpet, and tosses it into the corner. "And clean up after yourself for once!"

Riley's eyes are saucer wide, but Willa just sits down in front of her computer, ignoring her. It's still deliberating on that same screen, the cursor blinking, as if it can't make up its mind. She swears. Loudly.

Riley jumps down from the desk, her mouth fixed in a little purse. She doesn't say a word as she pulls on a pair of leggings, but Willa can see she's fighting tears. Guilt flickers at the edge of her frustration. Riley doesn't cry.

"Hey," she says softly.

But Riley's already running down the stairs.

# CHAPTER 32

## Finn

Finn's feeling good as she leaves the community centre. The sun's shining, she's got an idea to save the centre that the others like, and today she finished a painting she really likes in art club. And it's Thursday. Which wouldn't be as good as a Friday, except her school is having a pupil-free day tomorrow. Finn doesn't know who's happier, the teachers or the students.

Ready to plan her next move, she whips out her phone. There's a double-parental assault.

Dad: *I miss you, kiddo. When do you think you can make it for another visit?*

Mum: *I'll be stuck here until six. See you at half past.*

Finn's footsteps slow. Surprise. She's coming home to an empty house again. Instead of replying to either of them, she messages Willa.

*Okay if I drop by for a minute and say hi?*

Finn likes being at Willa's house, being around the chaotic, cosy groove Willa and her siblings have worn with one another. And she loves how patient Willa is with her brother and her sister. And they seem to love her like no siblings Finn knows. Not like Dan and his brothers, who are locked in constant combat. And just yesterday Rosie told Finn that she and her two older sisters never talk to each other, except to fight.

It's nothing like that at Willa's. Even Riley at her worst listens when Willa says the word. And Willa's so patient, considering how ratty Riley can be sometimes. She loves how Willa's always looking out for Jack too. Asking him questions to draw him out when he doesn't talk. Sitting with him while he does his homework, giving him a chance to ask the questions he won't seek out on his own. Watching weird cartoons with him because he loves them. Finn would never have believed that the forthright, take-no-prisoners girl she met at camp would be capable of such softness. But Willa is.

Her phone buzzes a response.

*Sure.*

Choosing to take the shortness of Willa's response as sweet, Finn changes course for her house.

Willa's hunched on her bottom bunk, still encased in her uniform. She's pushing loose strands of her ponytail back with one hand as she smacks at the keys of her laptop with the other.

"I don't think they like it when you do that," Finn jokes.

Willa barely looks up as Finn perches next to her. "There's something weird going on with my laptop. It's been starting up for, like, twenty minutes." She clicks her tongue. "I don't have time for this. I have an essay due tomorrow."

"Maybe it's doing updates. Just give it a minute." Finn curls her hands around Willa's arm. "Anyway, I won't distract you from your homework. I really just came to say hi. And to nag you."

"Nag me?" Willa drags her gaze from her screen. "About what?"

"Let's just say there's been a little pressure from the best friend department. And perhaps there's been a few conspiracy theories about you not actually existing, of my supposedly staging photos, etcetera, etcetera." Finn grins.

Wait, what?" Willa blinks at her, like she's still trying to tune in.

"Dan's dying to meet you. I know you're really busy, but I was wondering if you'd maybe have a minute to go for a coffee after school sometime? You know, so he'll shut up."

Willa taps at the keyboard again. "It's like it's just…stuck here." She shakes her head briskly, like she's trying to reset her thoughts. "So hang on. You want me to meet Dan?"

"Yes." Finn tries not to let the fact that Willa's barely listening bother her. Why did she even want Finn to come over if she's not going to talk to her? She sits up. "But you know what? We can talk about it another time."

This time, Willa doesn't even answer.

Finn frowns. Maybe she should just leave Willa to it. It's like she's not here anyway.

"I maybe can on the weekend," Willa says finally. "It depends on Riley and Jack."

"What's up with Riley, anyway? She barely looked at me when I came in."

"Don't ask."

"Okay." Finn leans against Willa's shoulder, staring at the laptop. It really is doing a woeful job of being a computer. "Can you force quit?"

"Tried it."

"Taken the battery out?"

"I don't even know how to do that." She lets out another exasperated moan and punches her fist into the mattress. "It was working fine yesterday."

Finn's phone buzzes. Another text from her dad.

*Seriously. Let me know which weekend, and I'll book you a ticket, pronto.*

She lets out a hiss. He's clearly not going to let this go until she answers.

Willa turns her computer over and peers at the bottom. "What's wrong?"

"Nothing. It's just Dad. He keeps hassling me about when I'm going to go over to visit him again." She shoves her phone into her pocket and goes over to the open window. It's so stuffy in this tiny room, cloyed with both the heat of a windless day and Willa's frustration.

Outside, Riley's pouting and digging a stick into the ground. Loud music thunders from one of the neighbours' houses. "Why do I have to fly to all the way to Tasmania because *he* wants to see me? Why can't he come over here? I mean, he's the one who left, not me. But somehow I'm the one who has to make all the effort."

"Oh, come on, Finn."

"What?"

Willa's frowning at her, the computer still clutched in her hands. "How often does your dad call and text you?"

Finn rolls her eyes. "All the time."

"And this is a problem because?"

"Because he just keeps nagging about me visiting." Has Willa even been listening? "I'm really busy with school and the community centre and stuff. I can't just run away every weekend that he wants to see me."

"Do you know," and now, suddenly, Willa's gaze is unrelenting, "that I've seen my dad seven times since I was eight? I counted the other day."

Finn presses her lips together. "I'm sorry," she mutters.

But it's like Willa doesn't even hear her. "You know what else? My dad lives in the same house as me right now and barely knows how to talk to me. In fact, ever since I told him you're my girlfriend, he barely even *looks* at me. So you should stop complaining just because—oh, poor you—your dad wants to hang out with you. I mean, what an asshole, right?"

"Okay, I get it. I'm sorry." Finn frowns, a perplexing mix of guilt and anger competing inside her. "But what did I do wrong?"

"Well, for starters, you're being a big baby about this."

"A baby?" For a second, Finn can only blink. Then anger wins, clenching her stomach like a fist. It clenches even harder when Willa just shrugs and starts to pound her finger on her keyboard, like she's done with the conversation.

Finn waits for her to apologise, but Willa just keeps staring at her computer, giving her nothing. She hasn't seen this arctic version of Willa since camp. And she hated it as much back then as she does right now.

"You know what?" Finn scoops up her schoolbag. "It's not my fault your computer's died. And it's not my fault your dad doesn't visit you. And it's definitely not my fault you're in a foul mood. Don't say I can come over just so you can take it out on me." She stalks out the door and dashes down the stairs.

Outside, the world is bright and clamorous as it battles its way home in the form of peak hour. Finn marches down the street, rigid with anger. But by the time she reaches the end of the street, it has faded to something else, something stiller and contemplative. And as she stands at the corner, waiting for the lights, recognition takes form.

She knows what this is. She's seen it before, at camp. This is just Willa shooting word bullets because she's afraid of the feelings that will consume her once she stops firing. This is Willa rubbed raw with stress.

The lights change, but Finn doesn't move. She remembers that day at camp, when Willa did the same to Drew in front of a crowd of people just because she was scared and worried about her sister.

Finn draws in a deep breath and turns slowly. Because her heart won't let her do anything else.

Riley answers her knock.

"Hey, thanks. I forgot something."

Riley just gives her a glum smile and stalks away into the depths of the house.

Finn frowns. Is anyone in this house happy today?

Upstairs, Willa's a demoralised hunch on the bed, her face pressed into her hands. The computer is now completely blank screened, like it's surrendered too.

She leans on the doorjamb. "Will, what's wrong?"

When Willa finally lifts her head, the anger has completely evaporated, and now she just looks miserable. Tears have turned her eyes liquid amber. "I'm really sorry," she whispers.

Finn crosses the room and sits gently next to her. "Hey, it's not like you were wrong. I know I'm lucky. I shouldn't complain just because my dad wants to see me."

"But I was being awful. You're not being a baby." Willa shakes her head, her eyes insistent. "I know it's hard with him gone."

"Don't worry about it." Finn tucks a fallen strand of hair behind her ear. "Are you okay? I mean, clearly you're not."

Willa presses her face into her hands again. It muffles her voice as she says, "I yelled at Riley too. Just because she wanted to go to the park and put her feet in the fountain."

"She'll live."

"But I *want* to take her to the park." Willa swipes at her eyes. "I never do anything with them anymore. Nothing fun. But I can't, because I have this stupid essay to write. And now my computer's broken. And I need to cook dinner because Dad never does. Then I have to help Riley with her spelling and finish my maths and figure out what to do about Eva, and then there's—"

"Hey, stop." Finn grabs her shoulders. "One thing at a time."

"But there never is." Willa lets out a charge of breath. "There's *never* just one thing at a time anymore. There are too many things. *All the time.*"

She looks so helpless that Finn just grabs hold of her and squeezes. Squeezes her like she's trying to push all the stress out of her. No one's head should be this crowded with worries. No one their age, anyway.

"I've never yelled at Riley in my life," Willa whispers.

"Which is why she'll forgive you for it."

She lets out a little moan. "And how am I going to get this essay done?"

"Is the only version on the computer? Please say no."

"No, I've got a print-out of the last draft in my bag. I could have handed that in, but I wrote all over the margins."

"Okay, listen," Finn sits up. "I'm going to go home and get my laptop for you. Do your maths, and by the time you're finished, I'll be back with my computer, okay?"

"Really?"

Finn smiles at the small bloom of hope in Willa's eyes. "Of course. Easy fix."

"But will your mum let you come back on a school night?"

"I don't have school tomorrow, remember? I'm a free agent." Finn goes over to the window and leans out. "Hey, Riles!"

"What?" Riley scowls up at her.

"Stop looking like that and come up here for a minute!" Finn points at the pile of textbooks next to Willa and puts on her best schoolteacher voice. "Maths. Do it."

You can hear the drama in every step as Riley plods up the stairs. When she finally appears, she's in full sulk mode, arms across chest, bottom lip out.

Finn pretends not to notice. "Hey, want to come for a walk to my house? You can meet my dogs."

"Yes!" Riley turns and plucks some sandals from the bottom of her wardrobe. Then she stops and slowly turns to Willa, her voice turning monotone. "Am I allowed?"

Willa's expression hovers somewhere between amused and sad. "Riles, come here." When Riley obeys, she clasps her sister's wrist and shakes it gently. "I'm really sorry I yelled at you before."

"It's all right," Riley says as if it's anything but.

"Hey," Finn says. "Remember last week when you dropped a whole glass of orange cordial on the lounge room carpet because you were too busy staring at the TV to watch where you were going? Remember how Willa didn't even get mad at you?" Finn jabs her side. "I'd have killed you."

Riley hangs her head and grins. Then she leans in and gives Willa a ginger, one-armed hug. "We cool?"

Willa laughs. "We're cool."

"Okay, let's do this," Finn says. "Go see if your brother wants to come."

"He's at Tyler's." Riley bolts out of the room and down the stairs.

"And don't worry about dinner," Finn tells Willa. "I've got a plan."

"What, no. It's okay. I'll make—"

"Spaghetti? Even I'm sick of your spaghetti. I mean, it's good, but there's such a thing as overkill, you know."

Willa gives her a dirty look, but Finn just laughs. "I'm making dinner, and you have to let me. To make up for you being evil before." When Willa's expression turns doubtful, Finn bends right over her and says, "I want to help, okay? I've got the day off tomorrow, I've got no homework, I get to be around you. *Let me help you.*"

Relief inches its way into Willa's smile. "Okay."

"Good. See you soon."

Finn trots down the stairs, feeling like a superhero.

# CHAPTER 33

## Finn

When they get to Finn's house, her mother's putting away the shopping.

"Hey, Mum. You remember Riley?"

Anita spins, a can of tomatoes in her hand. She smiles. "Of course. Hello, Riley."

"Hi." Riley goes all shy, sidling closer to Finn.

Finn drops an arm around her. "The dogs will be on my bed, probably. First door in the hallway. And on the bottom shelf of my desk there's a bunch of old DVDs. Pick one for us to watch. But be quick."

"Okay." She skates across the floor on her socks.

"Where did you acquire a child?" Anita asks from inside the pantry. "And will she be staying for dinner?"

"No. I'm going to Willa's." Finn pulls a snow pea from a bag and munches on it. "She's really, really stressed about an essay, and her computer's broken, so I said she could use mine while I watch a movie with Riley."

"Am I a broken record?" Anita pulls a box of muesli out of a bag. "What do I always say on school nights?"

"It's a student-free day tomorrow, remember?" Finn stares at the box of muesli in her mother's hand. Why is Anita even buying it? Finn hates the stuff, and Anita doesn't eat breakfast. She's always forgetting and buying things only her dad eats.

"Oh, that's right."

"So I'm going to teach Riles how to make pizzas and help her with her spelling while Willa does her essay." She grins. "Well, we're making pizza toppings on a shop base because I know my cooking limitations, which are many."

"Shouldn't you be out doing something fun?"

"Can't." Finn picks out another snow pea and frowns. "Willa's got school tomorrow, and we—"

"I meant *you*."

"Since when do you tell me to go out and have fun? My sadly early curfew suggests you're against it."

"There are plenty of things you could do and still come home early. Go the movies. Go out for dinner." Anita leans against the counter, giving her a sober look. "Look, I know Willa's got a lot of troubles at the moment, but you don't always have to be involved. You seem to be there all the time. What about your other friends?"

For a moment, Finn can only stare. "Why are you all of a sudden anti-Willa? I thought you liked her."

"Of course I do. She's lovely. I'm just not sure you need to be taking on someone else's responsibilities when you have enough of your own."

"Since when is helping someone who is having a hard time a bad thing?" Anger flushes Finn's cheeks for the second time tonight. "And what if I don't want to go out? I mean, I guess I could sit here in the empty house and wait for you to come home?"

There's a flicker of a warning look, but Anita opts for resignation at the last moment. "Look, I'm just saying that you need to have some of your own time too. You can't always be doing things for—"

She stops abruptly as Riley skips into the kitchen, a DVD in her hand and the dogs at her feet. "They're so cute. Can they come with us?"

"Sorry, mate. But we can take them for a walk on the weekend, okay?" Finn gives her mum a look, daring her to be annoyed by yet another babysitting promise. But Anita's staring at the counter, her fingernails drumming the dark-green surface. She looks tired and over it. So is everybody today, apparently. "Okay, I'm going to get my laptop, and then we'll go." Finn gives her mother a stony look as she passes. "And before you ask, I'm taking my bike. And, yes, I have my lights and helmet, and I'll be home by ten."

She stalks into her bedroom before Anita can reply.

# CHAPTER 34

## Willa

Willa stares at Finn's rough little drawing of the lamp-lit kitchen. She still cannot get over Finn's talent sometimes, the way she's sketched the window and the sink and the garlic plait with a soft grey lead. It looks so cosy and welcoming, like a picture in a book.

The real kitchen is not too bad either. The dinner mess has been cleared, and the dishes are all stacked on the dish rack. By sheer Finn miracle, Riley actually helped clean up without whining. It gets better too: there's leftover pizza in the fridge for school lunches, and both her brother and sister are in bed. Willa's hell day is nearly over. Only it doesn't seem quite as hellish any more.

She wants to flinch when she thinks about how she acted before, how close she came to messing up things with Finn. It was so dumb and so…*mean*, snapping at her like that. But it was like the stress was stealing Willa's brains and breath. And then when Finn left, clattering down the steps, there was this shipwrecked feeling in its place. But when Finn came back to her, Willa's breath came back too. And she knows just how lucky she is that her girlfriend and her gigantic heart came back at all.

Finn takes her time reading, her eyes slowly scanning the screen. After what feels like an eternity, she turns to Willa with a smile. "I can't see a single comma out of place."

"Are you sure?"

"I'm sure. It's time to put this baby in the ground." She pushes the laptop back to her. "It's really good too."

Willa's saving her essay to her USB when the front door opens and closes. She grits her teeth, a sitting duck to the coming awkwardness.

When he sees them, he pauses in the doorway.

Willa does her best to muster normal from somewhere. "Hey, Dad. You remember Finn?"

"Yeah, of course. G'day." He gives Finn a brief nod.

"Hello." Finn's greeting is not her usual off-the-cuff friendly, and Willa instantly regrets what she said earlier. Not that it matters. He's gone before it can turn weird. He cuts straight across the kitchen and out the back door. Seconds later, she hears the spray of the hose.

"Let's go to my room." Willa grabs up her books.

Upstairs, Riley's fast asleep, her arm dangling from the top bunk as she snores gently. Willa lifts it gently back onto the mattress and crawls onto her own bunk. She flicks a switch, and their small corner is filled with the sweet glow of the miniature chain of fairy lights dangling from the slats. Maida put them there for her on her birthday a couple of months ago. Willa loves reading by their twilit comfort, even if Nan's always saying she'll go blind.

"Cute." Finn touches the tiny bulbs. "Cosy."

Willa pulls down the little curtain she's fashioned at one end. "So the light doesn't wake Riley." She smooths a finger over Finn's cheek, even more freckled from all the sunshine lately, and whispers, "I owe you a million, zillion favours after tonight."

"No, you only owe me one." Finn's smile is instantly playful. "Two, actually."

"Which are?" There's no saying what Finn will come up with, with that look on her face.

"Come out with me and Dan and Rosie on the weekend. Even just for a quick coffee."

"Done," Willa says. "But just so you know, I feel totally awkward already."

"I know you do. But you're amazing, and they'll think you're amazing. Just try not to be shy-slash-surly Willa, and you'll be fine."

"So, what's the second favour?"

"Lie down with me for a little while before I have to go home."

"I would have done that anyway." Willa curls in close, and the way Finn smiles, indulged and sleepy, makes her feel fudge-y and warm.

"You look happier," Finn says as she strokes Willa's arm.

"I am happier."

"Good."

They lie there, wrapped in this new, potent calm. Willa's fingers dance the smooth tract of skin from Finn's shoulder up the side of her neck. She studiously tries to ignore the pale runnel of Finn cleavage, tempting her eyes down to the small swells of her breasts. This is probably not the time for lecherous Willa to be making an appearance. Not when her sister's asleep half a metre from them. And not when Willa's pretty sure such Finn terrains are still no-go zones. Still, she can't stop her mind going there sometimes.

"Hey, what's wrong with your friend?" Finn asks.

"Huh?" Willa wrenches her mind back to the room.

"You said something before about Eva."

Talk about a mood killer. She drops her head on the pillow and tells Finn about lunch today. Well, about Eva's non-lunch. And everything else. "Now I don't know what to do."

"Do you think her friends have noticed the same thing?"

"I have no idea."

"Maybe you could talk to one of them?"

"Maybe." Willa can't imagine having an actual serious conversation with Amira about something like that. How would she even begin?

Finn traces Willa's bottom lip with the very tip of her index finger. She always does that. "Why didn't you tell me your dad was funny about us?" she asks suddenly.

"Because it doesn't matter what he thinks." Willa picks at a splinter on one of the bunk slats. "I wish he wasn't here."

"Really?"

"I do. Because I know he hates being here. But sometimes I want to tell him he doesn't get to be pissed about it. I want to tell him to stop hiding out in the backyard and to pretend to want to hang out with us. I want to tell him to talk to Riley sometimes and to notice that Jack follows him everywhere. That he could at least pretend to be their dad for a couple more weeks."

"Then tell him."

"I can't." Willa swallows hard, staring at the tiny cluster of lights above her head. She forces herself to speak the thoughts that have swirled so long. "Because what if he hates me for it and he doesn't come back? What if something happens to Nan again and he doesn't come because of what I said?"

"He'll come back."

"How do you know that?"

"I don't, I guess."

Suddenly, Willa's assaulted by more hot, embarrassing tears.

"Oh, Will." Finn presses her face close to her cheek.

Willa swipes a tear away and takes a deep, steadying breath. She loves that Finn doesn't try to give her a solution. That she knows silence is a gift you can give too.

Finn's hand drops around her waist like an anchor. Warm air and the sounds of distant traffic float through the open window. Lulled by slow breaths on her neck, Willa lets herself sink back into this fragile little happiness for a minute.

When the outside world has completely surrendered to night-time quiet, Finn sits up. "I've got to go. I don't want Mum on my back again."

"Why is she on your back?"

"Never mind." Finn leans over her, frowning as she smooths Willa's hair from her forehead. "I'm sorry I have to leave."

"Don't be sorry. Thank you," she whispers again. "*Again.*"

Finn doesn't say anything. Just kisses Willa like she's fixing her, slow and soft.

～ ～ ～

Later, when Willa's still trying to search out sleep among the mess of thoughts, loud music crashes into the silence again. Her mind instantly turns to Kelly. Poor Kell. She'll have just finished work and is probably huddled in her bed, cursing her brother. Willa picks up her phone to tell her to come and sleep over here if she needs.

There's a message from Finn.

*I think you need to tell your dad what you're scared of.*

Willa draws in a breath. Maybe.

# CHAPTER 35

## Finn

Another Sunday, another drive to the eastern suburbs to endure her grandmother. Why couldn't Finn have won Nan in the great grandparent lottery, instead of a cranky, narrow-minded homophobe?

Every time they go to the seniors' village where she lives, Finn sits there, listening to the painstaking small talk, and tries to hunt out a redeeming feature. But she can't find one. Not a single one. Well, except for her dad. Finn's always trying to figure out how her super-chilled, lefty Dad came from this woman.

Finn's barely spoken to her mother since Thursday night. Mostly because she's barely seen her, but also because she's still kind of mad about Anita being weird about Willa. But trapped in the car speeding down the Eastern freeway, there's no escaping her mother's need to have a discussion about *everything*.

"So, how's Willa doing?" Anita asks finally.

And there it is.

"She's okay. Better." Finn gives her mum a sideways look. "Considering what a hard time she's been having."

Anita turns and smiles at her. "I sense I'm being taken on a guilt trip."

Finn doesn't answer. Pointedly.

"I'm also sensing that someone thinks it's completely deserved."

"Mum, do you know what time Willa has been getting up every day since Nan got hurt?"

Anita doesn't say anything, just glances at Finn like she's waiting, like she knows she doesn't need to answer this one.

"Five-thirty. She gets up an hour-and-a-half earlier than we do so she can finish her homework and her academic leader stuff. She does that so that at night, after she picks up the kids from wherever they are and does the shopping and cooks dinner and makes lunches and does washing, her homework's done. The only time she has to herself is after they go to sleep, and she never gets to go out. She's probably always tired, but she never complains."

"I get it, Finn. And I really do feel for her, you know."

Finn stares at the droplet of coffee rolling around the top of her takeaway lid. "I just don't get how can you find anything wrong with me wanting to help someone, someone who is a really good person and who doesn't deserve what's happened to her."

"There's nothing wrong with it at all. I'm sorry I made you feel that way. I was just being protective of *you*. You've always had a habit of taking on everything, and between Willa and that community centre project and Speech Night, all you seem to be doing is working."

"So? I like helping." How the hell has her mother managed to make an issue of this? Most mums would be happy their daughter's not being a selfish turd. "What's wrong with that?"

"Nothing. It's a gorgeous quality. But maybe I don't want you to turn out to be a workaholic like me. I know it doesn't seem like it, but I do want you to have *some* fun sometimes."

"Willa's not work."

She sighs. "I know. And I like Willa, I do."

Finn frowns into the sun's glare. Doesn't her mother get that it doesn't matter if she *likes* her or not? That they're way past the point of parental approval? Willa's a fixture. A delicious inevitability. Sometimes it's like there's this chasm between what her mother sees and Finn feels, no matter how hard Anita thinks she's paying attention.

"I also worry because things are going to get even harder to juggle when you start Year 11 next year. VCE is no joke."

"I know that." As if her teachers aren't already harping on it. "At least it won't be a complete shock to me like it will be for some of the other kids. Being a geek does have its merits."

Anita chuckles. "True."

"I think it's time we face the fact I'm never going to be a rebellious teenager. It's also a little weird that I'm more resigned to it than you are. But you'll get there. I've got faith in you."

"Very funny."

They drive into a tunnel, and the world turns dark and close for a moment. Finn blinks into the sunlight as they charge out the other side. "I love being with Willa, even if we don't always get to do fun stuff. And I like hanging out with Riley and Jack too. I like being at their house with them. It's nice there, even when Willa's stressed."

There's a silence as Anita negotiates the freeway exit. "You don't like being at home much right now, do you?"

Finn looks out the window so she doesn't have to see her mother's face when she says it. "Not really."

# CHAPTER 36

## Willa

The ball careens over the stubby grass, chased down by a crowd of kids, all elbows out and eyes fixed on the black-and-white rolling prize.

Dan claps as one of them charges the ball. "I never thought I'd get into soccer. The players are all too sporty and fit, and they make me feel like the pasty chunk I am. But this?" He waves at the game in front of them. "This I can do. Kid soccer is totally my speed."

"Look at that little guy." Finn points at a kid trailing the pack, his limbs going all over the place. "He's horrible, and I love him for it. Because I'd *be* him."

Willa laughs and feels a pinch of pride when Jack is the first to reach the ball, bringing it under control with some sleight of foot.

"I just can't get used to the soccer mums." Rosie stares at the gaggle of parents clustered by the fence next to them. "They're *so into* it."

The minute they arrived and found a spot to settle on the grass, a polite, officious woman marched over and requested that they please move to the side. Apparently, they'd inadvertently chosen the sacred site where the Mummy Cheer Squad gathers every single week to sit. And from the tone by which they were informed of this egregious invasion, Willa can only assume the Mummy Cheer Squad is a capital letter kind of thing and that it totally usurps Big Sister and her Bunch of Randoms Cheer Squad, even just by sheer numbers. So they moved.

"The only player I know is Beckham," Finn says. "But I don't even know if he still plays or just swans around advertising things and looking hot."

"And that Spanish one," Rosie adds, "with the tatts."

"Oh, yeah, he's *super* hot. Like, he knows it, but still." Finn turns to Willa and laughs, grabbing her hand.

"What?"

"You always look confused when I talk about guys."

"That's probably because I am."

Finn's smile is pure tease. "What if I say that a girl is hot?"

"Then I'm jealous. Actually…" Willa reconsiders. "I'm jealous either way. Doesn't matter who."

It's kind of a relief that Finn looks more excited by this statement than anything.

"Noted," she says with that same teasing grin.

Willa pulls Finn's hand into her lap. Because Finn looks like sunshine today in her cut-offs and yellow T-shirt, a pair of giant sunglasses covering her eyes. Like summer itself.

"Your brother's pretty damn good," Dan says to Willa after Jack gets another go at goal. "In my completely nonexpert opinion, of course."

"He is." She gives Dan the friendliest smile she can muster. She's been hyperconscious of smiling all day, trying to combat her salty Willa image.

Finn looks at her like she's amused at how hard Willa's working. Willa narrows her eyes, but Finn just laughs.

It's not so hard to smile with Dan and Rosie, though. For starters, they were totally okay with combining the meet-the-girlfriend event with kiddie soccer so Willa could still get to Jack's game. And they're really nice. Dan's funny and goofy, and Willa likes seeing him and Finn do their bff act. You can see all the history and love under the tease and banter.

Finn's already told her how Dan used to be much shyer. How he always used to pick on himself, and how he didn't even tell her about the YouTube channel he created in Year 8 to talk about his deep, abiding love of sci-fi. Didn't say a word until he had thousands of followers and had become some kind of geek-boy star. Only then did his confidence finally grow.

"Into outright ego," Finn had joked.

Willa and Jack watched one of his videos last night, her self-appointed homework for this meeting. She'd never seen the film Dan was talking about in it, so even though he was witty and animated, she got bored easily. Jack kept watching them all night, though.

The game's nearly over when Riley comes back from wherever she's been parading Banjo and Patter, her walk all high importance, now she has something to boss around. "I had to pick up poo," she announces.

"Thank you for sharing that information," Willa tells her.

"Not with your bare hands, I hope." Dan pulls a face and leans away from her.

"No," Riley says witheringly, hands on hips. "With the bags." She plops down on the grass next to Finn, eyes wide. "And they *both* did it. First Patter, then Banjo."

"Ah, yes, the great pooping chain reaction." Finn nods slowly. "It's a classic."

"It was so gross."

Willa hands Riley a donut in the hope that it will stop her talking. It works. She sprawls on the grass, feeding her face, surreptitiously passing morsels to the dogs.

A kid on the other team kicks a goal. The mums let out a cheer.

"You know, I didn't even realise they weren't cheering for Jack's team," Rosie says, eyeing them. "Now I resent them even more."

Riley turns to Willa, sugar all over her mouth. "Dad's here."

"Really?" Willa frowns and wipes it off for her. "Where? What's he doing?"

"Other side. Watching."

"Did you say hi?"

She shrugs and rolls over to pat the dogs.

Willa guesses that means no. She doesn't blame her.

When the game's over and Jack's team has won by a couple of goals, he heads straight for them. Willa can tell from his self-conscious half smile that he's pleased people have been watching. And that he can't wait to meet his new geek-boy hero. There's an instant flash of guilt that she hasn't come to more matches lately. If this is the way Jack expresses himself, she needs to be there for it.

He's still puffing when he gets to them.

"You were awesome," she tells him, passing him the donuts and a can of drink.

"Yeah, you were so great," Finn says. "Totally the star."

He ducks his head and grins as he opens the can.

"I wish I possessed an ounce of your coordination," Dan tells him with a shake of his head.

"Jack watched some of your videos with me last night," Willa tells him, because she knows her brother won't.

"You like sci-fi?" Dan asks him.

Jack nods, wiping his mouth with his arm.

"Good man."

"Have you seen *Stellarn*?" Jack asks him in his squeaky little-boy voice.

"*Stellarn*? That animation made from the Chinese graphic novel?"

Jack nods.

Dan looks around at them all, feigning shock. "We have a budding aficionado on our hands, people."

And Willa's heart swells at the pride in Jack's smile.

# CHAPTER 37

## Finn

Willa takes her hand and holds it tight as they stroll away from the soccer field. Finn smiles, remembering when Willa was too shy to show her feelings in public.

In the time it has taken them to pack up their picnic and say their goodbyes, the light's turned that pretty, late-afternoon golden. The breeze has abandoned them too, leaving something gentler behind.

Up ahead, Jack and Riley lead a dog each up the tree-lined path. Today's probably the best time Banjo and Patter have had in weeks, between the exercise and the attention and the doughnut scraps.

It's the best day Finn's had in a while too. She liked watching Willa and Dan quietly like each other, in the way she knew they would when they finally met. Finn had prepped Dan what to expect. She had to. Willa can be so tricky sometimes. The way her shyness so easily disguises itself as standoffish, and Finn didn't want Dan to be put off. Because Willa's not really like that. She's just like an animal freezing when it sees danger. Only the danger isn't something anybody else thinks of as danger.

"So what are you doing now?" she asks Willa hopefully. Because she doesn't want the day to end yet.

"Groceries. And then I have to finish my Geography assignment, an infographic explaining weather patterns, so that I've got time to visit Nan tomorrow. Boring. You?"

"I should probably go home and work on Speech Night, but…"

"But what?"

"I can think of a thousand things more fun." She yanks Willa closer until their shoulders are touching. "Like hanging out with you."

"I wish I could. Anyway, you can't be shirking your captainly duties."

"I guess not. Zehra's probably been working on it all weekend. Probably even decided what colour paper the programs should be." She sighs loudly. "I shouldn't complain. There's a lot to do."

"So why haven't *you* been working on it?"

"Because this is way more fun."

"But isn't that what you were worried about? That if you weren't focused enough, that Zehra might show you up?"

"I was…I am." Finn shrugs. "I have been working on it, but this Speech Night stuff is just so boring. It's not like we're doing anything to improve the school, really. I swear they only get us to do it so the teachers don't have to be bothered. They just act like it's some big honour so we'll take it seriously."

"Do you know what Nan says when Riley complains something is boring?"

"What?"

Willa gives her a sly grin. "That not everything was put on this earth to entertain you."

"Gee, thanks. And now I *feel* like an eleven-year-old."

"Sorry." She doesn't sound it, though. "I know, that stuff can be boring, but just remember where it's going to get you. When I'm in those painful curriculum meetings, I just think of how great it will be when I'm at uni, or applying for a graduate position, and I have this to list on my resume."

"You always say that. And that motivates *you* because you know what you want to do." Finn doesn't even know what she wants to study at university, let alone what she'll do after that. Who knows whether it will ever mean anything that she was a school captain or not?

"Finn, it doesn't matter if you don't know what you want to do yet," Willa says, squeezing her hand. "We both know it will be something awesome."

"Do we?"

"Of course we do." She says it with her special Willa brand of certainty. "And I guess I'm saying maybe you should be making sure you have every chance to do that awesome thing when you finally decide on it. And being able to say you were in student office is one of those things that could give you an advantage."

"I know." If it was Finn's mum or dad saying something like this, she'd just sigh. But if Willa has one power in this world, it's to make people listen to her. Besides, Finn knows she's right. It's so hard to make these things immediate, though. Things like university and job applications seem like centuries away. Especially while Willa and the sunshine are right, exquisitely, here.

Their steps slow as they get closer to the edge of the park. "I'm sorry if I was being a nag," Willa says.

"Don't worry." Finn swings their hands gently between them. "I probably need it."

Still, when they part ways, she finds herself heading for Dan's house. Partly because she doesn't want to face Speech Night boredom, but also because she doesn't feel like going home to no one.

# CHAPTER 38

## Willa

She finds him out the backyard staking the tomatoes.

"Nan asked me to do it," he says with a small grin. "She knew they'd be ready, even without seeing them."

"Of course she did." Willa fidgets with her jacket zipper as she watches him wrap binding around the stem of a plant. "Riley said you were at the park today, watching the soccer."

"Yep. That kid's quicker than he looks."

*That kid?* He makes Jack sound like someone else's child.

He nudges another post into the damp earth and picks up a mallet. It's driven into the ground with three short blows. "I was the same."

"Really?" she asks, even though she knows this already. Ninety-nine per cent of the photos of him in Nan's albums are action shots of him in shorts, charging around on grass, or holding a bat or ball. She asks because she figures she better make the most of it while he's actually offering up words.

"I played footy and cricket, though. Wish I'd played soccer, but only the Greeks and Italians in my neighbourhood played it back then." He gives the post a tap, testing it. "I was on track for the Vic Under-19s at one point."

"What happened?"

"Your mum happened."

She waits, hoping he'll say what kind of "happened" it was. Willa's never really known the shape of their marriage.

But that's all he says before he picks up another stake and hammers it into the ground. And because she doesn't know how to ask him a question like that, she leaves him there in the garden and goes inside.

# CHAPTER 39

## Willa

Willa's pen crawls over the page. She wishes she had maths or science to do today. Anything but this.

In English they read a short story about a girl who came to the Perth colonies in the 1800s. Within months, the girl has lost her mother and father to an accident and endured all kinds of hell. The story was small and sad and beautiful. Willa liked reading it. What she doesn't like is the "response" she has to write for homework.

She never knows what to say in assignments like this. She *feels* the things she knows she's supposed to write, but she never knows how to put them down on the page. Not in words she's willing to share with her teachers, anyway.

Usually, she just ends up treating the exercise like some kind of mini-essay, pretending she didn't quite understand the task. Homework evasion, geek-style. And Willa knows her English teacher will write what he always writes. *Nice analysis, Willa. However, this was supposed to be a response, not an academic treatment.* Then he'll give her a high mark anyway.

She's nearly finished it when Riley comes in, sliding her feet over the carpet, her lips pursed into a small frown. She stands there, her big toe nudging at a scuff in the carpet, like she's waiting for something. Her hair has gotten even longer, thinned out at the end to frizzy straggles. They're going to have to talk about getting it trimmed. But not today. It's Sunday. Willa's not in the mood for that kind of battle. "What are you up to?" she asks.

"Nothing." Riley perches on the edge of the bed next to her. She hugs her knees and stares at her feet. The blue polish Finn put on her the other night has already chipped at the top of her big toe.

"Why aren't you playing at Britt's or Lefah's?"

"They're both away." Riley's finger traces the edge of a scab on her knee as she frowns.

Willa stares at her. "What's up? You're quiet. It's weird."

"No, it's not." Her finger keeps working slow circles. "I'm quiet sometimes."

"Okay, whatever you say." Willa pulls gently at a strand of Riley's hair. "Maybe when I finish my homework, we can go somewhere. Finn said something about walking to the creek with the dogs this afternoon. Why don't you watch TV for a bit until I'm finished?"

"Dad's watching." Riley screws up her nose. "Car races."

"Where's Jack?"

"Watching too."

"Okay, so read a book or play a game." Willa tucks Riley's hair behind her shoulder. "I won't be long. Promise."

"Why doesn't Dad ever talk?"

Willa stares at her. Riley never talks about him. Never even seems to notice him much. "I don't know," she says finally. "He's just quiet, I guess."

Riley presses her finger hard into the middle of the scab. The skin turns angry around it. "He talks to us even less than Jack does."

"I know."

"And why doesn't he ever do anything with us?"

"I don't know." Willa's heart hurts a little. She watches Riley's fingernail edge under the ridge of the scab. "Don't pick."

The finger slides away.

"Do you *want* him to do stuff with you?" Willa asks her.

"Maybe. No." Riley shrugs, still staring at her bare feet. "I don't know. Maybe."

No matter how hard she searches, Willa can't think of a single thing to say to make her sister feel better, so she just folds an arm around Riley's shoulders and pulls her in close.

Riley leans into her embrace. "I wish Nan would come home."

Willa swallows hard. "Me too."

# CHAPTER 40

## Finn

The library is a sodden mess of purple-striped students avoiding the rain. It sounds like a football stadium, not a place of hallowed place learning. The librarians don't even bother trying to maintain the "shh" rules when the weather's like this.

Finn drags out her folder and pen and leans in so Zehra can hear her over the roar. "So I messaged all the kids who helped for Careers Night, and they're mostly willing to help with Speech Night. We just need to find someone for sound. And for social media, though we could probably do that ourselves."

"Okay." Zehra stares down at her notes. "I've been looking at the old run sheet, and I was thinking we should shuffle it a bit."

Finn pulls it out of her folder. She hasn't even looked at the run sheet again. She's been too busy with the filibuster at the community centre. They've been working on their version all week. "Really?"

"Yes. I was talking to some of the kids about how it went the last couple of years," Zehra explains, "and they gave me some good insights."

"Like what?" Finn wishes she'd thought of that.

"They all say that the worst part is the principal's speech at the end, that it drags on and on until even the parents' eyes are rolling back in their heads by the end. People are dying to go home."

"So it's just like all his other speeches, then." Mr Burgess is not known for his ability to read a crowd. Or his capacity for entertainment. He's mean with a signature, though. "We can't exactly tell the principal he can't speak on Speech Night. And we probably can't tell him to make it shorter or jazz it up either."

"That's not what I was suggesting," Zehra says in this tight voice.

Finn fights an eye roll. Then she reminds herself that Willa seemed this uptight when they first met, and look how awesome she turned out to be. Maybe there's some fun in Zehra somewhere. "So what can we do about it?"

"I think we should put him on right at the start. As the opener."

"But then people will be bored and annoyed right from the beginning."

"Sure, but then they have all the fun parts to enjoy after, like the awards and the student and alumni speeches. They'll leave happier—and with better memories of the night."

"That's true."

"And maybe he'll keep to his allotted time better if he knows there are lots of people waiting to go on after him."

"Maybe."

Zehra purses her lips and tightens her ponytail. "I think it could work."

A crowd of Year 7s are playing keepings off with a kid's phone. Finn stares at them as she pretends to think about it. Then she checks herself. Why is she being so resistant to this idea? It's a good one, and she knows it.

Actually, Finn knows exactly why. It's because she didn't think of it herself. And it's exactly the kind of solution she would usually come up with. Only she didn't because she's paid precisely no attention to Speech Night until now. Zehra, on the other hand, has been mulling over this stuff for weeks. *So get over yourself, Harlow.*

"No, you're right," she says finally. "It's a good idea. We should totally change it."

Zehra smiles and sits up straighter. "I thought of something else too. For the social media. We could use photos from last year to promote it on Facebook, and we could contact the seniors from last year and ask for their memories for captions."

Finn forces another smile. "Also an awesome idea. Let's do it."

# CHAPTER 41

## Willa

Nan's pensive frown turns to a smile when she sees Willa coming down the path. She's parked on a wooden bench in the yard, cornered by a silvery hedge of lavender, their purple heads scratching the air behind her.

Willa passes Nan the bunch of bright blooms she's carried all the way on the tram. "Your sweet peas are going mad."

"To think I'm missing the show." Nan twirls the flowers in her hands and tuts. "What are you doing here? You should be out in the sunshine enjoying yourself."

"I am in the sunshine." Willa stoops and kisses her cheek. "Besides, I'm pretty sure you can nag if I don't do my homework or if I stay out too late, but you can't nag if I bring my grandmother flowers."

"You wouldn't do those things even if I told you to do them, and you know it, my girl."

"I know." Willa settles on the bench next to her, a flicker of pleasure rising at the sight of Nan's wrist without a bandage. The bruise above her eye has faded to nothing too.

"What are the little ones up to?"

"Jack's at the pools with Tyler and his dad, and Riley's going to some hip-hop class with Bella."

"I have no idea what that means, and I don't want to."

"It means more impromptu dance recitals in the kitchen, probably."

"Wonderful," Nan says, pulling a face. "And how's Finn?"

"Good. She's coming to see you tomorrow."

"Good."

Willa hands Nan a plastic shopping bag from her backpack. "There's some spinach and lettuce and a couple of lemons from the tree too."

Nan peers into the bag, feasting her eyes. "Lovely. I'll make a little salad at dinner. You'd think a medical facility would feed people better, but look at us all." She tips her chin at all the people shuffling around the yard with sticks or frames. "The bionic hip brigade. Sad, aren't we?"

Willa laughs dutifully, but it *is* kind of depressing seeing Nan here. These people look so old and fragile, and she's never thought of Nan like that. She's always been so quick and strong. Always commanding everything on her own, wrestling her garden and her grandchildren into being. Now she seems more like them.

"So, how are things at the house? Are the kids behaving?"

"Of course."

"And your dad?"

"Yeah, he's behaving too."

"Very funny. I mean how is he?"

Why is Nan asking her? He visits Nan every single day. "He seems okay, I guess."

"Hard to tell sometimes, isn't it?" Nan smiles wearily and pulls her cardigan closer around her.

Willa picks a stalk of lavender and rolls it between her fingers. "He watched Jack play soccer on the weekend. Riley saw him there."

"Of course he did. Why are you surprised?"

"I don't know. He didn't say anything."

"When does he ever?"

"True." Willa holds the wounded flower to her nose and breathes in its rich smell.

Nan's silent for a minute, and Willa knows it's because she's deciding how to say something. "Listen, your dad might not say much, but he thinks and feels it. Remember that," she says finally. "You just have to look a bit closer."

"I guess." She's not sure she wants to look any closer. Or that she knows how to.

"You can be just the same sometimes."

Willa drops the flower onto the grass and changes the subject. "He said he used to be really good at football."

"He was. Quick on his feet."

"Then he said he gave it up because of Mum. Didn't she like it?"

"I don't think she cared about football either way, really. But she wouldn't marry him if he didn't have a steady job. So he gave up all the training and got himself a job.

He only played on weekends after that, even though he loved it. That's how besotted the boy was."

"I can't even imagine him having a conversation with a girl."

"He couldn't until the met her. But your mother talked for both of them." Nan grins. "She was a force of a thing. Bright and big and bossy. If Jack's like your dad, Riley *is* your mother. Sometimes when that child's telling me one of her endless tales, I can see your mother sitting in her kitchen, drinking tea and chatting that pretty face of hers off."

Willa smiles and watches a crane heft a slab of cement a couple of streets away. They never talk about her mother much. Mostly because Nan didn't know her that well. They only met five times in total before she died. There was the once when they first became engaged, once at the wedding, and then when Nan flew up to visit each time one of the three of them was born. It was too far and too expensive to fly to Northern Queensland more often, she'd said.

Her mother's voice is something Willa remembers well. The constant, relentless chatter and the lilting traces of her accent as she talked to the neighbours, to Willa, to anyone who'd listen. "I guess I'm not much like her."

"No, you're a little more like your dad. But more like your grandfather than anyone. Quick-minded and decisive. You look like Leela, though. You didn't get that face from us."

"Do you miss Granddad?"

"Of course. But grief softens with age, doesn't it?"

Willa nods. It's true. When her mum died, the pain was acute, like a physical hurt sometimes. Later it was a soft ache. Now it's just a twinge and a smudge of memories, and Willa knows she's losing her. But at least she had her. Riley and Jack barely remember her at all.

"Riley thinks Dad's not interested in her," she tells Nan. "Because he doesn't talk."

"He probably just doesn't know what to do with her." Nan gives Willa a shrewd look. "I don't suppose you two are finding much to say to each other either?"

Willa shrugs. She thinks of those other times when he'd visit and how it used to get easier. How it hasn't this time. And it's never going to now, not after the Finn thing. But Willa's not about to tell Nan that.

When she looks up, Nan's staring at her, her mouth thinned into a tight line, like she already knows things aren't okay. "I'll be home in a couple of weeks," she says, patting Willa's arm. "Then we can get back to normal."

# CHAPTER 42

## Finn

Finn idly sketches the shape of the white blood cells they've been studying in Biology in the margins of her History book. She draws in her books so often that sometimes her teachers comment on it as well as her work. Only nice things, though, because she gets good marks, and it's not like she's just sitting there, doodling and ignoring them. It actually helps her to listen.

Mr Granger's hunched over his desk is his tiny office, expounding on the spelling crimes witnessed in Year 8 English essays. "I suppose I shouldn't criticise too hard. How can a child whose parents think her name should be spelled k-a-y-e-t-e-e ever have a chance at attaining a normal human vocabulary? However, this essay is truly, deeply shocking. I'm not even sure she could spell 'string a sentence together' to save her own life."

Finn laughs. This is exactly what Granger will write in his comments too. Okay, maybe not the name-spelling part, but definitely the rest of it. She lifts her head. "Hey, question."

"Always. Question everything, fight the power, all that."

"Funny. What do you do if you're holding an event that requires people under eighteen to be out all night?"

"I thought that was what the bedroom window was for. A screwdriver will take care of the flyscreen." He lifts his head. "I never said that."

"Again, hilarious."

"Oh, you actually want the official, teacherly answer?" He twirls his pen between the fingers. "Am I allowed to ask what it's for?"

"Of course." She tells him about the community centre and the campaign. "We have a plan, but we need to be out all night for the last part."

"Are you coming out to me, Ms Harlow?"

"I guess I am," she says. "But not in the after-school special, 'I need help' way. More as a conversational by-product. In the matter-of-fact, happens-to-be-related way."

"Perfect. I think that suits our dynamic, don't you?"

She laughs, glad that Ms Lehrer isn't there. That would have kicked this a notch up from vaguely cringe-worthy to mildly excruciating.

"Tell me more. About your project, I mean."

She tells him about the filibuster idea which, with the help of Kayah and Rosie and the others, has turned into a plan for nonstop, all-night speech about why they need the centre to stay open. At first they were just going to record the whole thing and make a podcast to spread on social media, but Kayah has a friend who works at a community radio station, and he said they could use his graveyard shift to broadcast their stories if the station said yes. Which they did, thanks to Kayah and Bea's pleading visit to them last week.

The plan is to try and get enough of the kids involved that they can talk for six hours straight between songs, sharing their personal stories and talking about what the centre means to them. They'll hold a presentation at the community centre earlier in the evening, where they'll invite the media and local government people as well as parents and friends, and then they'll go to the radio station later as a group and start the filibuster. And the idea's just weird enough that they're hoping some media will want to come and write about it, like her dad said they might.

"That's a corker of an idea," Granger says when she's done filling him in. "Did you have anything to do with it?"

"Uh, kind of." She tells him about the filibuster article and the seed it gave her.

"I thought it had your name all over it." He taps his pen on the desk. "Well, I imagine all you'd need for the event is permission slips and a promise of no naughty stuff. Ask some of the parents to chaperone, maybe?"

"Good idea." She flips open her notebook and scribbles it down next under some Speech Night notes.

"So this is what's been keeping your brain so busy lately?"

"What do you mean?"

"You seem to have a lot on your mind," he says.

She frowns. "Is this some teacher-y way of saying I'm slacking off?"

"Harlow, if I thought you were slacking, I'd just say it." He points his pen at her. "All I'm saying is that you seem like you've been going through the motions around here a bit. None of your usual marching around, firing on all cylinders with your big ideas. But it looks like you are. Just not here. And honestly, I don't care where that energy goes, as long as it's still out there in the world, doing its thing."

"Oh, okay." The bell sounds. She grabs her things. "Maths. I better go. See you." She gives him a wave and takes off down the hall. How come, then, if he's not telling her off, she still feels guilty?

# CHAPTER 43

## Willa

Amira looks ragged. Her eye make-up is slim to none, and her hair is a wilderness. Willa didn't even know Amira had curly hair until right this moment. She looks so different. Younger.

"I know," she says, holding up a hand as she joins them on the quad. "Don't say it. I know how bad I look. It was this or be late."

"You don't look bad. You look pretty," Willa tells her. "It's just different."

"Quit flirting with me, Brookes." Amira cackles at Willa's shocked look. "Joke, dude. You can come onto me whenever you like."

"Guys, let's get on with it." Eva pulls out her script. "Last run through."

"Good. I'm sick of this thing," Amira moans.

Eva flaps the paper at her. "Says the girl who doesn't need as much practice as the rest of us."

They settle at one of the picnic tables. "I brought donuts." Willa pulls the greasy bag from her schoolbag. "I thought they would help."

"You thought right, lady." Amira takes a donut and yanks Eva's script from her hand. "No prompts, missy. We're doing this in half an hour, remember?"

Eva sighs. "Okay,"

"Want one?" Willa pushes the bag of donuts towards Eva.

She shakes her head. "Thanks. I already ate."

Willa's stomach starts to swim. Because that's strike three. It's the third time she's offered Eva food this week, and the third time Eva's offered up an excuse not to eat it. Willa promised herself she'd do something if it got to three. Only, now that she's here, she doesn't know what the hell that will be.

Anyway, she can't think about it right now, because Amira's whisking them through the dialogue. Willa knows she's improved since they started, mostly because she did as she was told and watched a bunch of Japanese cartoons with Jack. He was beyond excited to have someone watch with him. He tirelessly explained entire plots and background stories to her, even though she didn't need them. And she let him because it was nice to hear him talking so much. She even promised to watch some more with him on the school holidays.

When they've finished two uninterrupted run-throughs, Amira pulls a make-up case out of her bag. "Okay, we're good. I'm going to fix this." She circles her head with her hand. "Meet you outside the classroom in ten."

Willa shakes the bag of donuts at Eva. "Last chance."

"No thanks."

"You sure?"

"I'm sure."

They trudge towards the languages building, walking gallows-slow.

"So what did you have?" Willa asks finally. She flinches. Interrogation much?

"Huh?"

"Um…for breakfast?"

Eva gives her a funny look. "Why?"

"Just curious."

"You're curious about what I ate for breakfast? Your life must be packed with thrills right now."

Willa shrugs, swallowing hard. She's started it, now she has to finish it. "I don't know. It's just, every time I offer you food, you say no, and…well, you haven't really been eating lunch much, and—"

Eva stops and turns. She stares at Willa, her expression incredulous. "I thought it was weird, you constantly pushing food at me lately. Have you been…*testing* me or something?"

"I…I was just worried." Willa grips her bag. "You look skinny."

"I *am* skinny. I always have been."

"Well, skinnier. And stressed, and you never seem to—"

"You know what? You should probably mind your own business." Eva says it lightly, but as she strides ahead of Willa across the courtyard. Her spine is ramrod straight, speaking her annoyance.

Willa's stomach begins to turn in a slow, sickening roll. Yep, she should probably have minded her own business.

Outside the classroom, girls are lined along the wall, noisily going over their dialogues. It reminds Willa of the birds on her street, perched along the power lines in the mornings. Eva pointedly stares at her phone while they wait.

Amira comes back from the bathroom, her eyes and lips painted back into being, her hair pulled into a messy bun. She tries to heckle away the sullen silence. "Oh, come on, we're not marching to our deaths. Cheer the hell up. Think of my party this weekend. It's going to be killer." She turns to Willa. "You're going to come, right? With Finn?"

"W-what party?"

"You didn't get my Facebook invite?"

"I don't have Facebook."

"Oh, well, you're coming. It's my sixteenth on Saturday. I'll send you a text."

Willa glances uneasily at Eva. She's either not listening or pretending not to. "Um, I'll probably have to babysit my brother and sister that night."

"Get someone else to do it. It'll be fun. My cousin's playing tunes. And she's good too. We'll get our dance on."

Before Willa can conjure another excuse, the classroom door opens and three girls walk out, looking green. A finger beckons them into the room.

# CHAPTER 44

## Finn

They're back in the centre for the second night in a row.

"What are you going to talk about for the filibuster?" Finn asks Bea as they all fold and slide invitations into Finn's hand-decorated envelopes.

"Clothes."

"Clothes?"

"Yeah, about how I used to feel funny because my grandmother and my parents used to always say 'but you can't be gay. You don't *look* gay'. I think they thought you had to have the short hair and wear dude clothes, or you couldn't be a real lesbian."

"My kind of clothes," Nona says.

"Basically. My parents think all lesbians dress like you. Which is so old-fashioned."

"Are you calling me old-fashioned?" Nona pouts.

"No." Bea leans in and kisses her. "I'm calling you hot. I love what you wear."

Now Nona's grinning.

Finn rolls her eyes and laughs. Like Nona needs any more ego. Nona just gives her the finger.

Bea turns back to Finn. "It was confusing, because they were saying that stuff, but then all the gay girls I saw on TV looked like everyone else—straight. I didn't know *what* I was supposed to look like. I just knew I liked what I already wore." She waves at her dress, yet another fifties concoction decorated with bright blue flowers. "It wasn't until I came here and met other actual, real-life gay kids that I realised that everyone just looks like whatever they want to look like. I mean, Kayah looks more like the old lesbian cliché than I do, and she's got a boyfriend."

"I just don't like dealing with my frizz," Kayah says, running her fingers through her short curls.

"And I," Nona points at her slouchy jeans, plain T-shirt and razor-short hair, "am making a statement. Gay as."

"I don't think you need your outfit to achieve that," Kayah tells her. "The obnoxious flirting pretty much tips the girls off."

"You love it," Nona says.

"I do love your game," Kayah agrees. "I wish I'd had that kind of moxie when I was sixteen."

"Oh, because you're such an old lady now," Rosie teases.

"You know," Andy says, "maybe gay girls get to do what they want when it comes to style, but gay guys my age have to look a certain way. Like it's compulsory to have this clean-cut, preppy, shiny look. You can't be grungy or indie, or even have long hair."

"So?" Rosie pulls a face. "As if you would be grunge or indie anyway? Preppy is totally your look."

"I know *that*." He frowns at his twin. "But I'm just saying, what if I wanted to?"

"You'd look ridiculous."

"Shut up."

Rosie sticks out her tongue.

"I get what you're saying," Bea tells Andy. "The stereotypes are crappy and anxiety-making. Which is why I'm going to talk about clothes. How I dress is really important to me, but it took me until I got here to say *stuff it*, I can wear what I want."

"That's really cool," Finn tells her. She turns to Kayah. "What about you? What are you going to say?"

"How just because I have a boyfriend doesn't mean I'm not queer."

"What about you, Finn?" Bea asks.

"Finn's making the introduction speech," Kayah says as she drops a fresh pile of invites onto the middle of the table.

"I am?" It's the first Finn's heard of it.

"Yep. We need someone who's used to public speaking. Then after, Andy's going to do his filibuster piece, to give them a taste of what's happening later." She pulls a mock-apologetic face. "Oops. Did we forget to tell you?"

"Uh, you did. But why me?" Finn looks around the table. "Why not you? Or someone who's been here longer? Or what about Costa? He runs the place."

"It has to be one of the kids," Kayah says. "And I can't. I'll be with the journalists, giving them the info they need, remember?"

"I'm not even gay," Rosie says. "So I can't. It'd be like cheating."

"And I'm just *not*," Nona says. "Anyway, what's your problem? Aren't you like captain of your school? Don't you have to make inspirational speeches all the time?"

"You watch too much TV," Finn tells her. "It's not really like that."

"But you do have to do public speaking, right?" Kayah asks.

Finn has to nod, because just the other day she had to get up at assembly and remind the school to donate to the uniform drive. But this is different.

"Then you'll be fine," Kayah says. "Besides, no one else wants to do it."

Finn lets out a sigh. Because it feels strangely like Camp Nowhere all over again.

"So what are you going to say?" Nona asks her.

"You do realise that I *just* found out I'm making a speech. I have absolutely no idea."

"Better get on that, then." Nona gives her a cheesy grin. "Remember, you have to say something about how great this place is and how much we need it. For kids like me, escaping from my homophobic parents."

"Of course I will," Finn says. "Hey, are you back at home yet?"

"Yeah, a few days ago."

"Now she's just not allowed at mine," Bea says.

"Why not?" Rosie asks.

"Bea's dad caught me outside her window the other night." Nona grins. "Now I'm not allowed over there for a month."

"And that's getting off lightly," Bea adds. "I thought it'd be a year."

"I thought it would mean no getting off," Kayah says with a grin.

"Oh, don't worry about us," Nona says, waggling her eyebrows. "We have our ways. And our places."

"I do not want to know," Kayah says.

"There's no way I'd ever bring a guy to my house," Andy says, looking glum. "Mum and Dad might be *just* coping with my gay status, but I don't think they'd cope with that."

"Definitely not." Rosie pulls a terrified face. "Mum wouldn't know what to do if you brought a guy home for dinner. He better be into Vietnamese. Actually, he probably better *be* Vietnamese."

"Is Willa allowed over at your place?" Andy asks Finn.

"Yep. Mum basically invited her for dinner the minute I told her. She loves playing supportive Mum."

"Wow," Nona says. "Is she allowed in your room? Bea and I have to stay in the living room the whole time."

"Yeah, but there's a strict door-open policy."

"So they're cool about the bi part, but not so much about the sexual part," Kayah jokes. "That's how mine used to roll too. So annoying."

Finn laughs, but her chest tightens. She could never admit to anyone that she's actually grateful for the open-door policy. Because it saves her having to figure out why she's still stalling with Willa, keeping things very much in the kissing zone. Why she's stalling even though she finds everything about Willa so mind-bendingly hot.

She hasn't talked to Willa about it either. Mostly because she's not sure if she wants to know how Willa feels about it. Because what if Willa's secretly really frustrated but doesn't want to say? What if she's sick of waiting for Finn to get over this…whatever it is?

"Hey, Finn, you have to say something about the holiday programs we have too," Kaya says.

"Um, sure." She shoves the thoughts back and opens her notebook. "What else?"

# CHAPTER 45

## Willa

Willa had forgotten about the morning History excursion. She swore loudly last night when she found the permission slip in her diary and had to trudge downstairs to ask her dad to sign off on it. But once they're on the bus leaving the suburbs behind and a cool blue day is eking its way into being, it doesn't seem so bad. Better than double Japanese, anyway, a class where Eva will probably ignore her, just like she's done since the presentation.

Camp Nowhere must have had some effect on Willa, because there's this weird sense of nostalgia flooding her as they take off along the steep bush trail. She feels alive and awake as fern fronds brush at her legs and the huddled trees share their clean, cold breath. She even almost enjoys the dull ache in her calves from the uphill climb. *Almost*.

They're walking a bush track that was built into the mountains to commemorate the Australian soldiers who fought and lost their lives on the Kokoda trail in New Guinea during World War Two. It's this week's Australian History topic. Possibly Willa's least favourite subject.

But as she trudges up the rough steps, she imagines the slow march of soldiers through mud-thick jungle somewhere across the water. So many of them died on that track, in conditions so bad that more of them died from the jungle terrain and illness than in actual battle. It's weird. She knows all the facts of that wartime corner of the world, thanks to the test she studied so hard for last week, but she still can't imagine such a brutal experience. Some of those soldiers were only a few years older than her, and they were sent to this strange place to watch their friends die, and maybe to die themselves.

And now Willa's watching her supposed friends march up the track ahead of her with Holly and Ling. If it was this time last week, maybe she would have caught up to them, latched onto the chatter. But not now. Not when Eva gave her the weakest of smiles this morning but kept on walking straight past her and onto the bus.

It's her own fault. This is exactly why Willa didn't make friends at Gandry. She has no idea how to do this stuff, how to make and keep friends. And she had no business trying. Even Kelly and Maida were an accident. They were just those two girls who were always playing on the street together until Nan started minding Kelly sometimes. That was back when Kelly's grandfather was still alive and someone cared if she was looked after.

Kelly would come to their house after school a couple of nights a week and even stayed on weekends sometimes. At that relentless proximity, even the impossibly shy nine-year-old version of Willa managed to make friends. And with Kelly came Maida, always. But it was easier then, when friendships were forged on games and dares and the sharing of discoveries about the world. Not feelings and girl things and trust.

Now Willa wishes she had stuck with the plan and kept Gandry Girls High strictly workplace. Get in and get out with accolades, the reputation of the school, and the marks to get into her choice of courses. Friendship was never part of the plan.

It bugs Willa that now she wishes she *was* walking with the girls. That she feels like she's missing something she didn't even want a few months ago. She should have kept her head down and minded her own business. Then she would have stayed the hell out of Eva's too. Then there'd be no guilt. And no annoying *feelings*.

At some point near the top of the track, Amira turns around, spots Willa straggling, and waves for her to join them. Willa just pretends to misinterpret it and waves back like she's saying hi and puts her head down again. On the way back to school, she sits with a girl she barely knows from English who argues on the phone with her boyfriend all the way home. Willa shuts her eyes and wishes she was anywhere but on this bus.

All through lunch, which she eats in the study lounge alone, and then in her afternoon classes, she tries to tell herself to let it go. That she hasn't even been friends with these girls that long. She has no responsibility to Eva or Amira or any of them beyond school stuff. Still, the harder she's tried to push the worry away, the harder it works to sneak right back in.

After school, Willa hangs back and watches Eva and Amira say goodbye at the gates. They kiss each other's cheeks, Gandry-style, and Eva trudges away, her arms folded over her chest. Willa watches her move down the hill, willing herself to just head for the bus stop like she's supposed to.

Instead, cursing herself, she turns and dashes to the tram stop instead. Amira's on the bench, waiting. She's staring at her phone, one headphone jammed in her ear. She grins when she sees Willa. "Hey! Where the hell have you been all day? You getting the tram?"

Willa shakes her head and stares at the stragglers at the bus stop across the road gossiping and laughing and shaking off the day.

"Check out this." Amira holds her phone up in front of Willa. There's a model staring boldly at her, trying to sell her some kind of mascara. "Do you know what depresses me?" She doesn't wait for Willa to answer. "That eyebrows have turned into these ugly painted streaks, instead of the fluffy random scribbles they used to be. It's sad." She holds up another photo of a girl with two thick, black-arrow shapes painted over her eyes. "I mean, whatever happened to subtlety?"

Willa shakes her head, because she has no clue what Amira's talking about. Only that she wants it to stop. "Hey, I want to ask you something."

"Sure. What?"

"It's about Eva."

Amira looks up, frowning. "What about her?"

Nerves push at Willa, but she pushes them back. Because she can admit to herself now that her conscience isn't going to let her leave this friendship behind without doing the right thing. And that means at least being sure that someone else knows about Eva. She drops down next to Amira and lets the story out in a thick rush, skirting the things Eva told her about her brother, because she promised not to tell. She doesn't skimp on the rest, though.

"Now she's not really talking to me," she says. "So I can't say or do anything. But…but I thought I should tell someone."

A tram slides up to the stop, picking up the clusters of girls standing around them. Amira doesn't get up. Instead she lets out a sigh through her nose. "Bloody Eva."

Willa stares down at her hands. "I feel bad for talking behind her back, but—"

"Dude, don't feel bad." Amira loops an arm through hers. "You did the right thing. If there's one thing that girl sucks at, it's cutting herself some slack. *And* getting help when she needs it. She just needs a kick up the butt every now and then." She gives Willa a weary smile. "That's where I usually come in."

Willa smiles back, rushed by relief.

"I didn't even notice anything. She's been hanging out with you, studying at lunch, and saying she's busy out of school." Amira clicks her tongue. "I kind of feel like a shitty friend now."

"So do I," Willa says. "Maybe I should have said something to her earlier, but I don't know her that well, and I wasn't sure if I was imagining it."

"It doesn't matter. You said it to her now. And now she knows people are paying attention." Amira pulls her bag onto her shoulder and gets up. "I'm going to go and talk to her."

Willa stands too, breathing easier now. Even if Eva is never her friend again, at least someone will be on her case.

"And don't worry," Amira tells her, like she knows what she's thinking. "She'll get over it. Then you two can be geek buddies again, and I'll keep trying not to be jealous."

"What?" Willa's eyes widen. "*Really*? Of me and Eva?"

"Maybe a little bit sometimes." Amira shrugs. "It's no big. I know she's still my girl. And I'm glad someone hunted down the human inside the Willa bot. Turns out she's kind of cool."

Willa can't help smiling at her. Because whether she likes it or not, Amira is her friend now. And she probably likes it. A lot.

Amira grins back at her, shading her eyes from the sun. "I better go."

"Hey." Willa bites down hard on her lip. "Please don't tell her I told you."

"Try and stop me." Amira shrugs at Willa's horrified look. "Don't worry, Willa. She'll get over it, I promise. It's pretty poor form to hate on your friends for trying to help you, and she knows it. She's just too caught up in her crap right now to remember." She grabs Willa's wrist. "Look, Eva's kind of tense, but she doesn't do grudges. Trust me. I've been putting up with that freak show since primary school. I'll see you Saturday," she says pointedly, squeezing her wrist and dropping it. And then she's off.

Willa watches her saunter down the hill, looking anything but like she's about to solve the problems of the world. But that's the awesomeness that is Amira, she's discovering.

# CHAPTER 46

## Willa

Willa can't help it. She's nervous. Even though Eva texted her this morning and apologised for snapping, and told her she hoped she'd see her at the party tonight. Even though Willa's going to the party with Finn, who is completely, annoyingly okay with walking into a room full of strangers in the name of supposed fun. Even though both Kelly and Maida say she looks hot in her silky sleeveless top and with her hair all out for once.

"Seriously, *gorgeous*," Maida says as she carefully adds mascara to the eyeliner Willa lets her apply because she knows it's *that* kind of party.

And when Willa looks in the mirror, she almost believes them.

The babysitting excuse went out the window when Riley asked if she could stay over at Lefah's on Saturday and Jack reminded her he's going to Tyler's slumber party. Suddenly Willa was whisked free of responsibility.

When she joked to Finn about how close she came to getting out of the party, Finn pulled a face. "Why are you trying to get out of it? Parties are fun. You're supposed to want to go. You do know that, don't you?"

"Um…" Willa shrugged. "*May*be?"

Finn grabbed her hands. "Oh my God, Willa, we're going to the party. I want to see the girls from camp. And seriously, you need to learn how to be a normal teenager. Nan will be home soon, and you'll be required to leave this house after dark from time to time. By *me*. So let's practise, huh?"

Willa pulled a face, but Finn just squeezed her hands even tighter, like she was going to drag her then and there. "It'll be fun. I promise."

And somehow, Finn's enthusiasm made her believe it would be. Until now. Because now it's Saturday night, and she's staring down the barrel of forced socialisation. Now she's wishing she could just hide somewhere, preferably under a rock, instead of standing here, blinking at the mirror and waving away Maida's proffered lipstick.

"Nope, down, girl," Kelly says on her behalf. "Too far. Willa's not a lipstick kind of girl. Nice try, though."

"I'm really not," Willa says. Besides, how's she supposed to kiss Finn with lipstick on?

Maida's face falls. "It was worth a shot."

The doorbell rings, and Willa runs for it.

Finn's eyes widen the moment Willa opens her front door. "You…look…amazing," she says.

"I'll just be one sec," Willa bites down on a smile. She dashes down the hall, following the sounds of cricket commentary.

"I'm going out," she tells the back of his head. "Lefah's mum has my number if there's any trouble with Riley. Jack should be fine. They'll call me if he isn't." She takes off before he can even turn around. She grabs Finn's hand, waves goodbye to the girls, and slams the door behind her, feeling the instant, intoxicating rush of freedom. Maybe this isn't so bad at all.

They eat dinner in a buzzing little café that smells like baked bread and spices. Restaurants and cafés at night have never been part of Willa's existence. Nan prefers her own cooking to everyone else's. It's healthier, she always says. They probably don't have the spare money to eat out anyway. So Willa's never really done this, she tells Finn— eaten a proper dinner in a place where she wants to eat the food, with someone she wants to eat next to.

"Don't worry," Finn tells her as she fills her water glass. "It's just like dinner at yours, only you don't have to cook and we can actually talk to each other without gagging Riley."

But later, when they jump off the tram and follow the street numbers east, the jittery sensation returns. Because she's about to be thrown to the Gandry Girl wild.

The party is huge, taking up an entire restaurant. The huge part was expected. How could it not be, with Amira's relentless social butterflying? But Willa had just assumed it would be some kind of super-cool school thing, full of all the glam girls and their dates dancing and being shiny. She wasn't expecting the giant family gathering, with adults filling the front tables, eating and drinking and talking, or the little kids chasing balloons and each other between them. Beyond the seated crowd, she can see girls from school standing under shifting lights in small groups.

"You came!" Glitter falls from Amira's hair as she pounces on Willa. "And you look so pretty! I mean, you're always stupid pretty, but even more than usual—I hate you!" She turns to Finn. "Hi!" Finn too receives smacking cheek kisses.

Amira drags them along with her, stopping every now and then at family tables to chat and joke and accept an army of kisses. She leans over to listen to a little boy telling her something, then engulfs him in a cuddle. Willa watches her friend throw her exuberant warmth around the room and likes her even more than she already did.

Eyebrows raise slightly at the sight of Willa, but the Gandry girls act chill, like Gandry girls do, and smile and say their hellos. Daunted by small talk, Willa stands at the edge of the crowd, clutching Finn's hand as she chats to Holly. How does Finn just know how to talk to people? And how does she always find something to say? Willa has no idea what she's supposed to talk about.

A hand lands on her arm. "Hey, Brookes." It's Eva, looking delicately pretty in a green, sixties-style dress.

Willa feels the tingle of nerves but forces a smile. "Hi."

"I'm really sorry about the other day. I get lashy when I'm stressed."

"And I'm sorry I told Amira."

"Yeah, I guess should be mad at you, but…" She shrugs and smiles, looking around at the crowd.

"I didn't tell her about your brother, I promise."

"I know. Thank you. I ended up telling her anyway. She's kind of pushy, if you haven't already noticed."

"I've noticed. She's great, though."

"She is." Eva stares at the ground for a moment before finally looking up to meet her eye. "You know, I'm not deliberately starving myself. This is not some eating disorder thing."

Willa stops herself from raising an eyebrow. It isn't?

"I'm just not great at talking about things, and I guess when it gets too much, it comes out other ways, you know?"

Willa nods, thinking of that moment of panic in the hospital hallway. She remembers how Finn said that was about Willa's feelings finding their way out, even if she didn't want to let them. She wonders just how similar she and Eva are.

"And when I get stressed, I don't eat," Eva says. "I'm not *trying* to lose weight. I'm just trying to…" She sighs. "I don't know. Anyway, that's stuff for my counsellor. It's a party, right?"

"So I've heard. I'm unfamiliar with such events."

"Oh, well, if you need any explanations of cultural practice, let me know."

"You're too kind."

They exchange the kind of smiles that tell Willa that it's going to be okay.

Eva goes to say something but flinches as a song erupts from the sound system.

Amira shrieks and jumps. "My cousin's on. We dance!" She waves everyone towards the dance floor.

And Willa finds herself being carried with the tide of people that obediently follows the birthday girl to the spot where the lights beat brightest.

It doesn't take Finn long to get to her. And when she finds Willa marooned in the thick of it, her smile lights up, all cheek and "fancy seeing you here". She stretches her hand out through the crush of bodies and lets Willa pull her the last few steps towards her. And there they are, in a forest of towering high-heeled girls and athletic guys with haircuts.

Propelled by Finn's smile, Willa dances for the first time in her life. And it's not that hard, it turns out. You just make space for yourself in the sweaty, electric throng and let the music happen to you.

That's when Willa feels it, this brimming of goodness. Because in this moment, under the hot pulse of the lights, there's nothing to worry about. Nothing but not losing Finn in the current and what the next song will be.

And it reminds Willa that this is what life could be like. She loves studying next to Finn and hanging out with the kids with her—she likes doing anything with Finn. But now she wants to be out in this new electric world with her too. And maybe, just maybe, when Nan comes back and Willa's world tilts back to normal again, there'll be more moments like these. She hopes so. Because suddenly she's greedy for them.

# CHAPTER 47

## Willa

One minute Finn's lips are a hot force on Willa's, and the next thing she knows, they're gone, leaving her breathless and bereft.

"We should probably go in," Finn whispers. "I have to be home soon."

"Okay." Willa eases her shoulders from where they've been pushed against the rough brick of the side of her house. She exhales slowly, taking a moment to adjust to being just one person again.

"What's wrong?" Finn asks.

"Nothing." Willa drops another kiss on her. "Except that you're about to leave."

Instead of smiling like she usually does when Willa says something like that, Finn frowns. "But why did you sigh?"

"I think I was just breathing." Willa runs a finger along Finn's neck, right on the spot she was just kissing a few minutes ago. "You happen to make me breathe hard."

"Are you annoyed that we aren't having sex?"

Willa just stares at Finn, too thrown to speak. Not just because of what Finn's asking, but because of *how* she asks the question—as if Willa somehow provoked the need to ask. Willa hadn't even been thinking about that. She hadn't been thinking at all. "What do you mean?" she manages to ask

Finn shrugs, her lips pressed into a thin line, and takes Willa's hand from where it rests on her collarbone. She holds it tight between them, more like she's taming it than an act of affection.

"Why do you think I'm annoyed about it?" Willa asks her.

"Just tell me if you are." Finn folds her arms like a court lawyer demanding the truth.

Willa blinks, like she's trying to make this moment come into focus. Trying to make it make sense, but it won't.

The whole time, Finn stares at her, waiting, and Willa can't tell if she's angry or sad or something else. And it's horrible because she always knows how Finn feels. How is Willa supposed to navigate this moment? To find the right things to say to assuage whatever this tension is that has suddenly crept up on them? She feels like the guy in the movie trying to decide whether to cut the blue or the red wire to defuse the bomb.

This moment needs light, Willa decides, if she's going to have any chance of defusing it. She grabs Finn's hand, leads her back down the side of the house, and pulls her down onto the wooden bench under the back light. Then she asks the question as gently as she can. "Why are you worried?"

Finn draws small circles on her jeans with the tip of her finger. When she finally speaks, her voice comes out husky and thinned. "Because I know it's me that always stops things from happening."

"That's okay." She clasps Finn's wrist. "I figured you're still not ready."

"But are you?"

"I won't be ready until I know you are."

"Well, that's the right thing to say, isn't it?"

Her sarcasm stings, but Willa pushes back at the irritation as she leans closer, speaking softly. "Please don't be mad at me, Finn. Just tell me what's happening."

Finn hugs herself tighter. "I just don't want you to get frustrated with me, and I don't know what you're thinking."

"I didn't know you needed to know." Willa pulls Finn's arm away from where it's wrapped tightly around her and grips her hand, feeling like she's missed something completely, something she was supposed to do but didn't know she should. Why is she so bad at this?

She leans in a little closer. "But I'll tell you. Yes, I want to sleep with you. Of course I do. *One day.*" She ignores the blush storming her cheeks. "And I think about you naked. Sometimes at inappropriate times. But that's normal, right? And it doesn't mean I think anything *should* be happening yet." She watches the words settle around Finn and squeezes her fingers. "And I guess it doesn't really matter if I'm ready or not, because I know you're not."

"I'm not. I'm sorry." Finn meets her eye for the first time since they sat down. "Not that I don't think about you like that too. I do. It just doesn't feel…right yet."

"Okay, then we wait," Willa says, like the problem's solved.

Finn stares at her. "Okay."

It takes Willa a minute to work up the courage to ask the question. "I'm not…doing anything to make you feel like this, am I?"

"No." Finn shakes her head. "I guess I'm just worried you'll get sick of waiting."

"I'm not *waiting* for anything." How does Finn still not know what a revelation this relationship is for Willa? How it's the one thing that has kept her sane and happy and would probably still be the best thing in her life even if things weren't as messy and hard as they are right now? "I just want to be with you. And I am." She drops a kiss on Finn's shoulder. "I'm actually pretty easy to please."

Finn gives her a small, grateful smile, and Willa lets herself relax a little. Maybe she's not so bad at this girlfriend thing. She kisses Finn's shoulder again and whispers, "And of course I'm going to think about you naked sometimes."

Finn lets out a small laugh and leans into her. "You can do that."

They sit in a small silence, the sounds of TVs and parties and traffic washing around them. Sounds of a Saturday night still playing itself out.

"You know," Willa tells her as she plays with the bracelet Finn gave her, turning the tiny silver leaves over and over. "I still don't feel that great about sleeping with Freya."

Finn turns to look at her. "Really?"

"Have you ever gotten the feeling while you're doing something that it might not be a great idea but it's too late and you're too far in it?"

"Sort of."

"It was like I could feel Freya feeling that, even though she was the one who started it. And even though I felt it too, I didn't stop, and neither did she." Willa flinches at the memory. "But it made me feel weird. Like *I'd* pushed her into it. Only I hadn't. It was her that started it."

When Freya had started flirting so obviously and so out-of-the-nowhere at the party that turned out to be her farewell, Willa didn't know whether to doubt her sudden attention or to enjoy it. Even in the thick of her happiness, it seemed impossible, her dreams crashing true like that.

Willa will never know for sure why that night happened. Now that she's far enough from the hurt to let herself think about it, she's decided Freya was probably just looking for another thing to add to her list of worldly woman intrigues by sleeping with a girl. Whatever it was, Freya was relentless at that party, dragging Willa into corners, demanding she stay at her house afterwards and drink champagne snuck from the fridge. She was energised by something Willa hadn't seen before.

And she was relentless until they were under the covers, half-stripped of their clothes. That's when Willa could feel the two glasses of champagne turn from giddy to sickly. And she could also feel Freya's bravado being shaken by this unknown territory they were in. And Willa couldn't help her either. It was all just as new to her.

Willa knows now that she probably should have stopped things at that moment. But she didn't, because that would have required talking about what was happening. She didn't know how to do that. And she knows Freya didn't either.

The next morning, Freya acted like it was some stupid drunk thing. Something they could now go about the business of poking fun at for a couple of hours and then forget. And in those jokes was a silent demand for an agreement that it was a definitely mistake, one that needn't take up too much of their time or energy. Freya didn't care— or didn't care to know—if Willa felt the same.

Now that whole night is a regret Willa will keep forever. Especially now. Because imagine if instead she could look back one day and remember Finn as the first girl she was with? Willa can't imagine that memory will ever be anything but incredible.

Willa turns to Finn. Her face is peaceful now as she stares into the darkness. "Do you regret sleeping with Matt?"

Finn thinks for a moment. "I don't know if I regret *sleeping* with him. It's not like it was a bad experience. I think I just regret ever going out with him."

"Did it hurt?"

"Going out with him? Not 'til after."

"Ha-ha." Willa blushes. "You know what I meant."

"Not as bad as I thought it would. Anna says it's different for everyone."

"Well, I'm never going to find out."

Finn curls her hands around Willa's arm and grins. "Going to be a gold star?"

"A what?"

"A gold star. Nona taught me that the other day. It's some name for a lesbian who's never slept with a guy."

Willa nods. "Then I guess I'll be a gold star."

"You know, I couldn't talk about this with Matt," Finn says. "The sex thing, I mean. We never discussed it. Or *anything*, really. I felt like it wasn't...I don't know...hot to talk about this stuff. But maybe if I'd been able to have that kind of conversation with him, I'd have known him better. Then I'd have known what was going to happen."

"Well, don't worry, you can pretty much say anything you want to me, and I'll still think you're hot." Willa squeezes her hand. "And I want you to tell me this stuff. And I want you to feel good about everything."

Finn sighs loudly, and for a terrified moment, Willa thinks she's annoyed again. But the next thing she knows, Finn's clambering over her legs. Then she's sitting on her lap, facing her, her smile pushed in close to Willa's. "Stop it," she whispers.

"Stop what?"

"Being so lovely and incredible."

"No," Willa says, rushed by pride.

"Okay." Finn presses a fierce kiss on her and then rests her cheek on Willa's shoulder, breathing softly against her neck.

Willa smiles, wallowing in the soothe of Finn's weight on her. She smooths her hands up and down her back. *This* is happiness. And there's a little bit of ego too. Because Willa somehow navigated this moment.

"I bet you look really hot naked," Finn suddenly whispers and laughs into her neck.

~ ~ ~

Willa lies under her doona, still feeling the warm waves of getting something right for once. When Finn kissed her goodbye at the side gate, they felt stronger somehow. More invincible. And Willa felt the same after assuaging Finn's fears.

The truth is Willa does get frustrated with Finn's reticence sometimes. But it's only ever for a fleeting moment. It's hard not to feel a flash of impatience when Finn calls a halt to things in the thick of one of those moments that only makes Willa wants to take it further. And maybe it hurts a tiny bit that Finn doesn't entirely trust in them.

But the rational part of Willa's brain also knows it's not about her. It's about Finn. And about Finn and Matt. Finn had no reason to think that her boyfriend would go off her the minute she slept with him. What happened to Finn is a particular raw and bruising kind of betrayal, and Willa knows she needs time to get over it.

Willa would probably be careful too if that happened to her. With Freya, the warning signs were always there. Willa just chose to ignore them, so it's her own fault. She knows that. Knows it enough to never let Finn see the flickers of impatience that dog her when a kiss ends abruptly or when Finn leads her somewhere, only to drag Willa back to safety before she's ready. After what happened with Freya, Willa knows there are some things that are worth waiting for until it's right.

# CHAPTER 48

## Finn

Even though Finn feels better after talking about this stuff with Willa, she's still not one hundred per cent sure why she's still being so weird.

"It's so dumb," she tells Anna as they sprawl on the couch in her living room, avoiding a random viciously hot day. "I mean, I find her hot. Incredibly hot. And I like her more than I've ever liked anyone. So what's up with me?"

"Psych 101, dude." Anna takes a handful and passes her the packet of chips. "You did something out of character with Matt. It went wrong. And now you're scared. It makes perfect sense in the context of brain weirdness."

Finn shakes the packet, peering inside, searching for the perfect folded-over chip. "But I know Willa wouldn't do what Matt did. She wouldn't. *Couldn't.*"

"Fear knows no rationality. Besides, it's not about Willa, or about Matt. It's about you. You're the kind of person who knows herself well. And you shocked yourself a bit. Just let yourself get over it. It'll happen when it happens."

Finn bites down on a chip, wishing she'd inherited her sister's Zen-like ability to just take life as it comes. Finn's way too much of an overthinker to exist in that kind of chill. It must come from Anna's mother.

"I felt like such a prude, though, freaking out on her the other night. It's not like I'm some virgin."

"You know, the thing with my job is that I wind up in a lot of conversations with girls your age about sex. Mostly because they're too terrified to talk to their mums. I don't know how many of them don't get that just because you do something once doesn't mean you have to do it every time. By which I mean sex." Anna grins and tosses more chips in her mouth, chomping loudly.

Finn totally gets the whole not wanting to talk to your mum part, even if her own mother usually leans towards the open and supportive side instead of the freaked-out and authoritarian one. Finn always found it easy to ask her all the embarrassing "what the hell is my body doing" questions, but she has no plans to talk to her mother about her sex life. Or lack of it.

This is just another reason why she's incredibly lucky Anna turned up in her life. Her sister will talk about anything. *Anything.* Sometimes it's kind of alarming, but at other times it's a relief. "You missed your calling, by the way," Finn tells her. "You should've been a counsellor."

"No way. Not enough pay. But at least the counselling session distracts them from what's happening downstairs, right?"

Finn pulls a face. Why would anyone want to be a gynaecologist? Actually, she does know. Because Anna told her. Why wouldn't she want to work in a specialty that is completely devoted to women's health and wellbeing? Just another reason to admire her fierce feminist of a sister.

"Besides, you know what?" Anna says, staring at some soap on the TV, the sound muted against two characters deep in an intense conversation. "I know that you youth are an impatient lot, but there's something to be said for dragging this stuff out, you know." She grins. "Taking it slow can be its own special kind of fun."

"I hope Willa thinks so."

"What does she say about all this?"

"That she's happy to wait for whenever I'm ready."

"Does she mean it?"

Finn chews her lip, thinking of Willa's sweet patience the other night in the face of her mini freak-out. "Yeah, she definitely does."

"Then she's the perfect person for you right now."

"She is anyway."

"Aw, that's cute." Anna snatches the chips back from her.

# CHAPTER 49

## Finn

Finn surfaces to the melody of small, sonorous grunts. She rolls over, dislodging a dog. The sound stops.

"Were you snoring?" She narrows her eyes at Banjo. "Because that's a new trick. And not a good one."

Banjo just flicks open one eye, curls up tighter, and goes back to sleep. Finn's about to do the same when there's a tap on her door.

Her mother's already buttoned into a neat green blouse and her sensible work heels, her jasmine perfume trailing her into the room. "Time to get up." She pulls the curtains aside, letting the sunlight seep in through the ivy outside.

"I'm all over it," Finn fibs, stretching her arms above the doona. "Banjo was snoring."

"He's getting old." Anita sits on the edge of the bed and runs her hand over his head. "Poor boy."

"Poor *me*, you mean."

Anita picks him up and puts him on her lap. He blinks sleepily and licks her hand.

"You're going to get hair all over you," Finn warns her. "You'll look like a mad dog lady."

Anita shrugs and cuddles him. "Listen, I was talking to your Dad last night. About Cup Day weekend."

Finn loves that weekend. Well, she *used* to love that weekend. Every year they go away with her parents' old friends, Angela and Matteo, and their little girl, Belle, for the Melbourne Cup long weekend. It's the closest they've got to a family tradition. They rent side-by-side cottages right on the beach and stay there for three days.

"Your Dad's going to fly over for it."

Finn just blinks at her mother for a moment. "Really?"

"Yep."

Finn watches Anita croon at the dog for a moment, trying to calm the ripple of excitement. This has to be a good sign, right? "Hey, Mum?"

"Mm?"

"Do you miss him?"

It takes Anita a moment to answer. "Of course I do."

Hope springs again, and Finn wants to smile and grab her arm and tell her to keep missing him. To miss him so much that she can't live without him.

"Listen," Anita says, "I thought maybe you might want to bring a friend? I know it was tough for you in Tasmania. Maybe Dan might want to come along?"

"He's going to Adelaide to see his grandparents. What about Will?" Finn sits up, wide awake now. "Could she come? Nan's coming home this week, so she wouldn't have to look after her brother and sister."

Anita frowns. "We've never let someone you're dating stay over."

"I know, but it's not like we're going to be sleeping together." Finn blushes. Hard. "I mean, she would stay in the other room, just like Dan would have. And you guys will be there the whole time. She could totally use a weekend away."

"We'll see. I'll talk to your dad about it." Anita stands, brushing down her pants. "You should get up for school."

Finn lies there for a minute after her mum leaves, electric with the thought of the long weekend. It has to happen. The beach. Both her parents in the same place by choice. Willa there with her. She's *got* to make it happen.

# CHAPTER 50

## Finn

Finn wants it so happen so badly she rings her dad at lunch.

"Finno!" he cries down the phone, the same way he does every time she calls. Her regular dose of overcompensatory parental enthusiasm.

"Hey, Dad. I'm sorry I haven't been over," she says dropping onto a bench outside the locker bays. "Things have been crazy. I have school stuff, and Speech Night to prepare, and the filibuster."

"A filibuster? Have you turned into a politician in my absence?"

"No, well, it's kind of a repurposed filibuster." She tells him about the community centre event.

"I like it," he says with relish. "That's got to attract some local attention. Am I a bad dad if I tell you that I might be more impressed with this than I was with your last school report?"

"Probably. But it's okay. I'm sure Mum will pick up the slack the other way."

He laughs. "True."

"So, you're coming over for Cup weekend?"

"Sure am. I can't wait to see you."

"Mum said I could bring someone, and I asked if Willa could come."

"Good-o."

She rolls her eyes. Typical. It hasn't even occurred to him that he's supposed to be parental about this. "She said she has to discuss it with you first."

"Oh, well, she already mentioned that she was going to tell you that you could bring a friend."

"Dad, catch up," Finn teases. "She wants to talk to you because Willa's my *girlfriend*."

"Oh, right."

"But I told her we'd be on our best behaviour," she says quickly. "And you want to meet her, don't you?"

He laughs again. "Ah. I see your divide and conquer tactics for what they are, child."

Typical again. He's a clueless dad when she doesn't want him to be, and then he decides to get a clue right at the moment she *doesn't* want him to.

"But you're right," he says. "I do want to meet her."

"You'll like her. She's smart."

"Of course she is. Otherwise you wouldn't like her."

"Maybe." She thinks of Ruby Shipman, or Luke, that guy from Pender's College she dated briefly last year. Cute and funny, but definitely no mental giant. It's probably lucky her dad didn't meet Luke. He thought Australia's first female prime minister was Margaret Thatcher.

"I'll chat to your mum, and we'll see. But you know she has the final say on these things."

She sighs. "I know."

# CHAPTER 51

## Willa

Willa drops down under the apricot tree, the phone pressed to her ear. "Riley too?"

"Yep. That was my idea," Finn says. "I figured Riley could play with Bella, and my parents would be more likely to say yes if your little sister is sleeping upstairs with us, being, like, a buffer."

"You really are a genius." Willa waves at Maida, who's coming through the side gate with a ragged clutch of hand-picked flowers in her hands.

"So my mum said that your dad said he'd talk to Nan and that they'd let her know."

"Your mum talked to my Dad?" Willa's eyes widen as Maida sits down beside her.

"He said Nan had people over and couldn't come to the phone."

Willa can't even wrap her head around the idea of that conversation happening "What did he say?"

"That he'd talk to Nan, remember?"

"Oh, right. Sorry."

"So, do you think he's said something yet?"

"Probably not. She's had visitors all afternoon."

"I hope you can come," Finn says.

"Me too. I'll tell you as soon as I know. I've got to go, though. Maida's here."

"Okay. Say hi. And tell Nan I'll come see her soon. Bye."

Willa drops her phone on the grass and turns to Maida. "Finn says hi." She points at the flowers. "For me? You didn't have to."

Maida grins and hugs them to her. "They're for Nan, and you know it."

"She's in the living room."

"It's ridiculous how happy I am that she's home. You must be totally excited." Maida climbs to her feet, clutching her bright gift.

"It's pretty great." Willa follows Maida inside the house and hunts out yet another vase. The house is already bursting with blooms brought to welcome Nan home. She fills a jar at the kitchen sink as chatter spills in from the next room.

"I was just about to do that." Nan leans on her walking stick in the doorway, clutching Maida's flowers.

"Well, it's done." Willa puts the jar carefully on the table.

"Thank you, my girl." Nan thrusts the flowers into the jar and fusses at them until they're arranged the way she likes them.

Willa can't help smiling. Because Nan is calling her "my girl" again. Because Nan is in the house again, being Nan, making everything the way she likes it.

It was amazing how good it was to hurry home and find her holding court from her armchair throne. There was the usual game show on the TV with the sound down as she chatted to one of her community garden cronies. Jack was perched on the arm of Nan's chair, letting Nan smooth out the wrinkles in his school shirt as she chatted. Riley was thumping around in the kitchen, crafting some after-school snack, yelling her opinion into the next room. It was all so utterly, blissfully, loudly normal it made Willa want to cry.

And she nearly gives into it as Nan turns from her flowers and gathers her into a brisk hug. "Thank you, my girl, for taking such good care of things. I'm proud of you. *Prouder.*"

Willa swallows hard and says, "Want me to start dinner?"

# CHAPTER 52

## Willa

Kelly comes over after dinner, carrying an armful of artfully arranged pastel blooms. "The lady at the florist next to work gave me a huge discount," she says. "Otherwise it would have been el cheapo carnations."

"She's in the lounge room," Willa tells her.

When Kelly comes back outside, she's shaking her head. "Christ, it's like a jungle in there. I should have brought weed killer instead." She drops onto the end of the bench next to Maida. "You must be rapt she's back, huh?"

"I am," Willa says for what feels like the millionth time.

"Now you can have a life again," Kelly says. "Such as it was."

"Poor Willa," Maida says, smoothing out a strand of Willa's hair. "Our Cinderella. All you've done is cook and clean and study for weeks."

"She does all that anyway," Kelly says. "So are you going to finally party now you don't have to play sister-mum all the time? Or are you going to return to your nunnish ways?"

"Leave her alone," Maida tells her. "She's had a hard time."

"Dude, I know. Now I'm saying she should have a *good* time."

"I'm trying." Willa tells them about the beach weekend possibility. "If I'm allowed."

"A weekend away with the gf?" Kelly raises an eyebrow. "Sounds saucy."

"Separate bedrooms. And they've invited Riley. I'd be sharing a room with her."

"Okay, sounding less hot now. So what did Nan say?"

"Finn's mum spoke to Dad on the phone. He said he'll ask her."

"She'll say yes," Maida says. "She has to. You totally deserve a holiday."

Kelly leans against the brick wall and sighs. "So this is how the other half spends its long weekends? I'm working. Double time pay, though."

"We're going back to the new farm block," Maida grumbles. "Another four days with no electricity."

"What do you even do up there?" Willa asks her.

"I watch stuff until my laptop runs out of juice, and then I read and pray for it to be over."

"That sucks," Kelly says.

"It does." Maida picks up her textbooks. "Anyway, I better go." She hugs them both and dashes down the side of the house. "Night!"

Kelly jerks her thumb towards the back door. "So when's he leaving?"

"Dad? He's staying another week so he can take Nan to her hospital appointments. Around Cup Weekend."

"You looking forward to it?"

Willa shrugs. She still has no idea how to feel about it. About him leaving, specifically, or his existence in general.

Kelly slowly nods. That's the thing about Kelly. She knows that ambivalence is a thing you can feel about a person. Not like Maida. Maida feels everything for everybody.

They sit there quietly, the night air lulling Willa back into a laziness she hasn't felt in a while. She's still got maths to do, but it can wait. Maybe it can even wait until morning. Because tonight she's celebrating the return of Nan. The return of her world.

Kelly sits next to her, dreaming too. Willa loves that. Kelly will talk about anything you want to talk about, but you can also just be with her in silence too, and it's fine. Willa's gotten used to the night-time quiet, to the silence strung out, thick and indifferent between her and her dad after the kids go to bed, that the sound of voices in the kitchen makes her jump.

"I told her I'd talk about it with you," she hears her dad say.

"Why?" Nan says. "You could have said yes. I'm happy for them to go."

There's the sound of cups clattering and the kettle being switched on.

Just when Willa's thinking that's the end of the conversation, her dad says, "She told me that this Finn girl is her girlfriend. As in she's..." He starts but trails off, like he doesn't want to say the word.

"See?" Kelly nudges her. "Homophobe."

"I'm aware that Finn's her girlfriend." Nan says it in that gruff tone she gets when she thinks someone's talking rubbish. Usually Riley. "What's your point?"

"I'm so glad I was never in one of her classes," Kelly whispers, snickering. "She would have been terrifying."

Willa ignores her, straining to hear what comes next. There's no answer, though. Just more clattering of dishes and the purr of the kettle.

"Oh, don't tell me that you've lived in that conservative, parochial state for so long you've become a narrow-minded fool like the rest of them," Nan suddenly says. "People are gay. Always have been. Including your daughter. Now, kindly get over it, and join us in this century. I'm halfway to seventy. If I can handle it, so can you."

Kelly's shoulders shake with held-in laughter as she leans against Willa, listening. "Go Nan!" she whispers.

"Would you let her go away for the weekend with a boyfriend?" he asks.

Willa's eyes widen. *Wow.* He's not letting this go. Maybe he really is a homophobe.

"Honestly? I don't know," Nan says. "She's never had a boyfriend, so it hasn't come up."

Willa doesn't know why that makes her blush, but it does.

"Look," Nan says. "They're going away with the girl's parents. The mother is a school vice principal and hardly likely to let either of your daughters do anything they shouldn't be doing. *And* they've been nice enough to invite Riley too. This is hardly something I'm going to worry about. Why are you?"

There's another spun-out silence.

Then Nan starts talking again, on a full Nan roll. "You know what? I won't even entertain this nonsense. That girl doesn't get close to people easily, and she's found someone she cares about. She does nothing but work and work and work. She gets top marks. She earned a scholarship to a school neither you nor I could afford, and she helps out around the house more than any teenager I've ever known. And she does it all without being asked to. You and Leela brought a good girl into the world. She deserves to have a nice time." The kettle turns off with a click, as if to punctuate Nan's last statement. "She's going."

"The queen hath spoken." Kelly smirks and wraps an arm around Willa. "Pack your bags."

Willa nods and smiles and does her best not to let on that she's fighting another round of tears. Because she loves Nan so much right now she doesn't even know what to do with the feeling.

~ ~ ~

Later, when she's in bed and the house is a contented silence, Willa pulls out her phone and texts Finn.

*We're allowed to come to the beach.*

All she gets in return is an explosion of happy emojis.
She tucks her phone under her pillow and smiles her way to sleep.

# CHAPTER 53

## Willa

It's hard to even look at her dad after overhearing that conversation with Nan. And she definitely doesn't want to talk to him.

Every time Willa thinks about what she heard, she feels gross. Maybe she's been lucky, or maybe it's because so few people have known, but no one's ever made her feel as if liking girls is wrong or weird. And she knows that for a lot of people, it's not always like that.

The best-case scenario is that he's not weird about her being gay, and he's just being prudish and fatherly about her going away with her girlfriend. But still, it annoys her, because why does he get to play Dad like that all of a sudden? He hasn't earned the right to have an opinion.

Now she just wishes he'd hurry up and leave, for their life to go back the way it was when he was just a voice on the phone and not a confusing, absent presence. Until then, she plans on avoiding him. She's polite, as usual, but she does her best to evade any encounters. When he enters a room, she finds a reason to leave. When she walks out into the garden and he's there, she goes straight back inside. On the few times they all eat dinner together, she keeps her eyes on her food, and lets the conversation trickle around her. She does her homework in her room, pretending she needs quiet, and only goes into the lounge room when Nan and the kids are there.

*One more week*, she keeps reminding herself.

"I wish I could have told him it's none of his business," she tells Finn one afternoon after school in the park. "That he's got no say in what I do." She rolls over onto her stomach and rests her head on her arms. "You know, I don't even know if I care if I don't see him again."

"Really?" Finn gives her a long look. "Are you sure?"

Willa stares at the grass, jaw clenched. "Really."

"But what if something happens to Nan? I mean, it won't, but what if you need him again?"

Willa shrugs and changes the subject. Because she doesn't want to talk about it anymore. And because she'd like to ignore the annoying fact that Finn is probably right.

# CHAPTER 54

## Finn

As Friday afternoon barrels on, Finn gets more and more fidgety. By the time she arrives at the centre after school, she's a twist of nerves. Because it's D-day.

She wouldn't be so nervous if she wasn't the one making the speech. All week, she's been working on it, jamming in writing sessions between homework and last-minute Speech Night planning. Of course, in the grand tradition of planning clusterfluffs, these two events just had to fall within the same forty-eight hours. But with the help of Zehra and the army of kids they have gathered, they've got Speech Night wrangled into shape for Saturday night. And now they've done everything they possibly can to make the filibuster happen.

They spend the afternoon cleaning and tidying the centre, music blaring from Andy's portable speakers. Finn sweeps up the ancient piles of dust and scrubs coffee stains from tables with Bea. An hour before they're due to start, Nona brings in a huge tray of cupcakes, decorated beautifully with rainbow flowers.

"Wow." Rosie leans over them. "These are amazing, Nona. Totally professional."

"Amazing," Finn agrees, leaning over to get a better look. They're like cupcakes you'd see in a shop, with small, artful flowers and detailed little leaves.

"And they'll taste as good too," Bea says, wrapping her arms around Nona's waist. "Nona is a secret-amazing cook."

"Not so secret now," Kayah says, jabbing Nona in the ribs. "Why didn't you let on you can cook while you were staying at mine? I could have used a week off cheese toasties."

Nona shrugs and grins. "Sorry, I only do baking. I'm going to leave school at the end of the year so I can study to be a pastry chef. I can't wait."

"Really?" Finn's never met anyone who's left school early. "Are your parents okay with it?"

"No, but what's the point in staying? I know what I want to do, and I don't need to study to do it. I'm crap at school, and I just want to get on with it and get a job. As soon as I have enough experience, I'll start my own place."

"That's cool," Finn says. Her mother makes it sound like leaving school's the worst thing you could ever do, but what Nona says makes sense.

Nona rearranges a couple of the cakes and sighs. "Righto, I'm going home to get changed. No one touch the cakes until the presentation." She points at Kayah. "Please, people. Watch her. I don't trust her."

Kayah holds up her hands in protest. "Why me?"

Everyone goes back to cleaning. Finn straightens some posters and mentally goes over her speech. She called her dad and read it to him last night, but he's the only one who's heard it.

"It's good, kiddo," he said, after making a couple of minor suggestions for flow. "Really good. I wish I could be there."

"Don't worry," she grumbled. "It's going to be recorded for posterity. Dan's filming the whole thing." The thought makes her insides clench.

But tonight she can't even think about the cameras or the journalists coming down. If she does, she might lose courage.

"You okay, Harlow?" Dan asks as he sets up his camera in the corner. "You look pale."

"Nervous," she mutters through clenched teeth.

"What?" He pretends to look shocked. "Don't be. This is your thing. Your amazing, righteous, do-gooder thing. You'll rock it."

"Gee, thanks." She stalks off, looking for the next thing to clean.

"I mean it," he calls after her.

He does mean it. She knows he does. But it doesn't stop the nerves. It doesn't matter that she does this kind of thing all the time. This seems bigger. Like there's more hanging from it. And nothing Dan says is going to change that.

People start to trickle in about half an hour before the presentation is due to begin. The crowd is made up of parents and friends and the people from the church down the road who donated chairs for the event.

Finn's sitting with some of the others, deciding which songs the DJ should play between speeches on the radio later, when she sees Willa standing by the door. She's scanning the room, her hands jammed in her pockets. Finn's barely seen her all week, and it feels so damn good to lay eyes on her that she scrambles out of her seat midway through Rosie's argument for her case for a Beyoncé track.

"You came," Finn says when she's standing in front of her.

Willa pulls a face. "Of course I came."

"You didn't have to."

"Yes, I did. I came to see you do another amazing thing."

Beautiful Willa. Finn grabs her hand. "Come meet my people."

"Okay." Willa presses her lips together and takes a breath through her nose, the way she always does when she's trying to beat down shyness.

Finn smiles at the sight of it. Smiles because she knows her so well.

"You'll be okay," Finn tells her. "They're nice." She slides an arm around Willa's waist, and they cross the room, the swing of their hips matching the same beat. As she spies Nona and Bea curiously watch their approach, Finn's full to brimming with the fact that this beautiful, smart, cutely awkward human is her girlfriend. And she's never felt more like she wants to be watched in the act of being someone's girlfriend.

She slides into the seat, pulling Willa down next to her. "Guys, this is Willa."

"So she does exist!" Nona looks over at Willa and then flicks her eyebrows up and down at Finn as if to say she approves.

Finn rolls her eyes and laughs, keeping a tight hold of Willa's hand under the table. "We're picking songs to play between our speeches on the radio tonight," she tells her. She turns to Rosie "So, did Queen Bey make the cut?"

"No." Rosie also rolls her eyes. "They picked some indie chick instead."

"It's a community radio station, Rosie," Kayah reminds her. "I'm not sure they play a whole lot of Beyoncé there."

"Well, maybe they should," Rosie says. "Then maybe people would listen. What about Rihanna?"

"Um, maybe pick someone local," Kayah suggests.

Rosie pulls a face. "*Local?*"

"As in Australian."

"Australian? No way. Yuck. Our music is crap."

"Wow. No wonder the industry fails to thrive," Kayah's boyfriend, Dominic, says. It's the first time Finn's met him. He's short, dark, and extremely hot, with identical cropped curls to Kayah's. But somehow they manage to pull the twinned dos off.

When the list is complete, Finn turns to check on Willa. She's chatting to Nona. Well, Nona's talking to her. And she's also got that Nona look on her face.

"So, how'd you two meet?" she asks Willa. "Finn's never told me."

"Our schools were at the same camp."

"And you thought she was hot straight-up?"

Willa blushes. And Finn has to smile, even as she tells Nona to leave Willa alone. But Nona just gives Finn a sly grin and turns back to Willa. "You're gay, right? Like, totally gay?"

Willa face turns even redder as she nods.

"So, does it freak you out?"

"What?"

"Having a girlfriend who's bi? I mean, don't you worry she's going to meet some dude she's hot for?" Nona folds her arms. "I couldn't do it."

Willa stares at Nona for the longest time, her brow furrowed, like she's trying to comprehend her words. Finally, she says, "If you don't recognise the fundamental lack of logic in what you just said, I can't help you." She shakes her head. "No one can."

Nona actually deigns to look uncomfortable.

And Finn grins. That's one of the things she adores most about Willa. The staggering simplicity of her reactions to stupidity.

"Take that." Kayah grins at Willa. "Don't worry, even Nona doesn't believe half the crap she says. She just wants the attention."

Nona sits there and squirms, and all Finn can do is sit back and enjoy the mini takedown until it's time to make her speech. Because that's when the panic sets in. Finn stands at the front of the room, looking at everyone from the small platform they've made with wooden pallets, a rug, and Bea's mad budget-decorating skills.

Her stomach starts its slow roller-coaster ride. From here, she can see everyone: Kayah with two journalists off at the side, gesticulating as she talks. Bea and Nona at the meeting table with some councillors, smiling as they serve the cupcakes with coffee and tea. Dan's in the corner, fussing around with his tripod. Andy's at the side of the stage, waiting his turn. Even her mum and Anna are there, standing at the back of the room, flanked by Willa and Rosie, looking proud and expectant. Finn quickly looks away, clenching and unclenching her fists.

At the nod from Andy, she moves to the front of the stage and pulls in a slow, steadying breath. The room quiets as she taps the microphone to check it's on. *Just pretend it's a school assembly*, she tells herself.

"Hello everyone," she says, hearing the slight squeak of her nerves. She clears her throat and starts again. "Thank you for coming tonight and for taking the time to listen to what we have to say about the centre. This place might not look like much, but it means a lot to us." She looks around at everyone, making sure her smile lands on the councillors and journalists. "And given what it represents, maybe I should be talking about gay rights tonight. Maybe I should be talking about the marriage equality vote and the fact that politicians seem to think they and the rest of Australia has the right to decide on our equality as human beings. Maybe I should be talking about *human* rights. But I'm not. I want to talk about community."

She takes another breath, feeling steadier now. She shoves the speech in her pocket and wings it from memory. "You know," she continues. "There are only a few things in this world that most people seem to agree on. Like the fact that education is important. That flowers smell nice and pandas are cute. Beyoncé," she adds with a grin, seeing Rosie snicker down the back. "But another thing I feel like everyone believes in is the power of community. The need to feel like we belong. To form bonds with others that we share something with for support.

"Some of us might take it for granted, but community *is* important," she continues. "*So* important. Especially when you find yourself in a world where if you're different, even in just one way, you can feel like an outsider, and that's never a good feeling. This is when you have to go and find your own community. Because for some people, finding it can be lifesaving." She pauses. "But the thing is, for it to be found, that community first has to be able to form. It's places like this that make it possible.

"And, you know, maybe it's because everyone's talking about us right now, making decisions on our behalf about whether or not we get to live with the same rights as the rest of the world. But it feels like we need this sense of community more than ever. Because if the polls predicting the outcome of the marriage equality vote are right, out of every ten people who walk past me on the street, only two and a half of them don't believe in our right to equality. Yet those two and a half have been given the right to speak their minds about this as much as the seven and a half who do."

"And you know what?" she says, looking around the room, trying to keep people engaged. "Maybe hearing what they have to say will be easier if we're together. Our community will protect us from some of that, but only if places like this make it possible for us to be together. And that's why tonight we're going to gather together to speak for ourselves, to tell the world why we need this dank concrete room." People laugh quietly and shuffle. "So we can find each other."

She smiles again, hoping she's made some sense. Hoping that at least a part of what she wanted to express has come out right. "So, now, one member of our little community, Andy Nguyen, is going to come up and tell you his story, one of the many stories we'll be telling tonight on the radio in the hope that we're heard. Stories about why we need this centre, and each other. And why we're scared we might be about to lose it. Thank you again for coming. And for listening to us. It means a lot."

She gives them a quick smile and scuttles off the stage as the applause rises around her.

# CHAPTER 55

## Finn

When Finn finally drags herself up to the surface of sleep, the house is completely silent. Not even Banjo's newfound snore, keeping time with her breath, can be heard.

From the slide of light through the blinds, she can tell as she rolls over that it's late. Still, it's a shock to see the time on her watch. Two-thirty pm.

But instead of crawling out of bed to get ready for round two, she just lies there, eyes shut, going over last night in her head. After the speech and the cupcakes and making polite conversation, they all had marched over to the radio station. That's when it got fun. Because then it was just the community centre kids and Costa, their long-suffering youth worker, and a few supportive parents willing to supervise.

Some of the kids had been nervous about going on radio, but the DJ who did the graveyard shift was super chill and lovely. He showed them how to use the headphones and keep the microphones close to their mouths as they told their stories, and cracked jokes to stop nerves in their tracks. He was always ready to jump to a song if a story finished too quickly or to wait patiently when kids found out they had more to say than they thought they would.

While everyone took their turns, the rest of the group sat in the small, stuffy green room, offering encouragement as each pale-faced kid walked into the booth. They gave out rounds of applause whenever someone emerged, triumphant.

In the green room, they snacked and bantered their way through the six hours. And as the night wore on and she drank more coffee than was probably safe for any human, Finn listened to Nona's story and to Bea's and to Andy's again. When Kayah went in, Finn smiled her sympathy as Kayah talked about being bisexual and about the stupid assumptions people made about her because of it.

"Sounds kinda familiar," Finn said to Nona, who was curled up next to her on the couch, eyes half-closed.

Nona gave her a lazy smile. "You know I'm just messing with you when I say that stuff about you being bi, right?"

"I know." Finn said. Then she shrugged and gave her a weary smile back. "But I also wouldn't mind if you stopped doing it, you know."

Nona looked at her for a long moment and nodded slowly. "Okay. I'm sorry."

"Oh." Finn blinked at her, not expecting that. "Thanks."

"So this night has been pretty cool, huh?"

"Yeah." She kicked her socked feet up onto the coffee shop and smiled. "Once the speech part was over."

"You did great."

"Thanks," Finn said again. But she preferred this part, really, where it felt like they were all a team, making this thing happen together.

"So, you going to hang out with us now? At the centre? If we manage to save its butt?"

"For sure." The ceiling was completely covered with music posters. Finn frowned at it. "You know, I don't really have any gay friends, which is weird."

"Well, you do now. A lot of us," Nona said. "We should all go to the movies or something these holidays. Or there's usually some all-ages queer parties happening."

"Okay." Finn wondered what Willa would say. But she figured if she could convince Willa to go to a Gandry party, she could convince her to do anything. "Sounds fun."

"Your girlfriend is gorgeous, by the way," Nona told her with a grin. "And utterly terrifying."

"Yeah, I know."

"How long have you been together?"

"A couple of months now. What about you and Bea?"

"Six months next week. I'm making her a totally lush picnic and taking her to a play in the park."

"That's really sweet." Finn chewed at her lip. "Hey," she said slowly, "can I ask you something?"

"I bet I know what it is." Nona gave her another one of her lazy grins.

"Does that mean it's okay to ask?"

She shrugged. "Of course."

"Are you sleeping together?"

"One point to me." She winked at Finn. "Yeah, for a few months now."

"Right." Finn stared at a chip in her nail polish.

"What about you and your ice queen?"

Finn hesitated.

"Hey, I'm a loudmouth, but I'm not a gossip," Nona looked her straight in the eye as she said it, and Finn chose to believe her.

"We haven't. Not yet."

"Well, I can highly recommend it."

"That's a relief," Finn said, "because the reviews are kinda mixed online."

Nona laughed. "Is that so?"

Finn smiled but then turned serious. "At first I wanted to wait a bit, until I was ready. Last time I slept with someone, it didn't work out so well." Part of her couldn't believe she was telling Nona this stuff, but she ploughed on. "But I'm also nervous. I've never slept with a girl. It's kind of unknown territory. Okay, well, it's not, really." She blushed. "But you know what I mean."

Instead of laughing at Finn's gaucheness, Nona just sat up and held out her hand.

"Give me your phone. There's this cool website." She grinned at Finn's suspicious look. "Not *porn*. It's this forum where girls talk about this stuff."

"Oh."

"Trust me, it's great. I went on there a lot when I first started hooking up with girls. It actually helped."

"Is it really that hard to figure it out?" Finn asked, only half-joking, as she passed over the phone. "Now I'm even more nervous."

"No, of course not. Like you said, you're not exactly dealing with unknown anatomical territory, but there are some areas where a little guidance doesn't go astray, you know?" She types something into Finn's phone. "And if you're anything like me, you'll like knowing other girls felt as dumb and clumsy as you at first."

Finn grinned slyly at her. "And here I thought you came onto this earth knowing how to pull."

"Bea was the first girl I ever slept with, actually. And I was terrified. I didn't even tell her until after." Nona put her fingers over her lips. "Don't ever tell anyone I told you that."

"I won't," Finn said, guessing she owed Nona one by now.

Nona passed back the phone. "Check it out. Seriously."

"Wow." Finn sighed loudly. "There's even homework for sex."

"Well, have you slept with a guy?"

"Yeah."

"Did you fly blind the first time?"

"God no." Finn spent way too much time online in the week before sleeping with Matt, freaking herself out. She even read the dumb sex book her mother gave her when she was thirteen, in case she'd missed something the first time round. "I'm way too much of an overthinker for that."

"So it's the same." Nona handed her phone back. "I mean, just use it if you need it. You don't have to write anything, just lurk and read. There's so much crap on the net by horny guys and crazies out there. This forum's different. I mean, why have these awkward conversations when you can have them anonymously online?" She grinned. "And you know what the best part was?"

"What?"

"Finding out how terrified so many other girls were. I don't know, when you're on Tinder or at queer nights, everyone seems so cocky and experienced. They're really not as confident as they seem."

"Like *you* seem," Finn said.

"Like I *seem*."

Finn smiled and tucked her phone into her pocket. How did she end up having this conversation with *Nona*? Not only was it totally random, it was also weirdly reassuring. "Thank you."

Nona just shrugged and pulled her cap down. "No prob. Here for all your lesbian needs. Or bi needs," she corrected herself. "Or whatever."

When the night was finally over and the Saturday breakfast presenters turned up and kicked them out, they all trooped out into the grey dawn, feeling like they'd conquered the world. They ate eggs on toast in a tiny café and toasted themselves with coffee before trudging home to sleep.

Now they just have to wait and see if the filibuster gets any attention. The writer from the local paper promised there'd be an article in the next issue, and the journalist from the *Melbourne Daily* said they'd have an article online, possibly as early as Monday. One of the councillors also said she'd raise the issue. So maybe it will work.

When Finn can't put it off any longer, she drags herself out of bed, rescuing her phone from the pile of last night's clothes. There are eight missed calls and a bunch of messages—calls from Dan, Willa, an unknown number, and Zehra. Five calls from Zehra.

Finn sighs. It'll probably just be some last-minute reminder or worry. Finn had planned on having the longest, hottest shower in the world, eating some food and drinking a whole lot of coffee before she thought about Speech Night. She definitely didn't plan on dealing with Zehra and her relentless, nervous energy. After last night, Finn's got just enough energy in the tank to get tonight done and nothing more. Still, guilt wins. She dials Zehra's number.

Zehra picks up before the first ring is even done. "Hey. I'm sorry. I just panicked when I couldn't get in touch. It was getting so late, so I just asked her to do it. I'm sorry if—"

"Asked who to do what?"

"You didn't listen to my message?"

"No. I just woke up and saw all the missed calls, and I thought I'd just call straight back. What happened?" Finn asks, pulling on some socks.

"That lawyer guy, the one who was doing the alumni speech, can't make it. His daughter's in hospital with appendicitis. The principal tried to call you to let you know, but you weren't answering, so he called me."

"Seriously?" Finn stalks into the kitchen and checks the machine is on. "This is bad." She spots her mum through the sliding doors, out in the back terrace, working at the wooden table, the dogs at her feet. "Everything is organised around that speech." Something snags as she tries to untangle her brain. "Hang on, but did you just say something about sorting it?"

"Yeah. I was freaking a bit when I couldn't get in touch with you, so I made some calls."

"I'm sorry I didn't answer." Finn tells her briefly about last night. "I didn't get to bed until seven this morning. But you found someone?"

"Yeah. Hana's cousin, Naila, went to our school. She finished about nine years ago, and she and her husband own this really successful adventure travel company. They started it from scratch. It sounds pretty cool. And, I don't know, I thought it might be kind of cool not to have a middle-aged white man do the speech for once."

Finn laughs. "Agreed. She sounds great."

"Anyway, I'm sorry for finding someone without talking to you, but I ju—"

"Don't be sorry. Listen, I can meet you in the hall in, like, an hour?"

"I'm already on my way, actually," Zehra says. "Naila said they might show a couple of videos, so I thought I better go in early and check the system."

"I can do it." The guilt chafes. "You've been stressing out all morning. It's my turn."

"How about we meet there? We can stress together."

"Okay." Finn flicks off the coffee machine. "I'll see you as soon as I can. Just got to shower."

"Okay. I'll pick up coffee. You sound like you need it."

"Not going to lie. I do. And Zehra?"

"Yeah?"

"Thank you. For saving the day. I'm *really* sorry I was asleep."

"Don't worry about it. See you in a bit."

Finn hangs up and dashes for the shower. So much for relaxing. "Mum," she yells out the window, "can you please give me a lift?"

# CHAPTER 56

## Finn

As soon as the adrenaline drains from Finn's system, the exhaustion slams her. Hard.

It happens during the second-last speech. One minute she's all awake and attentive, the next she's considering sitting down in the wings of the school auditorium and giving in to the million yawns gathering in her throat.

From the moment they arrived at the centre, she and Zehra have been on the run, putting out fires and calming nerves. And now it's nearly over, Finn feels like she could go home and sleep twice over and still not be caught up.

They stand elbow-to-elbow at the side of the stage as the senior school captain winds up his speech with the school cheer. The principal waits in the opposite wings, ready to hit the stage for a last goodnight. Finn watches him brush down his suit and check his notecard.

"You were so right about putting his speech on at the start of the night," she whispers to Zehra. "He actually ran to time."

Zehra gives her a wry grin. "It's a pity we couldn't do anything to make it more interesting."

"Well, there's such a thing as aiming too high."

"Still, Speech Night done and dusted." Zehra claps her hands together, like she's cleaning them off. "Just the Year 10 Formal and Awards Night to go for the year."

Finn's shoulders sag. She can't even bear to think about the last two events. Not tonight. Monday. She'll think about them on Monday. Luckily, Zehra loves the formal, so she'll be all over that one.

"Thanks again for today," Finn tells her. "Hana's cousin was amazing. I'm kind of glad that other guy dropped out."

Naila and her husband's speech was easily the best part of the whole night. They were smart and funny. It was a change from the usual stiff, pompous people who come talk at the school on these kinds of occasions. They told incredible stories of their travels together and of the first crazy years of running the company. After showing a couple of videos, Naila talked about some things she learned while she was at Brunswick Hill that helped her later. And the whole time she and her husband talked, the audience was silent, smiling and laughing at the funny parts. Finn couldn't see a single light, signalling kids staring at their phones, waiting for it to be over. That's got to be some kind of miracle.

The more she thinks about it, Finn wonders why she didn't try and hunt out someone really amazing to speak in the first place, instead of just going along with the principal's boring recommendation. If she'd just asked around more, she could have found Naila in the first place.

As people clap the end of the senior captain's speech, the principal walks out to the stage.

"Come on, buddy, wrap it up quick," Finn whispers. "You know you can do it."

Zehra snickers. "But does he?"

He actually does for once, because he only says a few words about what a great night it's been and how the senior class has been such a valuable part of the school. Then he moves on to a list of thank yous. "We have a tradition here at Brunswick Hill," he says at the end. "Every year, the current Year 10 class stages this event for the senior school. It's part of facilitating respect and collegiality and the passing of tradition among the students."

"Or perpetuating slave labour," Zehra whispers.

Finn stifles a laugh.

"So," the principal goes on. "I'd like to say a big thank you to Finn Harlow, the intermediate school captain, for running the show. And to her team of helpers. They have staged a seamless and inspiring Speech Night. Thank you, Finn."

Finn stiffens as polite applause greets his words.

He presses his palms to the lectern and gives everyone a warm smile. "Thank you, everyone, for coming. Have a wonderful night, and drive safely."

As he walks off to another round of applause, Finn sneaks a look at Zehra. And even though she's smiling and clapping, Finn can see the tightness of her smile. And she doesn't really blame her.

# CHAPTER 57

## Finn

The article doesn't appear on the website until Monday morning. But when it does, there's even a photo. It's of Andy, wide-eyed and smiling on the stage as he talks to the crowd. Finn sighs with relief it's not one of her. There are quotes from her speech, though, which is nice.

She sips her coffee, kicking her legs happily against the counter, as her mother reads it on her iPad.

When she's done, Anita beams her most embarrassingly motherly smile at her. "I'm very proud of you. You did a fantastic thing."

Finn shrugs, but she can't stop her smile. "It wasn't just me."

This, of course, brings on yet another wave of guilt over Speech Night. Why did the principal have to make it sound like Finn did all the work? With the assistance of some helper monkeys? No wonder Zehra barely spoke for the rest of the night as they packed up. Her work was basically ignored. Finn kept trying to think of something to say to her, some way to apologise, but she couldn't. And they'd had such a fun night working together too.

"Well, it was partly you too," Anita says. "And I'm proud that you worked hard to make something you want to happen, happen. Most kids are perfectly happy to spend all their free time crafting the perfect selfie, not thinking of making the world a better place."

"Let's not make a paragon of me yet, Mum," Finn says. "I've got a bunch of questionable selfies of my own."

"Maybe. But you also do things like this. I know I wasn't one hundred per cent excited by it at first, but you've managed to help out with the community centre and keep your focus on school and on your captain responsibilities. You never stop impressing me." She drops a kiss on her forehead and picks up her briefcase. "Make sure you send the link to your dad."

~ ~ ~

By lunchtime, Finn's already received a message full of Dad pride. Anita clearly couldn't help herself, because Finn hadn't even sent him the link yet.

Finn's texting him back when she hears her name being shouted across the outdoor lunch area.

It's Hana, sitting outside the canteen with Zaki and Amy.

She veers towards them. "Hi! How are you guys?"

"Fabulous," Zaki says, holding out a container of almonds to Finn. "I just got an A-plus for my maths test, and that never happens."

"And I got a B-minus, which always happens if she doesn't help me study," Hana grumbles, patting the seat next to her. Finn sits, resting her elbows on the table and stealing one of Amy's chips.

"I offered to help," Zaki protests. "You were too busy looking for bridesmaid dresses with your cousins and buying three-month anniversary presents for the boyfriend. Don't blame me for not helping."

The Hana and Zaki show makes Finn laugh. She's missed this.

"We need to catch up properly," Hana insists, ignoring Zaki's dig. "Let's do something soon. I want to start looking at dresses for formal."

"Oh yeah, let's go shopping," Zaki says.

Finn nods. This year, they're hosting the formal for a bunch of schools, not just their own Year 10s. It's basically an old-school dance, but because the idea's so twee now, people kind of get into it. It's one of the few occasions Finn doesn't mind putting on a dress that's not her school dress. She wonders what Willa will wear. Does she ever wear dresses? Finn has no idea. Camp Nowhere didn't exactly call for frocks. She'll have to ask her.

But first Finn has to organise it all. She's planning on calling the first meeting next week. After her pathetic Speech Night effort, she's put planning reminders for every single upcoming event in her phone, weeks in advance. She's going to get the rest of this year right, even if there's only a month to go.

"Well, there's no way on this planet I'm going to the social," Amy says, tongue out. "But I do love to shop, so I can be the second opinion girl."

"I want something maroon," Hana says. "I've decided it's my colour."

Before anyone can say anything else, Zehra drops into the last remaining seat. "Hey, did you guys get your Maths test back?" When she notices Finn sitting there, she just blinks for a moment and then gives her a polite smile. "Hi, Finn."

Finn sighs inwardly as she smiles back. "Hi." It looks like they're back at square one.

"Hey, so I heard my cuz rocked Speech Night," Hana says. "As in everyone stayed awake for it."

"More than stayed awake. She was awesome." Finn turns to Zehra. "Everyone loved it, didn't they?"

"They did," Zehra says lightly, staring at her phone.

"We were just talking about the formal," Hana tells Zehra. "The next thing on the agenda for the intermediate school mafia."

"That's got to be way more fun to organise than Speech Night." Zaki nudges Zehra. "I'm guessing you're all over it?"

Zehra shrugs. "Not really."

"What?" Hana pulls a face. "You love organising them. Last year's was amazing."

"We'll see," is all she says.

Finn stares at her. She didn't even think Zehra was capable of anything less than total enthusiasm when it comes to organising things. "But didn't you take the lead on the Year 9 one?"

"I did." She finally looks up, meeting Finn's eye for a moment. Then she looks straight past her. "But I just don't know if there's any point this year."

"Why not?" Zaki asks.

Zehra just shrugs.

And Finn's stomach sinks. Because she knows exactly why. Knows exactly what Zehra's not saying aloud. What's the point in doing it if she doesn't get any credit for it?

She can see her point. Still, she pushes back at the guilt. Because it's not exactly her fault, is it? Finn can't control what the principal says. And it's not like she hid anything or tried to take all the credit. What was she supposed to do? March onstage and correct him when he only named her? Tell everyone that Zehra did at least half the work, if not more?

But still, the feeling won't budge. She makes a show of checking her watch. "Oh, hey, guys, I forgot. I have to be somewhere. I'll catch you later."

Breathing in deep, she hurries to the front of the school where she can hide until the bell rings. She parks herself on a bench and reads a text from Willa.

*Riley wants to know if she needs to bring a jacket with her. She doesn't believe it might be cold sometimes. Apparently her idol has to say it, or she won't believe it.*

Finn can't help smiling. Because that reminds her it's another day closer to their beach weekend.

*Tell her from me that unless she wants to freeze her butt off, she better bring one.*

*I shall pass it on to Her Highness.*

Finn tucks the Zehra mess away into a corner of her mind. Instead, she focuses on what's to come, a long weekend of beach and Willa and both her parents being in the same place for a minute.

# CHAPTER 58

## Willa

Riley does a little skip in the middle of the kitchen, her bag already on her shoulders. "I'm so excited!"

"I can tell," Nan says, shaking her head. "But you've still got twenty minutes until they pick you up, so you'd better settle down." She thrusts a shopping bag into Riley's hands. "Give that to Finn's mother. There's a loaf of my sourdough and some herbs and greens."

"There's no kale in there, is there?" Riley sticks out her tongue. "Nobody likes it except you."

"There might be. And now I know what you're getting with your dinner every night next week after that sass."

Riley's mouth closes instantly. It's enough to make Willa grin as she sits down next to Jack. He's bent over his maths homework, scribbling in the margins. "Need help?" she asks.

"Nope. It's easy. I'm just thinking."

"You're not upset you're not coming with us, are you?" She's been feeling guilty about it all week.

He shakes his head. "I've got soccer semis. And then Tyler's mum's taking us to the movies after."

"Good. Hey, we're all coming to the final, if you make it. Dan and Rosie too."

"Really?" He grins. "Cool."

She shoves his fringe back from his eyes. "Good luck for the game."

"Thanks. Dad says we've got a good chance. He says we're tight."

Willa nods. Her dad will be leaving soon. It's weird. Even though she's basically been waiting for him to leave since he got here, it's also strange to think of him not being here. She must have gotten used to it in some way.

"Well, sorry again that I can't come." She wraps arm around him and presses her cheek to his feathery, brown hair for a moment. "But Dad and Nan will be here to watch you."

He shrugs and wriggles away from her. "Dad isn't sure he's coming yet. Said he doesn't know what day he's going to leave."

"What?" Willa frowns. "Seriously?"

Jack shrugs. "Something about flights."

"What, he couldn't just stay long enough to watch you play first?"

He shrugs again, slower this time, giving Willa an uneasy glance.

"No, he's going to watch you play." She stands, her blood humming with this new urgency. "Is he here?"

"Out the back."

She stalks outside, arms crossed over her chest. He's down the side, setting up the ladder under the grapevine, where the vine has begun to sag under the weight of its new burden of fruit. She stands at a distance, watching him. "Wow, couldn't wait to leave, could you?"

He stops what he's doing and gives her the same uneasy look Jack just gave her. "I'm still here."

"Then why aren't you going to Jack's match?" She crosses her arms over her chest.

"I'm hoping I can." He adjusts the ladder again. "It just depends on flights."

"Get a later flight. Get one the day after. It's not that hard." She glares at him. "It's his semi-final, and he wants you to watch him."

He doesn't answer.

Heat spreads through her chest as the anger blooms. "Just be a dad for a minute. Watch him play, and then you're free to go."

Willa sees how he flinches as she says those last words, but she bites down on the guilt. Why should she care? Kelly's right. She doesn't owe him anything. She turns on her heel and marches back down the side of the house.

But before she even makes it to the back door, she's stopping in her tracks. She's not done. She knows it.

She hovers on the doormat welcoming her in, her determination beaten back by the part of her that hates confrontation. That hates asking for things. *Do it, Willa*, she tells herself. Because she might as well make things worse. She forces herself to turn and walk back to him.

He's still standing there, arms at his sides, frowning. She moves closer this time. He has to hear her. Because she's only ever going to have the courage to say it once in her life.

A breeze rushes through the vines, making shadows dance around their feet. Her stomach is a clenched fist, like everything is hanging, taut, from this moment. "Listen," she says. "I don't care if you don't like me or don't like that I'm gay or whatever. I've lived this long without you, and I'm fine. I don't need you. But them?" She jerks her thumb at the house. "They need you."

She begs him silently not to meet her gaze. He doesn't. He puts a hand on a ladder step, as if to hold him in place, and looks at the ground.

"So you have to come back," she tells him. "If anything ever happens to Nan and she can't take care of us anymore, you have to come back for them. Just for the next two years. When I'm eighteen, I'll look after them."

He finally looks up, his brow cleaved in that same way hers does when she's worried.

Shocked by the familiarity, she looks away. Her voice comes out smaller. "After that, you don't even have to think about us."

Now she can walk away.

# CHAPTER 59

## Willa

When Finn and her parents finally arrive to pick them up, Willa's still feeling the turbulence. Even though it felt like she had no choice in the moment, and that only her fear and her anger were operating her body, she can't quite believe what she just said to her father.

Part of her wants to sit down and cry it out alone. Another part is annoyed. Annoyed that these fine threads of guilt are weaving their way through her for talking to him like that. He's the one who's supposed to feel guilty.

As the adults go through the pleasantries at the front door, her chest is a tightness. On the footpath, Riley dances with impatience, her bag on her back. Willa pretends to listen to the polite chitchat and wonders if he's still standing there at the side of the house, hands at his side like he was when she walked away.

Finn takes her hand. "You okay?"

Willa manages a nod.

It's not until they're on the narrow highway that curls itself along the coastline that she finds some calm again. She presses her forehead to the window, Finn's hand cradled in hers, and watches waves assault the cliffs below. The talk seeps around her, but she doesn't listen. There's no room in her mind for it.

Finn rests her chin on Willa's shoulder and stares out the window with her. "When I was a kid, I was always scared that we'd go over the cliff. I still am."

"We won't." Willa squeezes her hand and tunes into the conversation flying back and forth between the front seat.

"He's going to spend all his money building a giant wall, my teachers told us," Riley says between mouthfuls of an apple. "That's so dumb."

"You know an awful lot about him, don't you? Tell me, kiddo," Finn's dad says, looking over his shoulder, "do you know the name of our prime minister. In Australia?"

"Um…" Riley frowns. "Is it Steve something?"

"No, it's not." He laughs and continues to fire questions at her like he's inviting her nonsense, getting a total kick out of her.

Willa surreptitiously watches him, turned around from the front seat, bantering with her little sister. She only ever saw him from a distance at camp. He and Finn look so similar, with their blond hair, brown eyes, and wide-open smiles. There's Finn's warmth and curiosity too. Willa knows she's going to like him. She already does. And Riley's so smitten with him she doesn't even care when he laughs at her. And Riley *hates* to be laughed at.

It's dark when they finally arrive, but as soon as they squeeze out of the car, Willa can smell and hear the closeness of the ocean. The waves sound thunderous and close, as if bruising the sand as they crash. She can't wait to see it for herself in the light.

They pile into the tumbledown wooden house. Bags are stacked into the corner, and the kettle is switched on in seconds. Willa smiles when the first things pulled out of shopping bags are coffee and teabags. She's never met a family of such rabid caffeine consumers.

Riley hovers close to Willa by the door, gone shy all of a sudden. Willa wraps an arm around her shoulder, feeling a little the same.

At the kitchen bench, Anita pulls a pile of folders from her bag and dumps them on the wooden surface. "Reports," she says to Willa with a sighing smile. "No escaping them."

Willa stands in the corner, enjoying watching this small family dynamic. They laugh a lot, Finn and her parents, and talk nonstop as they set up everything, like they've done it a thousand times before. Martin puts groceries into the fridge while Anita digs out towels, and Finn runs bags upstairs, looking purely happy. Willa knows it's because she has both her parents here.

Martin slides the glass doors open, letting the wind rush in. He sniffs the air in deep. "I missed this smell."

"Haven't you been living by the ocean for the last few months?" Anita reminds him as she goes over to stand beside him.

"Yeah, but the air's different here."

Willa notes the way he automatically places a hand on the small of Anita's back as she leans out, saying something to him about a tree outside. They don't seem like a couple on a break. They seem cosy and blended together in a way she wasn't expecting after everything Finn has told her.

Things get louder when Angela and Matteo come over with their little girl, Bella. Soon the house rings with conversation and the clink of wine glasses. The smell of garlic takes over from coffee and fire smoke as Finn's father makes pasta with an elaborate sauce with the fresh herbs that Nan sent along. Bella and Riley, completely over her shyness now there's someone her age, stand at his elbows, playing kitchen hands.

"She's definitely not that enthusiastic about helping at home," Willa says as they set the table for dinner.

"I think she might have a crush on my dad," Finn says with a grin. They settle at the bench, watching the cooking show in action.

"So you don't like green stuff in your sauce? That's okay," Martin tells Riley, holding up a spoon and a bunch of herbs. "You can have it with just cheese and oil like this one." He points his spoon at Finn. "She's a fussy eater too. Won't eat any of my sauces if they've got olives or capers or anything even mildly exotic. And never, ever, dare put in anchovies." He shudders.

Willa turns to Finn. "Really?"

"I just like things simple," Finn says.

"Boring, you mean."

Finn just shrugs and grins, like she's happy to own it.

"You didn't know that?" Martin asks Willa. "Until she was eight, she basically only ate bread, apples, and cheese. I couldn't even convince her to try a banana." He calls out to Matteo. "Remember when Finn was about four, and you tried to make her eat an avocado?"

Matteo laughs. "I wore it."

Willa turns to Finn, an eyebrow raised. How can someone so curious and brave be so unadventurous? About food?

"I have no comment," Finn says with a grin.

"My sister makes yummy sauce," Riley tells Martin as she hacks through a tomato. "Better than Nan's, even."

Finn's mouth drops open in mock shock. "Did Riley just…compliment you?"

"It's been known to occur. Maybe once a year. Don't tell Nan what you just said," Willa warns Riley.

Riley just grins and keeps talking as she chops. "My nan makes her own bread too."

"I know. We're going to be eating it for breakfast tomorrow morning," Martin says. "I can't wait."

"Please don't use the kale," Riley begs. "Just put it in the bin. No one has to know."

"I'm not so much of a fan either, kiddo, but we don't waste food. I'll bury it so deep in a dish you'll never find it, I swear."

"I'll find it," Riley says.

He laughs. "Game on."

As she watches her little sister hold her own in the crowd, Willa's consumed with this feeling. It's pride, or something like it. And happiness. Because she knows that Riley will always hold her own. That she'll always be okay. Willa knows it the way she knows only the certain things in life, like sunrises and grass growing. And with that knowing comes the certainty that all is left for Willa to do is to enjoy the ride of being Riley's sister and to be there to help her in the handful of moments when she's needed. And she loves knowing this.

～ ～ ～

That night, Willa can't sleep, even with the familiar sound of Riley's snuffles in the bed next to hers, even with the soothing of the waves and quiet warmth of the house that should bring calm but doesn't.

Her mind keeps flinging itself back to this afternoon and what she said to her dad. Every time she tries to make an escape from these thoughts, they inevitably slink back. And each time she remembers Jack's wary expression, or her Dad staring at the ground, she gets this sharp, unnameable feeling.

Part of it is because Willa has no idea what he's going to do with what she said to him. Which means, when it comes down to it, she's no better off than before she opened her stupid mouth and let fly.

She rolls over, staring at the shadowed ceiling. Why didn't she wait for him to answer her? If she did, she'd have something to go on. But maybe he wouldn't have said anything anyway. Maybe there'd just be that familiar, bruising silence.

She shuts her eyes, but they just float open again before she realises it's happening. She's too nervous to put the lamp on and read, though. What if she wakes Riley or if Finn's parents see she's up? She's finally starting to drift when she hears the sound of footsteps padding to the upstairs bathroom. It must be Finn. Pangs of longing assault her. If only she could go crawl into bed in the next room and be wrapped up in the comfort of Finn. Then she could sleep. She knows it.

The toilet flushes, a tap turns on and off, and the footsteps pad back across the landing. Willa blinks into the darkness, not moving. She can't break Finn's parents' rules. No way. Not when they've been so lovely and let them come here.

As the house settles into silence again, she squeezes her eyes shut and wills sleep to come. Because the sooner she sleeps, the sooner it's tomorrow. And tomorrow she gets the morning light, the sea, and Finn.

# CHAPTER 60

## Finn

Finn opens her eyes to grey light and the unfamiliarity of floral sheets. When she remembers where she is, she snuggles deeper into the covers, instantly overtaken with the delicious feeling that comes with waking at the beach house. Especially this time. Her parents are downstairs, acting like nothing ever happened between them—a fantasy Finn's totally willing to indulge in. Willa's in the room next door with Riley. There's the beach and coffee and walks to be had, and she's going to find a moment to paint today. Today is going to be a great day.

She tries to hunt down sleep again, but she's pulled by an awareness she can't quite place. When she opens her eyes, they instantly land on Willa. She's perched at the end of Finn's bed, her arms wrapped around her knees, as she stares out the window. Patter sits by her side, upright and alert as if he can see something he wants out there.

Finn reaches behind her, patting the covers, waiting for her hand to land on Banjo. It doesn't.

Outside, the sun is barely up, the grey sky only just tinged with the early blush of sunrise. Willa's so locked in her reverie she doesn't seem to notice that Finn's awake. There's a small almost-smile on her face. It makes Finn smile too.

Last night, after Riley went to bed, Willa told Finn about the words she'd fired at her father before leaving their house. It turned out Finn was right, she said. She did have to tell him what she was afraid of. Unfortunately, she did it in the worst way possible, in the choke of a rage she couldn't control if she wanted to. Willa cried as she told Finn how she basically accused him of being a terrible dad and how he just stood there. But how she had to say those other things, to tell him he had to be there even if he didn't want to.

As Willa talked, Finn just held her close and let her shed quiet tears. It's so unfair, she thinks, the way Willa's life seems to hangs on ifs and maybes. No matter how hard she works to keep it steady and afloat.

"It's good you said something," she told her. "Even if it was hard. At least you know he knows."

"I guess," Willa said. But she just looked sad and scared, and it made Finn's heart hurt. Because you shouldn't have to tell your dad something like that. He should just know. And you should just know that he'll be there when needed. Even when her own dad is in Tasmania, Finn knows he would come running the minute she needed him.

Finn watches her a little longer, enjoying the chance to drink in her quiet contentment. If she were going to paint Willa, she'd be a bright, bold outline filled with smudgy, warm pastels and greys underneath, like a gentle light penetrating thick, bright cloth. That's Willa.

Finally, Finn can't resist. She reaches a foot out and pokes Willa in the hip. "What are you doing on the end of my bed while I sleep, you creep?"

Willa turns slowly and smiles. "You can see the water better from here."

"Right. So it's the beach that you're stalking, not me." Finn smiles her way into a yawn. "What time is it?"

"You probably don't want to know."

"Probably not. So why are you up?"

"I'm excited."

"About what?"

Willa holds her hand out in the direction of the sea and pulls a face as if to say "duh".

"You're cute." Finn holds out a hand. "Come here."

Willa shakes her head. "I've been waiting for you. Let's go."

"Where?"

Again, Willa points at the window.

Finn just blinks at her for a moment before she can muster words. "To the beach? Now?"

"Now." Willa smiles and stands, her hand held out.

And there goes Finn's dream of snuggles and slow waking and coffee on the couch before dressing. Gone. All because she cannot resist this entreaty to make Willa happy. Couldn't if she tried. She scrapes the doona back and stands there, yawning and getting used to upright. "It's going to be freezing, you know."

"I like the cold."

"Of course you do." Finn shuffles to the bathroom. "Two minutes and I'll be ready."

When they're tucked into thick jackets and jeans and heading for the stairs, a voice calls out from the other upstairs bedroom.

"Will?" It's Riley, rubbing her eyes at their bedroom door. Banjo darts out from between her feet.

"So that's where you've been, traitor." Finn crouches down to pick him up. "Want to come to the beach?" she asks Riley, pressing her face into Banjo's ruff. "We can take the dogs."

"Mm," she mumbles from a yawn. "Okay."

"Then get dressed. We'll wait for you downstairs."

Outside the house, the world is a flurry of wind and waves and cold. They dash across the empty road towards the wet sand, the ocean coming at them hard.

Finn grins into the bracing wind, holding both her and Willa's hands deep in her pocket. The dogs and Riley tear towards the water and those crashing waves.

"I haven't been to the beach in so long." Finn practically has to shout to get her words to Willa before they're snatched up by the wind.

They stroll the stretch of sand, Willa leading her over to the rocks at one end of the cove. They tramp over a jigsaw of boulders and rock pools until they're standing on the edge, just shy of the spray. Willa looks like happiness itself as she gazes at the waves rolling towards them.

When she's done staring, they explore, peering into crevices and jumping over clumps of seaweed and water trapped between rocks. They watch the waves rush in and out of small channels, doing the work of carving stone and marking time. Crouching beside a rock pool, Willa's fingers plunge into the water. She pulls out a spongey red something, maybe seaweed or flesh. Her nose wrinkles as she inspects it. It falls back with a small splash, making her laugh.

Staring at that nose-crinkled smile, Finn is suddenly awash with this bright, amber feeling. All she can think is, *she is mine, I am hers.* The knowledge comes with a rush of pleasure and angst and inevitability. And suddenly Finn knows what she probably already knew: that there will be the summer soon and Willa's smile and everything beyond that. And that in that time, they'll know each other in all the ways they don't yet. She also knows that one day Willa will look up in a moment like this—probably one more spontaneous and sweet than staged and deliberate—and tell Finn she loves her. And it will make Finn's heart squeeze down even harder than it is doing right now.

This knowledge crashes through her as she hears herself saying. "Have you had your beach fill yet?"

Willa brushes her hands on her jeans and nods.

"Good. Let's go back."

As they jump from rock to rock, Finn swims inside a bittersweet memory of their creek walks at camp. At Willa's call, Riley runs across the wet sand towards them, chased by the dogs, their fur gone wild in the wind. Finn shivers, and Willa pulls her collar close around her neck and kisses her back to warmth.

# CHAPTER 61

## Finn

Her dad is leaned over his iPad next to the humming kettle. Another welling of happiness rocks Finn. He's here.

He holds a finger to his lips and points to the sofa. Her mother's curled up asleep, the TV on low. She always does this on holidays. Gets up early with them, as if she feels like she should, only to fall back asleep on the couch.

"I thought you three were all tucked up in bed," he says softly.

"Nope." Finn jerks a thumb at Willa. "This one was too hyper."

"Sorry," Willa says, not looking a bit sorry.

"I'm going out on the boat with Matteo in about half an hour. We'll try and probably fail to catch some dinner. You girls want to come?"

"Nope." Finn hates fishing. It's boring and cold, waiting for a bite. Then it's kind of gross when they finally do catch something.

"I knew you'd say that. I was just being polite." He turns to Riley. "What about you? Bella usually comes."

"Can I?" Riley turns to Willa. "I've never been on a boat."

"Yes, you have. With Dad. We went out on the mangroves, but you probably don't remember it." Willa smooths a hand over Riley's head. "Do what you're told, okay?"

Riley rolls her eyes. "I *know*."

"You girls want coffee?" Martin asks, turning for the kettle.

"Nope," Finn says. "I'm going back to sleep for at least two more hours, and no power on this earth can stop me. Come on." She grabs Willa's hand and pulls on it.

"You be okay, Riles?" Willa asks as Finn drags her to the foot of the stairs.

"Mhm." She doesn't even look up from the TV.

"She'll be fine," Martin says. "We'll have some breakfast, and then we'll go meet our fellow fisherman. What do you like on your toast, kiddo?"

Finn yanks harder on Willa's hand. She will not lose this tug of war. All she wants is Willa exquisitely, selfishly to herself, and this might be her only chance to get it today. She drags her all the way into her bedroom, with its sweeping view and unmade bed.

"It's freezing," Willa squeals as she sheds her thick jacket and sits on the mattress. Then she frowns. "Hey, will your parents mind that I'm in here with you?"

Finn shrugs. "The door's open." They're not breaking any rules, exactly. She pulls off her jacket and slides into bed, pulling Willa in with her. Willa's arm automatically curls around her and pulls her close. They hold on tight until they've built a stronghold of warmth.

"Better," Willa whispers. "Sorry I made you go out in the cold."

"No you're not." Finn smiles and shuffles in closer. "But I forgive you." She presses her face close to Willa's. They kiss, long and slow, and it feels like something's quietly unstitching in Finn somewhere. In the good way. She runs her hand under Willa's T-shirt, smoothing her palms over the silky flatness of her stomach. And then, because she can't resist, she glides it up between her ribs, dipping into that sweet hollow at the base of her chest. Bold now, she continues upward, swallowing hard when no bra strap stops her journey. Willa's not wearing one. Her blood swims harder as her fingers travel up the safe zone between Willa's breasts and up to her sternum. She's inching along the return journey, purposely veering off course, when Willa's brow furrows. She places her hand over Finn's. "Hey?" she whispers.

Finn doesn't know what to say. Or how to say what she suddenly feels secure in wanting. So instead she sits up, climbs over Willa, and smiles down at her.

Willa smiles back, but her eyebrows are a curious crinkle. Finn still doesn't say anything. Just pulls off her jumper and drops it on the bed next to her. Then her T-shirt. And then, in a manoeuvre more awkward than it's ever happened in her imagination, she unhooks her bra and throws it on the floor.

With that, Willa's eyes widen and then soften. She wraps her arms around Finn's neck and draws her down closer. Her gaze seems to shine a light to Finn's eyes, interrogating. "I thought we weren't going there yet?"

Finn can only smile. Because of beautiful Willa, who won't let her be reckless unless it's real. Not when Finn's made it mean so much. "We're not. Not really. I guess we're just taking a baby step closer?"

"Okay." Willa nods slowly, still scrutinising. Her hands stroke the bare stretch of Finn's back. "It just seems like a sudden, kind of large baby step, that's all."

Finn supposes it is, in context. Willa's never even let her hands stray *over* Finn's clothes. But because she wants Willa to hurry up and be okay with her sudden U-turn, she says, "Not really. It's just a second base kind of step. Or first base?" Finn frowns. "Actually, I've never been clear on the whole base thing, but we're here, wherever that is."

"We are." Willa's smile turns to tease. "Well, you are, anyway."

"You could fix that."

Willa takes her challenge, reaching down and takes hold of the bottom of her T-shirt. But as Finn sits up to make room for her, she suddenly stops and stares again, a small, smitten smile on her face. "You're so..." She shakes her head, like she can't find the right word.

A blush storms Finn's cheeks. She crosses her arms tight over her chest as her bravado starts to slink away. "Stop staring."

"Finn, if you want me to not look at you, taking off your top was not the ideal strategy."

Embarrassment makes Finn laugh harder than she needs to. Then she pointedly looks down at the scrunched blue cotton marooned under Willa's ribs. "Um, weren't you in the middle of something?"

She expects Willa to come back at that, to tease or challenge, but she doesn't. Instead her expression turns shy as she takes a hold of her T-shirt again. She doesn't move straight away, though.

Finn ducks her head, realising that she's recklessly thrown something at Willa and just expected her to catch it. "I mean, only if you want to."

"Of course I do." Willa's voice cracks as she says it, but she smiles. She begins easing her shirt up. Finn reaches down to help, sliding it up over her rib cage. When it's dropped on the floor beside them, Willa lies back on the pillows under Finn's gaze, a deep cleave between her brows.

"Hey, don't look like that." Finn leans down, her mouth close to Willa's ear. "You're *so* beautiful."

"So are you." Willa pulls her the rest of the way down until their skin is pushed close.

The sun slides further into the sky as they kiss and laugh and learn by heart the places they've bared for each other. The feel of Willa's skin under her is so unbearably good, and it's only the thought of her mother downstairs that keeps Finn from exploring even more.

The sun is higher and brighter when she pulls back from another breathless kiss and runs her hand up Willa's side. "Do you mind if we stop here?"

"Of course." Willa immediately moves off her, but Finn chases her, not ready to relinquish her altogether.

"I don't mean stop now," Finn whispers. "I just mean stop…here."

"I know what you mean. And I'm totally happy here." Willa pushes her lips to Finn's shoulder. "You know, I could *live* on second base," she says. "Or whatever base we're on."

Finn laughs. "I'm going to Google that later. As my history teacher always says, research first, research always."

"Somehow I don't think she was talking about this specific context."

"Definitely not." Finn pulls a face. "She's ancient."

Willa's hands are still roaming Finn's skin as she laughs, but her exploring is more languid and curious now than the urgency of earlier.

Finn smiles into Willa's shoulder. How could she have shied from this with Willa? It's all too perfect and hot and *right*. She already wants it to be next time they are alone together like this. "We should probably get up," she says with a sigh. "Before Mum comes looking for us."

"Okay," Willa says, but doesn't move. "We can ask her about second base. Maybe she knows."

"I dare you." Finn buries her face in the covers, laughing. "But maybe put your top back on first."

# CHAPTER 62

## Willa

That night, over their fish dinner, the adults chat about house prices and taxes and other grown-up boringness. At the other end of the table, Riley and Bella conspire and giggle and sneak food to the dogs, the best of friends now they're co-survivors of a bloodied fish gutting. Martin and Matteo did manage to catch something after all. Sandwiched between it all, Willa sits quietly, listening to all the conversations roving around her and trading smitten, silly glances with Finn.

They're eating dessert when Bella starts a chant of, "Mum, Mum, Mum, MUM!" over the adult chatter.

Angela finally drags herself away from the conversation and answers. Bella wants to know is if Riley can stay at their beach house tonight with her. But she needs to know in that way eleven-year-old girls need to know *now*.

"I don't mind. Is it okay with you?" Angela asks Willa.

"Of course." Willa looks at Riley. "You'll be good?"

Riley just gives her a scornful look and turns to Finn. "Can the dogs come?"

Finn shakes her head. "Sorry. They stay with us, but we can take them out for a walk after dinner, okay?"

"Okay." She turns and high fives Bella.

Finn sneaks another glance at Willa across the table. And Willa knows exactly what she's thinking. With Riley gone, maybe they might get some more alone time. And suddenly Willa's full of memories of what they did this morning. Then she's thinking covetously of what they yet have to do. A thrill ripples through her. Maybe Finn's right. Maybe baby steps are better.

― ― ―

It's nearly dark when they get back from their after-dinner beach walk. Willa can't seem to stay away from that crashing ocean, even when the day turns to cold, and the wind picks up to a hurtling speed. She still has to take one final stride down that stretch of sand to watch the water roll in hard and fast before she's satisfied.

Finn pauses at the top of the steps, staring at the kitchen window. Her parents are inside, talking by the kitchen counter. Willa stops behind her, quiet, letting Finn examine this moment between them. She's already noticed how much time Finn spends keeping an uneasy eye on them, as if she's trying to gather cues. Poor Finn. All she wants to know is what's going to happen.

"How do they seem to you?" Finn suddenly asks. "My parents."

"Honestly?"

"Of course, honestly."

Willa slides an arm around Finn's waist. "Well, I'm not exactly the person to ask about normal parental behaviour, but…" She hesitates, not wanting to get Finn's hopes up. What if she's wrong?

Finn shifts impatiently in her arms. "But what?"

"They seem like a typical married couple to me. If I didn't know anything, I'd think everything was completely fine between them."

"Me too. That's what's so confusing."

"Do you think they're going to be okay?"

"I don't know." Finn watches her father laugh at something her mother says as he pulls milk from the fridge. "They're not sharing a room this time." She turns to Willa and blushes. "I checked last night. I couldn't help it. I don't know if it's because other people are here or if last time it was just a sex thing…" She pulls a face. "I don't want to think about my parents having sex, but I'd rather they were in the same bed, you know?" She pushes her face into Willa's shoulder. "I just wish they'd make up their mind either way. I'm so sick of everything just hanging."

"I know you are." Willa squeezes her hard.

"Hi there," Martin says as they shuffle through the sliding door. "We're about to watch a documentary about that guy who sailed around the world twice without stopping. You two interested?"

"Not even a little bit," Finn says. "Once is crazy, twice is just weird."

Willa smiles. She would have watched it to be polite, of course.

"We're going to watch something on my computer probably." Finn turns to Willa. "Let's watch a really great terrible movie, okay?"

"Okay."

"What exactly is a really great terrible movie?" Anita frowns.

"If you don't know, I can't explain," Finn tells her.

"I hate it when you say that."

Finn just grins and pats her shoulder.

Anita rolls her eyes and flicks on the kettle. "Who wants tea? Willa?"

"No, thank you," Willa says in her politest voice. She catches Finn's look and presses her lips together. She trying to loosen up around Finn's parents, but it's hard. There's something about their effortless warmth that makes Willa feel stiff and awkward. She can't help it.

"Come on." Finn grabs Willa's hand. "Let's go up and pick something."

"I'll come get you for sweets later, okay?" Anita tells her.

"Okay."

They climb the stairs. Finn squeezes her hand. "Once again, that's her saying she'll be checking on us," she whispers.

Willa smiles. "Already decoded that one."

Finn laughs and holds up her finger. "And...wait for it."

"Door open, please," Anita calls up the stairs.

"See?" She giggles. "I know all her moves before she does."

They climb onto Finn's bed and set up the laptop. Finn leans into Willa, snuggling as they flick through the possibilities.

"We probably better behave ourselves, with those two up," Finn says.

"I know," Willa says with a grin. "That's cool. I'm capable of hanging out with you without randomly stripping off. It's you we've got to worry about."

# CHAPTER 63

## Finn

The weekend is nearly over. Finn stares sadly out at the overcast sky. At least the weather is making it a little easier to leave.

They're on the front steps, bags packed. Her parents are having a final coffee with Angela and Matteo at their place, while Riley and Bella carve their last cartwheels into the wind on the beach. Next to her, Willa's doing her Japanese homework, her pencil making small marks on the slab of text.

School feels so far away, even after these few snatched days. Finn can't believe there's only three more weeks until it's over for the year. And a week until she knows if she'll be school captain or not. Her stomach does this small flip-flop. It's going to be either her or Zehra. It has to be. It's only a matter of which way it will go, captain and vice captain.

When Finn thinks of Zehra, the stomach feeling gets worse. And she knows it won't go away. Because it isn't fair, what happened with the principal, and it definitely isn't fair that Zehra's feeling bad about it. The only thing Finn doesn't know is what she should do about it. Or *if* she should.

"Can I ask you something?" Finn hears herself saying.

"Of course."

Willa listens, cheek on hand, as Finn tells her about Zehra and her Speech Night save. Then she tells her about the principal and the look on Zehra's face as he named Finn in his thanks and not her.

"I feel so bad about it," she says. "Especially since she was the one who got Naila to come. While I was fast asleep."

Willa hugs her book to her chest and shrugs. "But that's just how it is sometimes? The teachers have no idea what happens behind the scenes. It's like politics. Everyone claps the big guy, while all the little guys work just as hard."

"But it's not fair."

"I know," Willa says. "I've gone to two out of three achingly dull curriculum meetings for Stella already, and at the end of the year, she's the one who'll get the certificate. Because she's the senior, and I was just a servant fill-in."

"That's sucks."

"I know. But like I said, it's just the way it is. I'll get the kudos when I'm senior academic leader."

Finn frowns. But what if Zehra's never school captain? Does that mean she'll never be acknowledged? That would suck. Especially when she works so hard and wants everything so badly. More than Finn, maybe.

"Do you think I should do something?" she asks Willa.

"Like what?"

"I don't know. Tell someone?"

"I don't know."

"Well what would *you* do?" Finn asks.

"Me? Nothing. I mean it's not like he *only* named you. He thanked you and everyone else. He can't acknowledge everyone by name."

"I guess." Finn frowns.

"But do you know what?" Willa turns to her, smiling.

"What?"

"You wouldn't do what I do." She clasps her hands around Finn's arm. "You do what *you* do. That's what I love so much about us."

Finn's smile turns to a frown. "But what do *I* do?"

"You know."

"I do?"

"Yep. You do."

"Gee, thanks for the help, Ms Cryptic Crossword."

Willa just smiles beatifically, kisses her cheek, and goes back to her homework.

Finn rests her cheek against Willa's shoulder and forces it all to the back of her mind. Because right now she wants to stay snug in the final embers of goodness that was this weekend.

# CHAPTER 64

## Willa

Nan stands at the counter and listens patiently to Riley's word-vomit recap of the weekend. "I'm glad you girls had a good time," she says, already pulling washing from Riley's bags.

Willa hugs Jack to her side. "So, did you win?"

"Yep. Kicked two goals."

"He was excellent," Nan says. "Your dad and I both watched."

"Well done. My champion brother." Willa lets Jack go and looks nervously around for traces of her father's presence.

"He got a flight out last night," Nan says.

Willa feels an odd emptiness. Despite everything, it's weird to think he won't be here anymore, ghosting around the house. It's back to the four of them again. She knows she's supposed to feel happy about it, but now she just feels strange. Like there's a thread hanging loose. One she's too scared to pull in case of the damage it will do. She frowns at her stupid, unwieldy thoughts. How stupid to spend so long resenting the imposition of him, only now to feel the lack of him.

*Get over it, Willa.* She picks up her bag and heads for the stairs.

"Bring your washing straight back down for me," Nan calls. "Then it will have a chance to dry this afternoon."

"Okay." It's an odd little bliss, being ordered around again, to come home to the sunshine calm of their little house, where Nan presides once more.

Willa climbs the stairs slowly, still luxuriating in that feeling of being bleached and salted by the hours on the beach. Even though it was never quite hot enough, she swam anyway. Couldn't not. They walked too, hiking along choppy stretches of coast, exploring with Finn and family. It feels as if the wind has whipped right through her insides, cleansing her somehow.

In her room, there's an envelope propped against her pillow. She drops her bag on the bed and picks it up, frowning. Inside is a small piece of folded paper and a cheque for more money than Willa's seen in a while.

She unfolds the paper, her heart a ticking mess. His writing is a childlike scrawl that marches lopsidedly across the page. Just like Jack's.

*You don't have to worry. I promise you that if anything happens, I'll come back. You and your brother and sister will always be looked after. For as long as you need it. Never, ever worry about that.*

*This money is for you. It's not a bribe. It's not anything but the fact that I know you need a new computer. How else will you keep showing your teachers what a brilliant girl you are? Your nan sends me your essays sometimes. Maybe you don't know that.*

*Someday you three should come up here to visit. It's been too long. I'll take you camping in the forest where we went when you were little. There are waterholes and waterfalls and secret green places everywhere. Maybe you'll like it as much as you did back then, when neither your mum or I could get you out of the water for a second.*

*Love Dad.*

For a minute, Willa can only blink, awash with a sudden memory of a waterhole and brown water. The sounds of her gasping breaths and the feel of his hand under her belly, holding her up as she splash-kicked her inching way across the surface.

She drops the note on the bed. But then the next thing she knows she's picking it up and tucking it into a book in her bookshelf, because she needs it to be out of her sight. But she also needs it to be close, though she doesn't know exactly why. In fact, she doesn't recognise anything in the cocktail of feelings currently assaulting her. All she knows is it's making her throat ache and her insides hurt.

Shifting into the comforting automatic of doing, she pulls her washing from her bag and marches numbly down the stairs. Dropping her clothes on top of Riley's, she switches on the machine.

In the kitchen, Nan's straining something at the sink. She looks at Willa and frowns. "What's wrong with you?"

Before Willa even knows the storm is coming, it's on her. She sinks into a kitchen chair, rests her head on her arms and sobs. Sobs until it hurts. Suddenly, Nan's fingers are running soothing journeys through her waves of hair. Under the comfort of her touch, Willa somehow finds her breath. "I don't even know why I'm crying."

Nan pulls out the chair and sits next to her. "Yes, you do."

She does, a little. That clumsy letter let loose all kinds of feeling Willa didn't even know she had about him—that she *could* have about him. There's sadness. There's also something like guilt. Because maybe she could have tried harder too. She looks up at her grandmother, staring at the blissful familiarity of her ruddy, lined face, and her no-nonsense hair. "I'm so glad you're home."

Nan smiles, her fingers still busy with the job of smoothing Willa's hair back from her face. "Will you let me tell you some things about your dad?"

Willa nods slowly, and rests her face on her arms again.

"He doesn't seem like much of a father to you. I know that." Nan sounds sad about that.

Willa scratches at a mark on the table and wonders what it's like to watch your child be a parent. How strange.

"And maybe he hasn't been," Nan says. "It's a pity. But he never really got a chance to learn to be. It was your mum who loved babies, you know. Wanted a heap of them, and she wanted them young, and he would have done anything she wanted. So he took jobs in the mines, on boats, in factories, so she could have the thing she wanted. And I think he got to like it too when he was home. He was never going to be the chatty, share a deep-and-meaningful-fatherly-advice dad, but I think he would have figured it all out. He would have grown into the job if she'd been by his side, showing him how. But sometimes people are put in situations they aren't ready for." Nan plucks a tissue from her pocket and passes it to Willa. "No one knew what would happen to her. To him. To all of you. Suddenly he was in his twenties, alone with three kids. He had no idea what to do, but he did try."

"I offered to take you all back here right after the funeral, at least until he found his feet and a job he could do with you all in his care, but he wanted to see if he could do it himself. He thought he should. But in the end it was just too hard with the kind of work he was a fit for, and Jack and Riley being so young. He called me one day, and he was crying on the phone because he felt like you weren't living the life you should be, always with the neighbours or stuck in that house because he was too tired from work to do anything with you most nights."

Willa's chest squeezes, because the thought of him crying on the phone to his mother makes her want to cry again too.

"Even after I convinced him to bring you here, he felt terrible about it. He tried to get a job down here, but he couldn't find one and had to go back. But he's never missed sending money, not once. And this time, he used up every single day of leave he had being down here. He wanted to stay longer, to make sure we'd be okay, even if it meant losing his job. I told him to go back."

She takes a hold of Willa's wrist. "That's how he fathers you now. By supporting you. When you started at Gandry and we found out the bursary didn't cover the uniform, he found the money for it. I don't know where, but he did. Sometimes I'm worried that he doesn't leave himself enough to live on."

Willa can only sit there and blink at Nan. She had no idea. She didn't even know they had to pay for the uniform, and she definitely didn't know that he paid for it. She didn't know he wanted to stay longer. She didn't know any of this.

"This is how he takes care of you," Nan says. "Because this is the only way he knows how to. I know it probably doesn't feel like enough, but it's going to have to be."

"I know," Willa whispers. And maybe it is enough. He's promised he'll come if he's needed. Maybe Willa can let that be enough. She smiles at Nan through her tears. "I have you, anyway."

"You have me. Always"

"Do you really send him my essays?"

"I've been sending him your schoolwork since the day you came here. And if I don't send it, he asks for it."

Willa sniffs. "I didn't know that."

"I didn't tell you. Maybe I should have." Nan smooths another non-existent hair from Willa's forehead and leans in, her face serious. "You have me, of course. But maybe, with a bit of effort on both sides, you might be able to have each other too."

"Maybe," Willa whispers.

Maybe.

# CHAPTER 65

## Finn

Finn walks out of the classroom reading the text that's come from her dad.

*It was a treat to see you this weekend, kiddo. I like your Willa a lot. She's a quiet fire, I can tell.*

What he doesn't know is that sometimes Willa's a blaze too.

This weekend, her dad finally told Finn about the article he's working on, a piece about a war correspondent who reported so hard and for so long from war zones she forgot how to live in the real world. He almost seems glad he lost his job now. He says it's freed him for other things, things he feels are more worthy than the daily drudgery of political news. "I felt more like a gossip columnist than a reporter sometimes," he said to her.

She's glad for him, even though she wants him back. Even with the rift it caused, Finn will never stop admiring him for doing what he did. For standing up for people who couldn't do it themselves. Maybe it wasn't the best thing for his journalism career, but it was the right thing for his soul. She likes to think that she'd do the same thing he did.

And maybe that's why she finds herself heading towards Mr Granger's office when the lunch bell rings. She marches the familiar journey to his office as fast as she can, refusing every temptation to change her mind and go find Dan instead.

Mr Granger's hunched over his desk, a trail of crumbs guiding his sandwich from lunchbox to mouth. Ms Lehrer's there too, staring into space, her long legs crossed, a sandwich in her hand too. Looks like they still haven't cottoned on to the whole matching lunch giveaway.

Finn plants herself in front of his desk. "Hey," she says, already wondering how much she's going to regret this.

He looks up at, blinking. A fleck of something green is stuck to the corner of his mouth. She points at the same spot on her lip.

He swipes it away. "Are we meeting today, Harlow?" He looks at his desk planner. "Because if we are, I for—"

"No, I just have something to tell you."

He tips his head to one side, looking wary. "Okay," he says slowly. "Shoot."

She takes a deep breath, clenching and unclenching her fists. "Okay, so, on Speech Night, the principal thanked me for organising the whole night. But Zehra did just as much as me. Actually, maybe she did more in the end. The important stuff, anyway. I just think..." She feels herself losing momentum as regret begins its slow seep. "I don't know, I just think someone should know how hard she worked and that she had some really amazing ideas. And then she kind of saved the whole night when the alumni guy pulled out, by finding a replacement while I was doing something else. It was her, not me. I just think someone should know," she says. "That's all."

His stare lingers. Then he grudges a nod, like he's finally accepting something he's been talked into. "Copy that."

She stands there, waiting for something else to come. It doesn't. "C-cool," she says, her face flaming. "I'm out." She backs out of the room without looking at either of them and makes a dash for it.

When she's clear of the building, and clear of possibly the best or stupidest thing she's done all week, she hunts down Dan via text.

In the computer lab, she sinks into a seat next to him.

"What's with you?" he asks. "You look like you just witnessed a murder."

"The murder of my reputation, maybe. I can't believe I just did that." She blinks at the editing software on his screen. Her ribs feel tight, and all the righteousness she marched into Granger's office with is gone, leaving only a fizzing of nerves. "I might have done something stupid."

"How stupid?"

She tells him.

"What?" He drags his eyes from the screen again, his face scrunched in disbelief. "Zehra? Why'd you help out that suck?"

"Hey, don't be like that. Just because you've got some ancient, infantile beef with her." She glares at him. "I did it because she deserves to be acknowledged. So what if she can be a suck? She's really nice and she also works really hard and tries really hard. I mean, what's actually wrong with that?"

"Okay, okay. Nothing." He holds up his hands. "Don't get angry with me. Zehra deserves all the kudos in the world. But aren't you worried? You're basically acknowledging, to a teacher, no less, that she did your job for you."

Finn gnaws at a fingernail and shrugs. "Well, it's the truth, so…"

"Harlow, I swear…" He shakes his head at her. "Honesty has got to be your worst freaking trait."

"Shut up," she mutters. "I already know that."

# CHAPTER 66

## Finn

Finn tucks her hands under her head and stares at the ceiling. She can still see the places where the glow-in-the-dark stars her dad put up there when she was little used to be. They've all dropped away since, leaving only faint, sticky marks.

"Do you think I'm an idiot?" she asks. "For telling Granger about Zehra and Speech Night?"

"Finn." Willa gives her a wry smile. "I told you, you'll do what *you* do. So I already knew you'd do that."

"You did?"

She presses a finger to Finn's sternum, still smiling. "I know you, Finn Harlow."

"You do know me." Finn buries her face in Willa's neck, her favourite place to hide.

"So when do they announce school captain?" Willa asks.

"Friday." Finn's stomach does that flip-flop thing it does every time she thinks about it. She doesn't know if she's nervous because she wants it or just because she wants to know what's going to happen for sure. But she does know that she doesn't want to think about it right now, so she rolls over and kisses Willa. Because kissing Willa is the best kind of distraction there is.

Willa agrees, apparently, pulling her close and stroking a hand over her waist. And as Willa's tongue finds hers, Finn wraps a leg over Willa's and kisses her harder.

Since that morning at the beach house, Finn's only problem with Willa has been keeping her hands *off*. Because now that she's taken a baby step, she just wants more. Much more than the alone time they seem to be able to snatch lately. More than the hot, breathless minutes curled on her bed with the door open, alert for footsteps. More than hot kisses down the side of Willa's house because there's nowhere else to hide when they're over at her house. She wants more than the slide of Willa's legs against hers. More than the push of lips against her neck. Whatever it is that began to unfurl in Finn that morning at the beach is completely unravelling. And the best part is that it feels completely okay.

She rolls onto her back, making room for Willa's fingers to creep higher under her school shirt.

"Girls?"

Finn whips her hand out from where it's made a stealth slide under Willa's school dress, exploring the soft stretch at the back of her thigh. She sits up, yanking her brain back into being. "Yeah, Mum?" she replies, instead of screaming like she wants to.

Anita sticks her head around the door, frowning. "I'm afraid you'll have to get going, Willa. Finn's father's on Skype, and we want to talk to her about something important." She gives Finn a smile, but her eyes are serious. "Two minutes, okay, hon?"

Finn nods numbly. Then she just sits there, her stomach turning another lurching flip-flop. "I'm terrified," she tells Willa as she gets up slowly.

"Don't worry." Willa grabs her hand and squeezes it. "It'll be okay."

"Will it?" Finn chews on her lip. "What if they're going to say they're getting a divorce?"

"Well, at least you'll know then. And what if they're going to say your dad's coming home?"

*What if?* Finn yanks in a breath.

"Go find out." Willa pushes her gently towards the door. "It's easier to know, isn't it?"

"I guess."

At the front door, Willa kisses her and says, "Call me later? After?"

"Of course."

"Remember, whatever they say, everything will be okay."

Finn nods because she wants to believe her.

Her dad is all smiles on the laptop screen when she sits down on the couch next to her mother.

"Hey, kiddo," he says. "How's Willa?"

Finn frowns and folds her arms. Small talk? *Really?* "What's going on?"

He and her mum look at each other.

"Do you want to tell?" Anita asks him.

"Okay." He picks up a mug and takes a sip. "So you know I've been writing this article?"

"Yeah," Finn says slowly.

"Well it's going really well, but it's going to be a long one. I think I'm going to need the summer to research, interview, and write."

"Okay," she says slowly. What's this got to do with anything?

"But I'm hoping to be back with you guys by mid-January."

She stares at him for a second, her breath snagged in her throat. "Here? Back in the house?" She turns to her mother, blinking.

Anita smiles and nods. When Finn doesn't smile back, she clasps her wrist. "What's wrong?"

Finn yanks her arm away. "What's wrong? What do you think's wrong?" She turns to her dad. "You know how you always complain when people bury the lead? Well, don't do it to me! I don't care about where you want to write your damn article! I just wanted to know you're coming back." She swipes at her face, feeling the hot slide of tears under her fingers. "That's all I've wanted to know."

"Oh, Finn. I'm so sorry." He leans in, his eyes wide. "I'm coming back. Soon."

"Well, I know *now*, don't I?" She brushes her sleeve over another falling tear. Anita moves closer, but Finn shifts away. She's too mad to be comforted.

"I thought you knew it was happening," he says. "After Cup weekend."

"How the hell would I know that? You were acting all fine, but you were sleeping in different rooms. You weren't in Tasmania."

They exchange looks.

Finn rolls her eyes. For two such smart people, they can be so stupid, thinking they're being stealth when they are so unbelievably *not* being. "I know you were then. Then this time you weren't, but you were acting all normal, and then you just go off again to Tasmania like everything's the same." She glares at him. "I mean, what's confusing about that? Stupid me."

"Hey, hey." Anita starts to run her hand up and down Finn's back, the way she would when Finn couldn't sleep when she was little. "Calm down, honey."

"I *am* calm." Finn pulls her knees to her chest and hugs them. "Okay, well, no, I'm not. I just didn't know what you were going to tell me, that's all." She draws in a deep breath, trying to stop this embarrassing flow of tears. They won't let up, though. Not yet. Her voice comes out quiet. "I was scared because I didn't know."

"Oh, Finn." Her mother pulls her closer and presses a kiss into the side of her head. "I'm sorry things have been so uncertain."

"Me too." Her dad's leaned in all close to the screen, looking sad. "I'm sorry. And I'm sorry I didn't just say it just now."

Finn sniffs and looks between the two of them. "So are you two are going to be okay?"

"We're going to be okay," Anita says.

They look at each other for a moment and smile.

If Finn wasn't caught in a riptide of relieved tears right now, she'd tell them they're gross.

"Good." She gets up and leaves them there. "I'm going to bed."

~ ~ ~

Finn kicks her socked feet up against the wall and presses the phone to her ear. "I kind of unleashed the brat on them," she tells Willa. "But I couldn't help it. I was just so mad. It was like he was telling me he was planning on going fishing for the weekend." She shakes her head. "I still don't get why they thought I knew."

"You know what it reminds me of?" Willa says.

"What?"

"When my dad left. He told me was leaving, but he didn't *really* say it, and Nan had to tell me all over again later before I figured it out. It's like he just assumed I understood what he was *not* saying, or something. I thought your parents would be better at that stuff than my dad, though."

"Apparently not."

"Poor Finn."

Finn wriggles her toes and sighs. "Do you sometimes feel like playing the game at camp was easier than life is?"

"Definitely. We knew the rules at camp."

"And I think I'd rather deal with that douchebag Drew than face the school captain thing tomorrow."

Willa snickers. "I'd forgotten about Drew."

"Okay, so I might have acted a bit crazy, but I'm *so* happy Dad's coming home." Finn curls her arm around Banjo and rests her cheek against his head. He licks her wrist and flops back into snooze mode. "I can't wait to just sit around and eat toast and talk about nothing, instead of our time together having to be so *special* because it's the only time we've got. I just want to hang. That's what we do." Finn bites down on her lip. "I'm sorry."

"For what?"

"For saying stuff like that after what happened with you and your dad."

"Don't worry. It's not like it was much better before this." Willa says. She's quiet for a moment, though, and Finn wishes she was with her so she could read her face. Finally, she speaks again. "Nan says maybe I need to try harder. With Dad."

"What do you think?"

She sighs into the phone. "I don't know. I know I'm happy for you, though."

Finn pouts at the ceiling. "Why aren't you here on this bed with me right now?"

"Because I'd much rather be squashed into a bottom bunk under my snoring little sister than cuddled up with you. *Obviously.*"

"Of course you would."

# CHAPTER 67

## Finn

At the start of fourth period, her teacher passes her a note telling her to go to the principal's office at the end of class. Finn chest tightens as she stares at the slip of paper. Well, at least she knows for sure she's in the top two now. It's got to be captain or vice.

Luckily, they're watching a film, so she just fixes her eyes to the screen and lets her thoughts race until the bell goes.

Zehra's already there when she arrives at the principal's office. She's standing, hands clasped behind her in front of the principal's desk.

Finn's only ever been in the principal's office a few times, and it's the same as it's been since the first time: a fiesta of brown. Carpet, desk, paintings, books. Then there are the plants on every available surface. The desk, the shelves, the floor. A green trailing thing drapes from the curtain rail and over the window, cluttering the light. She wonders how much time Mr Burgess has to run the school between watering sessions.

"Ah, Ms Harlow, come on in." He beckons her through the door with his creepy, long fingers.

Finn edges in, giving Zehra a diffident smile. Mr Granger's in the corner, legs crossed, staring at the back of his hands like there's something fascinating there. He looks up to raise an eyebrow at her and smiles as if to say, "look at us in the principal's office".

She manages a small smile back, then turns to Mr Burgess, her hands clenched by her side.

He takes a tissue out of his sleeve and swipes at his nose, then sits back in his chair and appraises the two of them. "This is the first time we have had Year 11 students in this role," he says. "And I trust you understand what an enormous responsibility it is."

Finn nods. She can see Zehra doing the same in her periphery.

"Okay, so we wanted to let you know before we announce it to the rest of the school. After a long and lively discussion with some key faculty last night, we've decided that for next year, Zehra will be senior school captain, and, Finn, you will be vice captain."

The world stills for a moment and then starts again. Finn hears Zehra let out a sharp breath next to her. This is happening.

She forces herself to turn and smile and say, as lightly as she can, "Congratulations."

"Th-thanks." And Zehra looks so shocked and excited that Finn can't help feeling flickers of happiness for her, even as her own stomach turns in slow, sickening circles. It's not like Zehra hasn't worked for it too. Maybe she even wanted it more too.

Mr Burgess folds his arms on the desk and leans forward, tissue still clutched in his hand. "Finn, I want to thank you for your hard work this year. And I certainly don't want you to see this as any kind of demotion. Both of you girls have contributed so much to the school over the last few years, and it is simply a rewarding of hard work of both of you. For you to both have your turns, as it were. We're simply very fortunate in having two such hardworking, strong leaders among us. It will be a privilege to have you both run student affairs."

Finn's cheeks burn as she nods. "Of course. Thank you for the opportunity," she says politely. She turns back to Zehra, pushes out another smile, holds out a hand, and says, "I promise I will be as amazing a vice captain for you as you were for me." And she means it.

Zehra smiles, her eyes still wide with the shock. "Thanks."

"Now, that's what I like to see." Burgess stands, smiling beatifically, as if he orchestrated this moment. "We'll be making the announcement at the end of lunchtime. I'm sure you two will be wanting to enjoy your lunch." He picks up his mobile phone from his desk. "Now just let me take a photo of you for our social media. With your student advisor, of course." He waves them into the corner. "Under the window, perhaps. Beside my Devil's Ivy. That would be lovely."

Finn follows the principal's stage directions in a zombie shuffle, standing in the jungle of greenery next to Zehra. After a couple of misfires, finally he gets the photo he wants and sits again, busying himself with his phone.

"Thank you, girls," he mutters, one alien finger hovering over the screen.

Dismissed, apparently.

Mr Granger gives Zehra a grin as he moves for the door. "Congratulations, Zehra. I'm looking forward to you keeping me on my toes next year." His hand lands on Finn's shoulder as he passes, squeezing it hard.

That's when Finn throat constricts. "Hey, congratulations again," she tells Zehra, and hurries away, sliding through crowds of kids sitting in the covered passageway outside the office.

Dan's at the seats, waiting for her. She lowers herself down next to him, and clutches the edges of the hard wooden seat.

"So?" he says, his burger halfway to his mouth. "Don't keep me in suspense."

She draws in a slow breath, wishing she hadn't shown him the note after English. Then she could have had some time alone with this. Then she wouldn't have to say it out loud. "Zehra's captain next year. I'm vice."

"Oh." He puts his burger back down. "I'm sorry."

His soft tone pushes her to an edge she knows she can no longer come back from. "Th-that's okay," she stutters. She lets out a resigned breath. "Right, I'm just going to cry for a minute, okay?"

"Um, okay," he says, lowering his head as if she's suggested they pray.

"And then I'm going to be over it," she says with a hard nod. "Then I'm going to be big."

Dan doesn't say anything else. Just hands her the serviette that came with his burger and lets her sniffle for a bit. And when she can't bear her own stupid, ego-bruised misery any more, she blows her nose and shakes the feelings loose.

"Okay, I'm over it," she says, sitting up straighter. "I mean, fuck it. Not many people get to say they were vice captain of their school. It's not like it's a bad thing."

"*And* I get to call you veep now." He grins and leans into her for a moment. "But seriously, are you okay?"

Finn examines the feelings. "I think so. It's just the ego bruise more than anything. Burgess says it's not a demotion, but it still kind of sounds like one." She wipes her face and kicks her heels against the grass. "But, anyway, it's not so bad, maybe. I get time to do things now. I'm going to join the Greens this summer. I'm going to paint more. I'm going to help at the centre. I'm going to do all kinds of *stuff*." She smiles a little, because the more she thinks about it, the more she's not just telling herself this to make herself feel better. The more these things have a glitter of potential on them.

"Of course you will. Dude, you don't need to be boss to be boss. You'll do it anyway. That's the glorious thing about you, Harlow."

"Thanks." She tucks a hand through his elbow. Dan's a smart-ass a lot of the time, but he's also pretty fantastic at the whole cheerleader-best friend thing.

"Here to help." He picks up his burger.

She takes a deep breath and thinks of having her afternoons free to paint and study. And to spend time with Willa.

*Willa.* Finn wishes she was here right now. Because what she really wants is for her girlfriend to smother the last shred of disappointment for her. To do it with arms wrapped so tight that Finn can't feel anything else. She pulls out her phone.

*Can you meet me in the park after school?*

*Of course.*

And with those two words, Finn knows that Willa knows she didn't get school captain. Because she didn't ask. And somehow Willa knows Finn wants her to be there with her when she says the words. Needs the comfort to be her *presence.* And she loves that Willa knows that and does that.

Now Finn just has to get through the next couple of hours, and the announcement, and she gets to have that comfort.

～ ～ ～

When the final bell goes, she heads for the tram stop, but at the last minute, she just can't help herself and turns and strides to his office.

He looks up from the mess of his desk and gives her a weary smile. "Harlow. I'm glad you came."

Hands thrust deep in her pockets, she asks the question that hasn't left her brain since lunchtime. "If I hadn't told you about Zehra and Speech Night, would I have got it?"

He folds his arms and leans back in his chair, each movement feeling like it takes an eternity. Finally, he nods. "I might have fought harder for you if you hadn't. But you know what?"

"What?"

"I think you were telling me something more, even if you think you weren't."

Finn sighs. Examining what he might mean by that will have to wait until later. "Do you think I've been slacking off?"

"Honestly?" He stares at her. "Not at all. I think you have had priorities, and you've made decisions based on them. This is a good lesson to learn, Finn. An important one." He smiles up at her. "But don't worry. No one would ever accuse you of being a slacker."

All she can do is nod, because for some reason, hearing that make her want to cry again.

"Look," he says, "no one in that meeting thought for a moment that you didn't deserve it after everything you'd done this year. It was just a matter of whether Zehra deserved a shot as much. And I did tell them about what you said about Speech Night. And maybe that information pushed her across the line."

"Okay."

"But you know what else, Finn?"

"What?"

"At the end of the day, you don't need this as much as Zehra does. That's not the reason why she got it, but it's a reason to feel okay about not getting it."

She nods slowly and stares at the ground, waiting for the hurt. It doesn't come. "You know, except for the ego bit, I'm okay with it. I really am."

"Of course you are. You can handle this and so much more. When you're done with all this school stuff, you're going to hit the world with full force, no matter what." He smiles at her. "I'm quite looking forward to the moment of impact, actually."

"Thanks, I think."

"Well, I can't thank you." He gives her a grin.

"Why not?"

"Because now I've got to put up with Zehra nagging me all year."

"Good." She looks between him and Ms Lehrer, who's at her desk, politely pretending not to listen.

"By the way," Finn says. "A tip before Zehra starts coming in here a lot. If you want to stay on the down low, you should consider not bringing the same lunches."

Both their heads snap up. They look at their lunch boxes and then each other.

Granger tips his head back and laughs. "Boom."

Finn grins and makes a run for it.

Outside in the sunshine, she does a little shimmy, trying to shake it all off, to leave this defeat behind her. But then, as she crosses the yard, she spots Zehra, in a congratulatory huddle with some of her friends, including Hana and Zaki, and her steps slow again.

Okay, it's probably going to take a little longer.

# CHAPTER 68

## Willa

Willa's sauntering out of the school gates, already feeling the promise of the weekend, when she hears her name being called. She quickens her steps, worried that it's Miss Cassavetes, trying to hunt her down for another last-minute meeting.

"Hey Brookes! Get those hot legs over here!"

Okay, so not Miss Cassavetes.

Willa turns, frowning, but it turns instantly to a smile.

It's Amira, of course. She's slouched with Eva on a bench under the elm tree, their school dresses pulled up so their thighs catch the sun.

Hi!" Eva squints up at Willa. "What are you doing this weekend?"

"Not sure yet." Willa still hasn't got used to the idea of being able to make plans.

"We're thinking of going to see *Romeo and Juliet* on Saturday night for English," Eva says. "Maybe get some food before. You want to join?"

"It's come to this," Amira says. "You geeks have me doing homework on the weekend."

"You love it," Eva teases. She turns to Willa. "So, what do you think?"

"Sure. I might ask Finn too, if that's okay? Her school's studying it as well."

"Cool. I'll message you."

"And Willa," Amira says. "Do us a favour and get Facebook? I don't expect to you to stretch to Insta and or Snap, but make our life planning a little bit easier, would you? All this texting and actual talking on the phone. It's a lot to ask of a person."

"Nope." Willa grins. "Not even for you, Mir."

"You suck."

"I know. See you." She walks away, feeling light and airy. There is something pretty great about having friends at school.

Willa doesn't go home straight away. Because she doesn't have to. It's nice knowing she can take her time and that Riley and Jack will be okay. She can even go out at night now. Even if she didn't want to, Nan would make her. She's practically been forcing Willa out of the house on the weekends. Probably to make up for all the time she was stuck there. But also because Nan loves running her territory again.

When the bus drops her off, she crosses the road and goes into a small café opposite the park. It's nearly empty, like it might be about to close, but the waiter smiles her welcome, so Willa sits. She orders an iced tea and pulls a piece of paper and a pen out of her bag. It's time.

When the cold glass is clutched in her hand, she stares at the blank sheet and gnaws at her lip. This is harder than homework. Harder than writing those story responses. But Willa promised herself she'd do it, so she will. She's going to create a thread, however fine and however loose, between them.

She picks up the pen and hunches over the page. Then she writes her dad a letter. Not a letter full of feelings. Not even one addressing what has passed between them. Just an opening of communication. A thank you for the money for her new laptop. Life news. Simple things, like Jack's coming soccer final and Riley's part in the school play. How Nan's first apricots got eaten by parrots. Little bits of life's mundane. News that will render a normalcy between them. Because maybe all they need first is to form a habit.

Finally, she hits the end of the page, her self-imposed word length. She signs off, saying, *I think I might be as bad at writing letters as you are at small talk, but it's got to be a bit more interesting than one of my history essays. Love, Willa.*

And maybe Nan's right about trying. Because writing it feels like releasing a long-held breath. She seals the paper into the stamped envelope she bought especially this morning and tucks it in her bag to post on the way home.

When she looks out the café window, she spots Finn straight away, frowning as she walks to meet her in the park. It's amazing how Finn still grabs her eye like a beacon, even on a crowded street. The expression on her face confirms what Willa already suspected from her text earlier: Finn didn't get school captain. Willa hurries to find her wallet, because that girl frowning at the footpath looks like a girl in need of a hug.

But Willa has to smile too. Because even when she might be a little heartbroken, Finn still walks like a girl on a mission, like the girl capable of giving the speech she gave last week at the community centre. That's because a girl like Finn doesn't need to be school captain to prove herself. She proves herself just by being who she is, brave and believing. That's what Willa will tell her. Maybe some people don't know the full wonder of her yet, but they will one day. And right now, Willa's smitten with being one of those who do.

# CHAPTER 69

## Finn

Jack's team scrapes their win, 1-0. And without even kicking a goal, Jack wins the best on field. They all stand and yell and clap, trying to out-cheer the Mummy Cheer Squad, back at their peppy best for the finals.

When the coach is done with them, Jack trots straight over to them all.

"Superstar." Willa forces him into a hug. Nan does too. He submits, but he's looking to Dan the whole time.

"Total hero worship," Finn whispers to her best friend.

Dan just grins and smacks Jack's shoulder in bloke-y congratulations. "Great job, dude."

"Riley, congratulate your brother," Nan says as Riley wanders over the grass with the dogs.

"You didn't suck," Riley tells him, yanking on the leashes.

Finn pretends to strangle her. "Why do you have to be like that?"

"I just do." She shrugs. "It's older sister rights."

"I don't treat you like that," Willa says.

"Yeah, that's because you're weird." Riley grins and dances around with the dogs attached to her wrists.

"And you, young lady, are obnoxious," Nan says from her camp chair.

"I know," Riley says, sounding positively gleeful about it.

Dan and Rosie grab up their things.

"We have to go," Rosie tells Finn.

"Apparently I have to go home and put on something nicer," Dan says, yanking at his T-shirt.

"Yeah, you do." Rosie grins nervously at Finn. "He's meeting my mum tonight."

"Aren't I meeting your dad too?" he asks her.

"Yeah, but my mum is the only one whose opinion counts. If it was just Dad, you could turn up in a penguin onesie."

Dan looks at Finn and grits his teeth. "I'm meeting parents."

"Oh boy." Finn gives him an encouraging arm slap. "Don't be weird, okay?"

"Thanks. No, really."

Tyler and his dad come over, and Tyler and Jack high five like they didn't just see each other on the field five minutes ago.

"All right, kids. Our ride is here." Nan slowly kicks her feet from where they've been resting on the esky, which was full of sandwiches and fruit when the day started. "Get your things."

Riley pouts, clutching the leashes. "I want to walk home with Finn and Willa."

"With the dogs, you mean," Finn corrects her. "It's not our company you want."

"So can I?" Riley asks, smiling cutely at Finn.

"We don't know what we're doing yet," Willa tells her.

"You leave the girls be for a minute," Nan tells her. "They might like to spend some time without you."

"But they love hanging out with me."

"When you're being nice, we do." Finn gently yanks on her ponytail.

"Come on, my girl," Nan says to Riley, leaning on her walking stick. "They already took you to the movies last night. You come home with me. You can see if Brittany wants to come over for dinner, if you want."

"Can she stay for a movie?"

Nan shakes her head and smiles at Tyler's dad. "It's never enough, is it, with kids?"

"Nope. Give 'em an inch." He grins and hefts the esky onto his shoulder. "Shall we?"

"Yes," Nan says. She turns to Finn and Willa. "There's plenty if you both want to come back for dinner. The dogs are welcome if you promise they won't dig up my yard."

"Thanks, Nan," Finn says, giving them all a wave.

The group takes off slowly, accommodating Nan's halting stride. Riley drags her feet, turning and giving them the occasional mournful looks.

Finn shakes her head. "Such a drama queen. How'd that even happen with you and Nan around?"

"I have no idea. She was born like that."

"You two are drama queens too," Finn tells the dogs, who both strain at the leash as Riley, their source of fun and snacks, abandons them.

When everyone's gone, they wander down the path together, the dogs trotting behind them.

"Holidays in two weeks," Willa says with a slow smile. "I can't wait."

"We're going to Tasmania for Christmas," Finn tells her. "Anna's coming for a week too."

"Cool. We might go stay with Dad this summer. Just for a week."

Finn stops walking. "Really?"

"Yes." Willa's shoulders rise as she draws in a breath. "I wrote to him. And…and he wrote back. Sort of. It's awkward, but way less awkward, if you know what I mean." She looks so self-conscious and elated, and baffled by her own elation, that Finn forgets to be miffed Willa didn't tell her this. Maybe she just needed to sit with this one her own.

"I'm really glad," she tells her.

They walk some more, away from the soccer fields, towards the lusher, shadier part of the park where plane trees stand sentinel over the paths.

"I can't believe we start VCE next year," Willa says with a shudder.

"It can't be that bad."

"I hope not."

"Anyway, I don't want to think about it," Finn says. "Not yet. I just want to think about five long, lazy weeks without school."

"Me too. I can't wait to read whatever book I want to read, for as long as I want to read it."

"Geek."

"So are you," Willa shoots back.

"True. I also can't wait to paint in Tasmania," Finn says, thinking of the views she sketched last time, wishing the whole time she had brought her paints.

"That reminds me." Willa stops by a bench and reaches into her bag. She pulls out another smaller shopping bag. "I got this for you."

"What is it?" Finn inspects the bag, curious. It's flat and hard.

"I've got an idea. Why don't you look?" Willa teases.

Pulling a face at her, Finn opens the bag. Inside, wrapped in tissue paper, is a small picture frame. The wood is a light, sandy colour, the grain a series of fine swirls.

"It's for your painting in your bedroom. The one you keep forgetting to buy a frame for."

Finn smiles. How did Willa remember that?

"I hope the colour is okay. I took a photo of the picture to the man in the framing shop. He said a light colour would work best. But he also said you can change it if y—"

The only thing Finn can do to stop Willa's mouth is kiss her, so she does. "Don't worry, it's perfect."

Instead of smiling, Willa bites her lip and pulls her closer to the edge of the path. "I just wanted to get you something to say...I don't know...thank you. For being so amazing while Nan was in hospital, and being patient when I never had any time and when I got so angry. Anyway, um..." She keeps fiddling with the zipper of her bag, her cheeks flaming.

A honey feeling slides through Finn, because Willa's deer-in-headlights expression when she's using her words is the most awkward-cute thing she's seen.

She places her hand over Willa's fidgeting one. "Thank you." Then she gives her a sly grin. "So...you *do* want to go round with me."

Willa brow furrows. "What?"

"You do realise that you never answered when I asked you that time?"

"I didn't?"

"No, you gave me some shruggy answer."

Willa smiles playfully and shrugs again. "Okay, well, I guess I will, then." Then she laughs and grabs Finn's hand, pulling her down the path. "I totally want to go around with you, Finn Harlow."

"Well, that's okay, then." Finn smiles. "So, what do you have to do now?"

Willa's step slows as she turns to Finn, eyes wide. "Nothing. Nothing at all."

"It's a miracle!"

"What about you?"

"Nothing at all."

Willa tips her head back and lets out a breath like it's the best news she's heard all week. She grabs Finn's hand and leads her off the path. Dropping onto the edge of a tree shadow, she pulls Finn down with her. Her smile spreads as wide as her arms as she lies back. "Let's just do nothing for a bit, then."

The next thing Finn knows, she's lying too, her cheek resting on the warm denim of Willa's thigh, the dogs sprawled beside them. How could she resist? "Good plan."

Then she lets her eyes fall closed to the sunshine and the soft slide of Willa fingers in her hair.

~ ~ ~

# About Emily O'Beirne

Thirteen-year-old Emily woke up one morning with a sudden itch to write her first novel. All day, she sat through her classes, feverishly scribbling away (her rare silence probably a cherished respite for her teachers). And by the time the last bell rang, she had penned fifteen handwritten pages of angsty drivel, replete with blood-red sunsets, moody saxophone music playing somewhere far off in the night, and abandoned whiskey bottles rolling across tables. Needless to say, that singular literary accomplishment is buried in a box somewhere, ready for her later amusement.

From Melbourne, Australia, Emily was recently granted her PhD. She works part-time in academia, where she hates marking papers but loves working with her students. She also loves where she lives but travels as much as possible and tends to harbour crushes on cities more than on people.

**CONNECT WITH EMILY**

Website: www.emilyobeirne.com

# Other Books from Ylva Publishing

www.ylva-publishing.com

# Future Leaders of Nowhere
*(Future Leaders – Book 1)*

**Emily O'Beirne**

ISBN: 978-3-95533-821-3
Length: 353 pages (74,000 words)

Finn and Willa have been picked as leaders in the camp game. Finn doesn't know what's throwing her more, the fact she's leading a team of unenthusiastic overachievers or coming up against Willa. And Willa doesn't know which is harder, leaving her responsibilities behind or opening up to someone. Soon they must balance their clashing ideals with their unexpected connection. And find a way to win.

# Pieces
## G Benson

ISBN: 978-3-95533-805-3
Length: 292 pages (104,000 words)

Carmen is sixteen, homeless, and desperate to keep her and her kid brother out of foster care. Ollie, also sixteen, has a life that's all about parents, school pressure, and friends. One kiss changes everything. Ollie is captivated, but Carmen vanishes. When they cross paths later, everything is different.

A young-adult, queer romance about what we're prepared to sacrifice for those we care about.

*All the Ways to Here*
© 2017 by Emily O'Beirne

ISBN: 978-3-95533-894-7

Also available as e-book.

Published by Ylva Publishing, legal entity of Ylva Verlag, e.Kfr.

Ylva Verlag, e.Kfr.
Owner: Astrid Ohletz
Am Kirschgarten 2
65830 Kriftel
Germany

www.ylva-publishing.com

First edition: 2017

Credits
Edited by Astrid Ohletz and Michelle Aguilar
Proofread by Amanda Jean
Cover Design by Adam Lloyd
Print Layout by Allen at eB Format